6-15-88

Abbie Jarvis is an American woman

She's a bona fide success story, the small-town girl who sought her fortune in the big city and became a prominent Manhattan lawyer. Abbie is living her dream, but that dream has brought her to a crucial place in her life, a time of sitting back and taking stock, of seeing where she's been and where she's going. At thirty-four, Abbie has reached the age of reason.

After too many years of working around the clock, Abbie is wondering whether success is worth the cost. Having ended a long and unfulfilling relationship, she is asking herself what she wants from love. She hasn't found the answers she's looking for, hasn't found the happiness she seeks, but in asking all the right questions she's halfway there.

Dear Reader,

This is indeed a special year for American Romance: it marks our fifth anniversary of bringing you the love stories you want to read. Stories of real women of contemporary America—women just like you. This month we're celebrating that anniversary with a special four-book series by four of your favorite American Romance authors. Rebecca Flanders, Beverly Sommers, Judith Arnold and Anne Stuart introduce you to Jaime, Suzanne, Abbie and Marielle—the women of Yorktown Towers.

They've been neighbors, they've been friends, but now they're saying goodbye, leaving Manhattan one by one, in search of their lives, in search of happiness, carving out their own version of the American Dream.

Jaime, Suzanne, Abbie and Marielle: four believable American Romance heroines...four contemporary American women just like you.

We hope you enjoy these special stories as much as we enjoyed preparing them for you for this occasion. It's our way of saying thanks for being there these past five years. We here at American Romance look forward to many more anniversaries of success....

Debra Matteucci
Senior Editor

Harvest the Sun
Judith Arnold

Harlequin Books

TORONTO • NEW YORK • LONDON
AMSTERDAM • PARIS • SYDNEY • HAMBURG
STOCKHOLM • ATHENS • TOKYO • MILAN

Published August 1988

First printing June 1988

ISBN 0-373-16259-6

Chapter One

Looking at T.J. now, Abbie wouldn't have guessed that the doctors once predicted he'd never walk again.

He was standing behind the bar, so his legs were hidden from her view. His movements were graceful as he reached for bottles, tossed ice cubes and lemon peels into glasses, drew beer from the taps and mopped up spills on the laminated oak surface of the bar. He worked efficiently, saving himself steps whenever he could. But he was obviously a healthy man.

His face had lost the strain that Abbie had noticed in it the last time she'd seen him, which was at her mother's funeral seven and a half years ago. He had been leaning heavily on a cane that drizzly March day, and he'd scarcely been able to bend his left knee as he hobbled over to Abbie and her father to offer his condolences. He'd been much thinner then, almost gaunt. There had been shadows in his eyes, tension in his mouth as he'd contended with his bad leg. More than five years after the injury had occurred, he'd barely begun to recover.

He was still thinner now than he'd been in his heyday, back in high school and then at the University of Southern California, when his name was being bandied about as a possible candidate for the Heisman Trophy. Abbie had never cared much for football, but she'd followed T.J.'s career because he had been a classmate of hers, a local boy making good. She had figured that someday she would be able to turn to her husband during a Super Bowl game and say, "You know the wide receiver who just made that spectacular catch? T. J. Hillyard. I knew him."

That wasn't going to happen. Abbie was thirty-four years old and single, and T. J. Hillyard was an over-the-hill gimp running a bar on the western edge of town. Forget about husbands and Super Bowls—both Abbie and T.J. had missed the mark by a wide margin.

She dug her hands into the pockets of her slim-fitting denim skirt and surveyed her surroundings from the safety of the doorway. The walls of the bar were covered in vertical panels of birch; two wide front windows overlooked the parking lot and beyond it Route 20. The bar ran the length of the rear wall, and several neon signs promoting various brands of beer hung above a shelf built into the wall to display liquor bottles. The end of the room farthest from the door held a pool table, and smaller tables and booths occupied the remainder of the room. On the jukebox, Emmylou Harris was singing "Here, There and Everywhere."

For a Thursday night, the place was reasonably crowded. A couple of ranchers sat on barstools and a trio of farmhands monopolized the pool table. Two youngish women sat smoking cigarettes and conversing quietly at a table, and although a few of the male customers ogled them from a distance, nobody bothered them. Tyler's wasn't a pick-up joint, Abbie concluded with satisfaction.

Abbie's father had urged her to come here. Less than an hour ago, after they'd finished dinner, she had retired to the bedroom that had been hers for the first seventeen years of her life. Her father had found her there, sitting on her bed in a trancelike state, mutely holding the framed wedding photo of her parents which usually stood on top of the dresser. "It's hard, isn't it," he had murmured, crossing the room to sit beside her. "It was hard for me, too, at first—getting used to being in this house without her."

"You seem used to it now," Abbie had pointed out enviously.

"I've had seven years to get used to it," he'd reminded her. "This is your first time back home since she died." There had been no criticism in his tone, no reproach. He understood why Abbie hadn't been back to Wheeler in seven years, why when she'd wanted to visit her father she had arranged to meet him at his sister's house in the San Francisco suburbs or else talked him into traveling to New York. He had always accepted her explanations: she could make the trip to California only once a year, and she wanted to see Aunt Martha as well as her father, and without an airport Wheeler was awfully difficult to get to.... But they both knew the real reason Abbie had avoided her hometown for so long.

Ever since she'd arrived at her father's house that afternoon, she had felt disoriented. The neat ranch house with its sun-bleached stucco facade and its comfortably dowdy furnishings was far removed from her life in New York City, not just in miles but in atmosphere. For a long time she'd remained outside in the yard, inhaling the strangely odorless air, gazing at the almond and plum trees, the small vegetable garden bordered with a knee-high wire fence, the row of sunflowers at the rear boundary, wizened and drooping in the autumn phase of their cycle, and the pseudoantique wagon wheel fastened to the side wall of the tool shed. Once she'd mustered enough courage to enter the house, she had wandered from room to room, buffeted by memories.

She was confronted by too many physical reminders of her mother—the quaint, amateurish watercolors Grace Jarvis had painted and hung around the house, the matching towels, curtains and bath mat set she'd selected for the bathroom, faded with age to a pale blue, the wedding photo of Abbie's father and her now resting in Abbie's lap.

"Why don't you go out for a while?" Abbie's father had suggested.

"I just got here," she had argued halfheartedly.

He'd ignored her protest. "You hardly ate any supper, Abbie. I know it's difficult. Maybe you need some time to yourself."

She hadn't wanted to abandon her father so soon after arriving—but she *did* need some time to herself, time to adjust to where she was and what she'd left behind in New York City. Besides, she planned to remain in Wheeler for at least a week. She would have adequate time to spend with her father once she'd grown accustomed to where she was.

"Why don't you go to Tyler's and treat yourself to a drink?" her father had recommended. "Nice bar, run by T. J. Hillyard. You remember T.J., don't you? Of course you do. He bought Mike's Place, that old dive out on Route 20, some years ago. He fixed it up real nice. Ask me how many nails he bought to rebuild the place—I sold him every single one."

"I'll go if you come with me," Abbie had proposed.

Shaking his head, he'd taken the photograph from her and carried it back to the dresser. "I thought we just decided that you need some time alone."

"You decided that, not me," Abbie had countered with a smile.

Her father had smiled, too, but Abbie had thought he looked wan and edgy. "I've got to get back to the store, Abbie," he'd said.

"Why? You locked up at five." Abbie knew that for a fact; earlier that day, after the house had begun to get to her, she'd driven the car she'd rented at the airport over to the drop-off site at the Wheeler bus terminal and walked the block and a half to Jarvis's Hardware Store, where she'd loitered for the rest of the afternoon, shooting the breeze with her father and his two clerks until closing time.

"Well," her father had said vaguely, "there's some paperwork I want to go through."

Paperwork? One thing Roy Jarvis couldn't handle was paperwork. Abbie's mother had been the store's book-keeper until her death, and then Faye Hinkel had taken over.

Faye Hinkel hadn't been at the store that afternoon. When Abbie had innocently asked her father where the woman was, he'd mumbled something unintelligible and changed the subject. And—maybe it was just Abbie's imagination, but Joe and Stan had seemed awfully jit-tery, almost artificially cheerful. Sure, they were as glad to see Abbie after so many years as she was to see them. But why, when she'd headed toward the office at the rear of the store saying that she wanted to say hello to Faye, had Joe intercepted her and advised her not to go into the office?

Her father had never mentioned during their regular phone conversations that Faye was no longer keeping the books for the store. Nor had he ever given Abbie any rea-son to suspect that anything was wrong at the store. Jarvis's Hardware had been in business for over fifty years, ever since Abbie's grandfather had founded it, shortly after he'd settled in Wheeler after a long migration that had begun several years earlier in Dust Bowl Oklahoma. Jarvis's Hardware was a fixture in town, and Abbie was sure nothing was seriously amiss at the store.

Except . . . why wasn't Faye working there anymore? And why had Joe made that remark about how Abbie shouldn't worry, everything would work out? She *hadn't* been worried until he'd said that.

"What kind of paperwork do you have to do?" Abbie had inquired. "Maybe I could help."

"No, honey—it's nothing, really. Ten minutes with a pencil and I'll be done. I can walk down to the store—you take the van and check out Tyler's. T.J. did a fine job with the tavern. Turned it into a place where a person can kick back and feel comfortable. Why don't you go have a beer and say hello to your old school chum? He's doing real well, Abbie. Doesn't even use his cane anymore."

He wasn't using his cane tonight, she observed as she lingered in the darkened doorway, watching T.J. attend to his clientele. She concentrated on him in an effort to put out of her mind the suspicion that her father had been just a touch too anxious to get rid of her that evening—and to put out of her mind, as well, the difficulties that had compelled her to request a brief leave of absence from her job at the Manhattan District Attorney's Office, pack a few bags and flee to Wheeler in the first place.

It seemed hard to believe that less than fifteen hours ago she'd been in New York, boarding a plane to the West Coast. She still had the stinging scent of the city in her nostrils, the gritty texture of it beneath her fingernails. She still had the professional frustration of trying to work in an unworkable system simmering inside her, and the personal torment of having tried to change an unchangeable man. But she was here now, thousands of miles from all that, ready to clear her lungs and her head. She only hoped that she'd recover from her wounds as well as T. J. Hillyard had recovered from his considerably larger ones.

"Care to order?" a waitress asked.

Abbie jumped. Given that she was still standing in the doorway, she hadn't expected to be approached by a waitress. She eyed a vacant table not far from the entry and said, "I'll have a beer. An Oly," she specified, smiling as she spotted the Olympia beer logo attached to the wall above the bar. Olympia wasn't available in New York. If Abbie was going to drink beer in Wheeler, she was going to drink one of the local brews.

The waitress nodded, twirled her tray and strode toward the bar. She was chunky in build and wore a faded pair of jeans and an embroidered peasant blouse. Her dirty-blond hair fell in a braid nearly to her waist. Abbie didn't recognize her—but then, she'd been gone a long time. She could no longer expect to know everyone in town.

Drifting toward the empty table, she saw the waitress place her order with T.J. If appearance was a valid measure, Abbie had to agree with her father that T.J. was doing well. He'd always been a golden boy, someone who seemed to have too much going for him: athletic talent, a functioning brain, a handsome face and a beguiling modesty about his overwhelming assets. Even in high school, when nearly every girl in the school had had a crush on him and the Wheeler *Register* had considered him worthy of a dozen feature articles, when universities from around the country were sending scouts to this remote hamlet in the Sacramento River Valley of California to check out the hot prospect who could do it all on

the football field—especially catch impossible passes—
T.J. had never been particularly stuck-up.

He'd been confident, sure—but so, in her own way, had
Abbie. The one thing she'd had in common with T. J.
Hillyard when they'd been classmates at the regional high
school was that they'd both known they were going to get
out of Wheeler, to escape the small, stifling town and
stake their claims on the world.

He had been good-looking then, but Abbie thought he
looked better now. His hair was still a thick mane of dark
brown waves. His eyes were also dark, accented by laugh
lines and glinting with a mild humor. He hadn't had a
mustache the last time Abbie had seen him, but she liked
the shaggy growth of hair covering his upper lip; it
downplayed the sharp prominence of his nose and drew
attention to his mouth, which seemed to settle naturally
into an easy smile. His jaw appeared squarer and more
rugged than it used to, probably because of the weight
he'd lost. During his playing days, his neck had been
thickened with muscle. Now it was more normally pro-
portioned.

His chest, too, had lost some of its bulky muscular-
ity—and Abbie considered that an improvement. She
liked the bony shape of his shoulders beneath his loose-
fitting cotton polo shirt, and the sinewy lank of his arms.
He looked less like a football deity now, and more like a
human being.

He twisted the cap off a bottle of Oly, placed it and a
glass on the waitress's tray and glanced past her. Glimps-
ing Abbie, he arched his eyebrows in surprise. "Abbie
Jarvis?" he mouthed before breaking into a dimpled grin.

She returned his grin and wove among the tables to the
bar. It was silly, but even after all these years, after she'd
risen to impressive heights in her profession while T.J. had

seen his own career destroyed along with his knee, Abbie still responded to him a little bit like a schoolgirl, breathless and bashful and enormously flattered that the great T. J. Hillyard had actually acknowledged her, remembered her, bestowed his dazzling smile upon her.

"Abbie," he greeted her as she settled on the empty barstool nearest him. He had to walk a few paces to reach her, but he covered the distance without a hint of his former limp. He reached across the bar and engulfed her slender hand in his firm clasp, then pulled the bottle and glass from the tray and poured her beer for her. "You're looking great. What brings you to town?"

She was touched by T.J.'s congeniality. He had always been friendly, his affection for old acquaintances genuine and unreserved. But even so, to be welcomed so personally by him—to be told by T. J. Hillyard that she was looking great—warmed Abbie. "You're looking great, too," she remarked. "I like the mustache."

He ran his fingers over the fringe of hair, as if to remind himself of what mustache she was referring to. Then he laughed. "I've had it a long time, Abbie. Which gives me an idea of how many years it's been since you've been home." He leaned halfway across the bar and ran his gaze over Abbie, assessing her low-heeled pumps, her well-toned calves, her skirt, short-sleeved sweater, unmade-up face and straight auburn hair. "I like your lack of a mustache," he quipped, flashing her another dimpled grin. "Seriously, Abbie, you look terrific. The big time must be treating you right."

"What big time?" she snorted, then took a sip of her beer.

"T.J.? I need two Wild Turkeys and a rum-Coke," the waitress hollered from the far end of the bar.

T.J. responded with a nod and turned back to Abbie. "Don't go anywhere," he murmured, patting her hand before he turned away and ambled down the bar.

She saw it then, his slightly lopsided gait, his tendency to lengthen his right step and abbreviate his left. She also noticed that his legs, like the rest of him, were leaner and lankier than they'd been during his playing days, and that his faded jeans fit him in a supremely attractive way. Talk about looking terrific...

Sure, he looked terrific. But instead of using those looks to hawk exercise equipment or motorcycles as a famous sports figure, he had wound up tending bar in Wheeler. Fate could be awfully nasty sometimes.

She still remembered the day it had happened, and the game. She couldn't imagine why the moment was permanently lodged in her memory; it had been T.J.'s tragedy, not hers. Of course, the entire community of Wheeler had embraced T.J.'s tragedy as its own, just as they'd embraced T.J. himself as their own blessed son.

Even though Abbie had said goodbye to Wheeler, she hadn't lost her admiration for T. J. Hillyard, the town's claim to fame. Attending U.C.-Berkeley, she hadn't followed sports at all. But, as if pursuing a dark secret, she had sneaked glimpses of the sports section of the Sunday newspaper to read up on how U.S.C. had played the previous day, and specifically, how T. J. Hillyard had played. Perhaps it was the vicarious thrill of seeing someone she knew celebrated in print that inspired her to keep tabs on his progress. Perhaps it was that his success provided some reassurance that a person born and bred in Wheeler could soar to greatness in the outside world. Or perhaps it was simply a matter of her taking pride, however undeserved, in the superlative achievements of an old acquaintance.

When Abbie finished college, she was accepted into law school. When T.J. finished college, he was drafted by the Chicago Bears. No matter how detached she felt from the village that had been her home for the first seventeen years of her life, she wasn't about to miss the broadcast of T.J.'s very first professional game.

The apartment she was sharing with two other law school students in downtown New Haven had been oppressively hot and stuffy that Sunday afternoon. One of her roommates had appropriated for her bedroom the lone window fan they owned, and the other had gone out to cool off in an air-conditioned movie theater. Abbie had opened the living room windows, fixed herself a glass of lemonade and settled on the secondhand sofa in front of the television. Panicked by the amount of work facing her, she had brought her Constitutional Law textbook to the couch with her, determined to get a head start on her class reading while she watched the game. In truth, she planned to watch little of it; she figured she could listen for T.J.'s name, and when the announcers mentioned him she'd pull her nose out of the textbook and pay attention to the play of her renowned hometown chum.

He participated in the Bears' first offensive series. "A good, clean reception by T. J. Hillyard, the rookie out of U.S.C.," one of the announcers said. "I've got to tell you, Chicago is really high on this kid. They're expecting big things from him."

"Well," the other announcer said, "this is his first pro game, and he's off to an impressive start." This comment was followed by a commercial, and Abbie—unjustifiably peeved that the announcers had failed to say anything about Wheeler—resumed memorizing case studies.

"It's a long pass, into the end zone, intended for Hillyard," one of the announcers said a while later, prompting Abbie to glance toward the screen again. She had never understood football too well, but what she saw didn't look like a good pass to her. She could barely spot T.J. surrounded by three gigantic players from the opposing team. "He threw into traffic there," the announcer criticized the quarterback as T.J. and the three other players converged on the ball. "It looks like there's a flag on the play."

"Pass interference," the other announcer conjectured.

"I think so. They really came together hard, didn't they? We've got a man down—it's Hillyard, the rookie from U.S.C. He must have gotten the wind knocked out of him."

Abbie wouldn't be surprised if he had—the four players had suffered a massive collision. She went to the kitchen to add some fresh ice cubes to her lemonade. When she returned, the television screen was filled with a picture of several men in civilian clothes huddled around a motionless player lying on the grass. One of the men was wriggling the helmet off the player's head, and Abbie immediately recognized T.J.'s profile through the thicket of legs.

"We don't know yet how badly hurt he is," an announcer said. "He's conscious, talking to the team doctor, moving his head, moving his arms." The camera pulled away to a wide shot of the field, with T.J.'s teammates milling around, looking worried. Then another commercial was broadcast. When the game returned, T.J. was being carted off the field on a stretcher.

Abbie's father mailed her clippings from the *Register*, full-page stories about how the left knee of Wheeler's golden boy had been shattered into a zillion pieces, about how the lower half of his leg had been twisted a sickening number of degrees out of alignment—gruesome stories about how the great T. J. Hillyard would never walk again.

And here he was, striding back down the length of the bar to Abbie and proving the medical world wrong. Fate might be nasty, but sometimes, if you fought it hard enough, it couldn't crush you.

"Now tell me, Abbie," T.J. said, resuming his position across the bar from her, resting his elbows on the polished oak and relaxing into his familiar good-natured grin. "How've you been? How's New York?"

"It's dirty and crowded," she answered dryly. "That's why I'm here."

"Is that the reason?" he asked, his smile waning slightly.

"Can you think of a better one?"

His gaze met hers. There was an incandescence in his dark, deep-set eyes that she'd never been aware of before, a mesmerizing radiance cutting through the shadow cast by his brow. She tried vainly to make sense of the question inherent in his expression, then gave up with a shrug.

T.J.'s smile returned. "As I understand it, the Big Apple's been dirty and crowded for ages, and this is the first time you've visited your father in—how many years has it been? Since your mom passed away."

"Who told you that?" Abbie asked, taken aback. She knew that her father occasionally patronized Tyler's, but she never would have guessed that he confided about his daughter to a bartender who'd been his daughter's classmate. "I spend every Christmas with my father," she defended herself.

"Down south at his sister's house someplace," T.J. pointed out.

"My Aunt Martha's house in Richmond," she said, hoping her surprise at T.J.'s familiarity with the Jarvis Christmas routine wasn't too obvious. "Meeting in the Bay Area is easier for me, and my dad and I both like San Francisco," Abbie explained, wondering why she felt the need to justify herself to T.J. Wondering why they were even having this conversation. He was an old friend, but not a particularly close one.

T.J. scrutinized her, evidently able to sense that she was annoyed by his subtle accusation. "Your dad's real proud of you," he commented, clearly hoping to mollify her. "He talks about you all the time, Abbie. He goes on and on about how hard you work, winning cases in court and putting all those thugs behind bars."

"Is that what he thinks I do?" Abbie chuckled pensively at her father's erroneous image of her job. Yes, she won cases in court, but more often than not the thugs she prosecuted wound up with a suspended sentence, six months' probation and a useless lecture from some harried judge reluctant to remand them to the already over-crowded prisons. "So," she concluded after taking a sip of beer, "now I know how my father spends his nights— hanging out in bars and bragging about his daughter."

"Not *bars*," T.J. corrected her. "*Bar*. Tyler's. He's in here maybe once a week for a beer or a shot, tells me about how wonderful you are—" T.J. winked before Abbie could protest "—and then heads for home."

"Nothing personal about your establishment, T.J., but he ought to go somewhere where he can meet women." Abbie glanced around at the distinctly unromantic atmosphere of the bar. "It's high time he got remarried."

"Who's he going to meet around here?" T.J. asked. "This is Wheeler. Everybody knows everybody."

"How's your wife?" Abbie inquired, unsure of how she'd made that mental leap, or why. A picture flashed across her mind of the gorgeous woman with the lush blond hair and big blue eyes who had accompanied T.J. to Abbie's mother's funeral. She hadn't been a local woman—as T.J. had just observed, it wasn't easy to meet the right woman in a town as small and self-contained as Wheeler. "Forgive me," Abbie added, "but I don't remember her name."

T.J. laughed. "Neither do I." At Abbie's shocked expression, he relented with a wistful smile. "Her name is Mary-Jane, and we're divorced."

"Oh, T.J., I'm sorry," Abbie said.

He shrugged off her concern. "We were already on the rocks when you saw us at your mom's funeral. As a matter of fact—" he drifted for a minute, reminiscing "—we started falling apart a long time before then."

"I'm sorry," Abbie said again. Since T.J. didn't seem too broken up about it, she adopted his light tone and teased, "So, who are you going to meet around here, T.J.? This is Wheeler. Everybody knows everybody."

He grinned mischievously. "You'd be surprised, Abbie. I don't know everybody yet...but I'm working on it."

"T.J.?" One of the cowboys at the other end of the bar called to him, then lifted his empty glass.

"Duty calls," T.J. whispered before abandoning Abbie to see to his customer.

Divorced, she contemplated, gazing after him. She supposed that even in a small town like Wheeler people got divorced—probably at the same rate they got divorced everywhere else. But that thought didn't console her. She felt genuinely sad for T.J., and empathetic. She might as well be divorced herself—having wasted close to four years of her life on Bob, she often felt as if ending their relationship had been a divorce of sorts. Such situations hurt, no matter how flippantly one treated them. Abbie knew exactly how badly they could hurt.

T.J. suddenly seemed to be in great demand by his customers and the waitress. He filled two mugs with draft beer, mixed something pink and frothy in a blender, splashed whisky into two highball glasses and then sprayed seltzer into them from a hose attached to the bar.

Abbie sipped her beer and watched him work. There was a fluidity about his movements, an almost balletic quality to the motions of his hands and arms as he reached for bottles and glasses, utensils and garnishes. His face remained animated, too, his dimples deepening as he smiled in response to a comment from one of the cowboys, his brow creasing in a slight frown as the waitress informed him he was running low on peanuts, his affable smile returning as he sold a pack of Marlboros to one of the pretty chain-smokers. The young woman whispered something to him as she handed him some money, and he tossed back his head with a loud laugh.

Abbie wondered whether women in Wheeler still got crushes on T.J. She wondered whether, unlike her widowed father, T.J. had females fawning on him and sighing over him. Her father swore he wasn't lonely—yet he'd chattered up a storm over dinner, as though he was starving for company.

Once again, Abbie found herself meditating about Faye Hinkel. Why hadn't her father considered romancing Faye? Herself a widow, she had been awfully good to Abbie's father after his loss. She'd visited him, brought him hot meals, taught him how the vacuum cleaner worked. She'd volunteered to help him out at the hardware store so he wouldn't have to hire someone to replace his wife. He'd hired Faye. "She's a fine woman," he'd explained to Abbie during their frequent telephone calls, "and I'm not going to have her working for free. I could use someone to help me keep the books, you know. Your mother was always the bookkeeper around here. I've never been good at making the numbers line up."

So what was going on? Why hadn't Faye been at the store?

"Did something happen to Faye Hinkel?" Abbie asked T.J. as soon as he returned to her.

"Faye?" he asked, apparently puzzled. "Not that I know of. Why do you ask?"

Abbie shook her head. It wasn't fair for her to expect to be apprised of every detail in her father's life when she had willfully distanced herself from Wheeler for so many years. It wasn't fair for her to demand to know the reasons for his business decisions, or the choices he made in his personal life. Just because Faye Hinkel had been kind to him in his bereavement didn't mean he had to date her. Just because he was innately terrible at bookkeeping didn't mean he had to maintain Faye on the payroll at the store.

And just because New York City had temporarily gotten the better of Abbie and she'd escaped to Wheeler for some desperately needed R and R, didn't mean anyone owed her any explanations.

"How long are you going to be in town?" T.J. was asking. Abbie forced her attention to him. As he spoke, he busied himself filling nut dishes with peanuts. He emptied the jar into one dish and laughed. "You know what this means, don't you?" he asked, tossing the empty jar into a garbage pail hidden behind the bar. "It means it's pretzel time at Tyler's."

"How come you named the bar after yourself?" Abbie asked him.

He lifted his gaze to hers. His mouth softened into a gentle smile. "How come you keep avoiding my questions, Abbie?"

"What questions?"

"Why you came to Wheeler, how long you're planning to stay..."

"I told you," she replied, a touch sharply, "I came to Wheeler to get away from New York. And I'll probably stay long enough to get sick of Wheeler, and then I'll go back to New York."

"Sounds like a great life," T.J. said with scarcely veiled sarcasm. "Here, Abbie, have some peanuts." He nudged a nut dish toward her.

She smiled apologetically. "I was getting frazzled there," she explained. "I needed some fresh air. Seriously, T.J., that's why I'm here. Okay?"

"They'll be burning the rice fields around here soon," he reminded her. "It isn't going to smell too fresh."

"It'll smell better than the I.R.T. at rush hour," she insisted.

"You didn't come back because of your father?" he probed.

"What do you mean?" she shot back, mildly alarmed. "Is something wrong with him?"

T.J. held her gaze for a second too long. Then he busied himself opening a bag of pretzels, his grin firmly in place. "No, nothing's wrong with him, Abbie. I'm asking... I'm asking only because I'm sure he likes having you back. Maybe you ought to stick around for a while."

"Maybe I will," she said, puzzling over T.J.'s mysterious attitude, trying unsuccessfully to make sense of it. She knew nothing was wrong with her father; if something was, he would never hide it from her. He had kept her informed when he'd been having trouble breathing a couple of years ago, and she'd gone so far as to purchase a plane ticket to Oakland—but then he'd called her with the news that Dr. Fellowes had diagnosed it as a stubborn side effect of the flu and was treating it with antibiotics. And when her mother had been lying in a coma after the accident, her father hadn't concealed anything. He'd told her there were head injuries, there was no hope, and she'd better come home.

She'd come.

If something was wrong now, he would have told Abbie. Even if they lived three thousand miles apart, they didn't keep secrets from each other. They might gussy up the truth a little, play up the good news and tone down the bad, but if something were really and truly wrong, they would tell each other. Abbie kept her father posted not only on the thugs she convicted but on the cases she lost. Last March she had called him the very day she'd ended her relationship with Bob. She had told him that she'd been wrong in thinking marriage was in the cards for her and Bob, that Bob had removed his spare toothbrush and razor from her bathroom, that she was once again free and single and was doing her best not to get into a funk about it.

She expected the same degree of honesty from her father.

"He's lonely," T.J. went on, evidently sensing that Abbie required more of an explanation. "I like your dad, Abbie. Anyone who comes into Tyler's on a weekly basis I get to know pretty well, and I've gotten to know your dad. I like him. And I know he's lonely."

"Who isn't?" she snapped. She didn't want T.J. laying a guilt trip on her. It wasn't her fault that her father hadn't remarried, any more than it was her fault that her mother had been blinded by the headlights of an oncoming pickup on a county road one night and had veered into a ditch and flipped her car. It *was* Abbie's fault that she'd wasted close to four years of her life waiting for Bob to grow up and make a commitment to her, but she didn't blame her father for that, or make him feel guilty for her loneliness.

T.J. measured her touchiness before responding to it. "All I said was, it's nice that you came home."

"I'm not here on a permanent basis," she reported crisply. "I've got an apartment in Manhattan, and my job is waiting for me whenever I want to return to New York."

"Lucky you," T.J. muttered, although his eyes were glinting with laughter. "Think of all those thugs waiting for you to come back and prosecute them when you get sick of Wheeler."

It occurred to Abbie that T.J. could have taken her comments the wrong way. When he'd come home to Wheeler, it hadn't been on a temporary basis. The Chicago Bears hadn't been about to hold his job open for him. They'd honored his contract, of course, and paid his salary and his medical bills, but when he'd come home to Wheeler he didn't have his next escape planned, as Abbie did.

"Don't you get sick of it?" she asked.

"Hey, Abbie, you're talking to a local businessman now," he boasted. "Civic booster and all that."

"Don't tell me you joined the Rotary Club."

T.J. chuckled and shook his head. "I've been invited, but so far I've been turning them down. I'm not sure I can stand being that establishment. But..." He noticed that her glass was nearly empty, and he poured out the remaining beer from her bottle and cleared it away.

"Wheeler doesn't bore me. I'm not eighteen years old anymore, Abbie, and the world looks a whole lot different to me now than it did then."

Abbie wasn't a teenager either, but she was sure Wheeler would start to bore her soon enough. Where was the theater here, the array of movie theaters like those in Manhattan? What museums were there to go to? What could one do to hear good jazz or classical music on a regular basis? Where could one go to find the exciting variety of people, the heterogeneity, the clashes of ethnicity and culture...and the good restaurants?

T.J. may have made his peace with Wheeler, but Abbie couldn't imagine resettling here. A week, sure, maybe two—just enough time to regain her bearings, to grow restless and start yearning for the charged atmosphere and hectic pace of the city, to cleanse Bob from her system once and for all and gird herself for a return to the brutal social scene in New York—and then she'd kiss her father goodbye and take off again.

That was the plan. She would stay in Wheeler only long enough to grow sick of the tedium, sick of watching the farmhands cruise up and down Main Street in their pickups, sick of baking in the arid heat that gripped the town until nearly Christmas, sick of gazing out over the flat rice fields with their grid of soggy brown irrigation ditches. She would stay until she remembered every reason she'd had for leaving—by which time, ideally, she would have forgotten every reason she'd had for leaving New York.

And then she'd be gone.

Chapter Two

She didn't know.

T.J. loped down the bar to the cash register to ring up a bill. It was a calm night in the bar, a warm night outside—conditions that treated him kindly. Chilly weather—the raw February rains and late summer thunderstorms—caused his knee to stiffen up. So, as a rule, did Friday and Saturday nights, when Tyler's drew huge crowds and even three barmaids were scarcely enough to keep the customers' glasses filled. But tonight things were going smoothly. The customers were mellow and Lina wasn't having any trouble taking care of them. All of which gave T.J. the freedom to shoot the breeze with Abbie Jarvis.

He'd told her she was looking great and he'd meant it. Women in Wheeler had a tendency to wear too much makeup, a practice that had taken on a personal relevance to T.J. ever since he and Mary-Jane had split up. But Abbie, the city slicker, the big-town sophisticate, looked as dewy-eyed and freshly scrubbed as a kindergartner on the first day of school. Her evenly filed fingernails were unpolished, her eyelids unadorned by strange colors of eye shadow and her lashes only as dense and dark as nature had intended them to be. Her shoulder-length auburn hair was straight and shiny, with a slight fringe of bangs dropping across her brow. The healthy pink color in her cheeks wasn't a result of cosmetics.

That delicate flush had faded fast enough when he'd hinted about her old man's troubles. Her face had gone white, her hazel eyes had grown round—she'd looked genuinely panicked. T.J. hadn't done much to assuage her panic, either. He'd always been a lousy liar.

He supposed she would learn about the situation at Jarvis's Hardware sooner or later. But she wasn't going to learn about it from T.J. She would have to hear it from Roy Jarvis himself. Roy didn't seem to have too much difficulty talking to T.J. about it every week, over a shot or two of Jim Beam. If he could tell T.J., he could sure as hell tell his own daughter.

After shoving the cash drawer shut, T.J. sauntered back down the bar to Abbie. It was more than her being an old schoolmate of his that made him want to spend with her what spare time he had that evening, and more than the fact that he already knew most of the single women in town. It was more, even, than the pleasant shock of discovering that Abbie had aged into a remarkably good-looking woman. If she'd been such a knockout in high school, T.J. hadn't been aware of it.

He remembered her as being kind of skinny back then, intense and tenacious and inner-directed. She'd been too smart in school to be thought of as pretty. In their senior-year social studies class, he recalled, she'd been the only student willing to shoot her mouth off at the teacher when he had asserted that the Vietnam War was a good thing. She'd stood up and lectured Mr. Daniels for ten minutes about civil war and self-determination while the rest of the class snickered or snored or penned doodles in the mar-

gins of their loose-leaf paper. T.J. remembered being
awed by her knowledge, even more awed by her guts, and
all in all amused that she thought their pompous, slightly
addled teacher was worth expending that much breath on.

But he didn't remember being conscious of her beauty.

He tried to visualize her in New York City, dressed in
high-fashion apparel, turning heads with her shapely legs
and slender figure, her clear gray-green eyes and honeyed
complexion. He had never been to New York himself, but
he'd seen enough movies to be able to picture the place—
and to imagine Abbie Jarvis in the heart of it, surrounded by glass skyscrapers and flashing neon signs,
taxis and limos and hordes of rich, debonair men willing
to lie down and die for a glimpse of her lovely smile.

New York City. That was why he wanted to talk to her.
She was a Wheeler escapee, currently living in the great
big world. He, too, had escaped, but it hadn't worked out
and he'd come back. She had escaped and survived—even
triumphed, if Roy was to be believed. She was a visitor
from Out There, and T.J. was eager for firsthand news of
the universe beyond Wheeler's confining borders.

"Is it really that bad?" he asked once he reached her.

She had just scooped a couple of peanuts out of the
dish he'd left for her, but she froze before popping them
into her mouth. "Is *what* really that bad?"

"New York. It really smells worse than when they burn
the rice fields?"

Abbie laughed. Her voice had a sultry throatiness that
seemed to contradict her clean-cut beauty. T.J. remembered that she'd had a slightly raspy voice in school, too,
especially during those lengthy diatribes on justice and the
Bill of Rights, directed at Mr. Daniels and the social
studies class. T.J. hadn't considered her voice particularly sexy back then; like most teenage boys, he had

generally judged a girl's sex appeal by the dimensions of her chest and nothing more. But his tastes had become refined with age, and he honestly believed that if the circumstances were right, listening to Abbie recite a monologue about First Amendment guarantees in that innately husky voice of hers could be a real turn-on.

"The subways do. Imagine, if you will, a combination of axle grease, reefer smoke, urine and stale sweat," she described the odor. "Not that it matters much. These days, no sane woman takes the subway if she can help it."

"Is it really that unsafe?" he pressed her. He'd read news reports about big-city crime, and he'd followed with fascination the case of that guy who had shot four black youths who asked him for money on a New York subway train. But still, T.J. had to believe that the media sensationalized those stories somewhat. He himself had lived in Los Angeles for four years, and in Chicago for almost two months before the game that ended it all, and he'd never felt the least bit anxious about going out at night.

Abbie plucked another peanut from the dish and rolled it around in her palm. "If you're a woman and you weigh a hundred and twenty pounds, yes, T.J., it's that unsafe. I considered taking a course in self-defense, but I decided not to. I resented the idea that I should have to live my life like a paranoiac because the crazies have taken over the streets."

"I thought we were talking about the subways."

Abbie shrugged. "Them, too."

T.J. conceded with a nod. When he'd lived in Los Angeles and Chicago, it had been easy for him to be fearless. Muggers weren't apt to attack a wide receiver who stood six foot two, weighed two hundred ten pounds and ran a four-nine mile. And by the time those statistics were no longer applicable, once he'd become a semiinvalid weighing substantially less and taking ten minutes to walk ten feet, he had returned to Wheeler, where street crime generally meant nothing more serious than high school kids getting drunk and spray-painting their names on to the sidewalk, and where nobody would take advantage of a cripple—especially not a cripple like T. J. Hillyard, the onetime town celebrity.

"It can't be that bad," he argued, grinning. "You've lived there for how many years, and you're here to tell about it."

She smiled grimly. "Call me lucky," she said. "When it was my turn to get mugged, all the guy wanted was my money and my watch. He let me keep my credit cards and my driver's license, and after he waved his gun around a few times to impress me, he put it away."

"Oh, God." T.J. was affronted that anyone—especially an old acquaintance of his—should have had to endure a mugging, no matter how "lucky" she might feel about it. "Too bad you didn't get to prosecute him."

Abbie's laughter this time was genuine. "My office doesn't even waste time with muggers," she remarked. "We only try the really interesting cases—rapes, murders... I personally handled the case of the Bryant Park flasher-slasher—"

"What?"

"He'd open his fly, and instead of pulling out what you'd expect he would pull out a knife. Obviously, he had the element of surprise on his side."

"And you had the law on yours," T.J. remarked.

"Right." Abbie scowled. "We got a conviction, but Ossining was full to overflowing, so the flasher-slasher was sentenced to six months at a mental hospital."

"Maybe that's where he belongs."

"That's where they *all* belong," Abbie agreed sadly. "They're all nuts. One of my more recent cases..." She sighed and took a sip of beer, eyeing T.J. over the rim of her glass. "You don't really want to hear this," she guessed as she set the glass back on the bar.

"Sure I do."

"The woman was trying to sell her child—her own flesh and blood—for five hundred dollars. But that wasn't the worst part of it. The worst part was, she'd already been through the system once. We had been planning to charge her with child abandonment. But then Jaime—a social worker and a good friend of mine, I'm sorry to say— talked me into dropping the charge. Time passes, and the woman gets nabbed for child selling, and what does she say to me? 'At least I understand what my baby is worth now.' Can you believe it?"

T.J. grinned in spite of himself. "Did you get a conviction on that case?"

"I passed it along to an associate," Abbie told him. "I didn't want to deal with it. I didn't want to deal with any of it—so I've taken some time off, and here I am."

T.J. studied her thoughtfully. He recognized burnout when he saw it, and Abbie was obviously suffering from an extreme case. "There must be nice things about New York, too," he said, partly to salvage her mood and partly because he wanted to cling to his image of Abbie living a glamorous high-powered life in the big city.

Abbie lifted her glass and chuckled. "Sure. One of the nicest things about New York is that there's plane service out of there."

"Which is more than you can say for Wheeler," T.J. commented as Abbie drained her glass. "Can I get you another beer?"

"No, thanks," Abbie declined, lifting a stylish hand-bag of navy-blue leather from her lap and pulling out her wallet.

"It's on the house," T.J. insisted, closing his fingers around her wrist before she could unsnap the wallet. Her wrist was narrow; it felt almost fragile against the broad, slightly calloused surface of his palm. For a brief, irra-tional moment he didn't want to let go of her.

He did, of course. As soon as she raised her eyes to his and smiled, he let his hand fall away. "Thank you, T.J.," she said.

Her appreciation seemed to extend beyond the simple statement. It glittered in her multicolored irises, it shone in the deepening color of her cheeks, it expressed itself in the generous fullness of her smile. "My pleasure," he mumbled, inexplicably embarrassed by her unspoken gratitude.

"You still haven't told me why you named the bar af-ter yourself," she reminded him, tucking her wallet back into her purse.

"What was I supposed to call it?" He shrugged. "Not too many people around here even know my name is Ty-ler, anyway. I'm surprised you do." Even in school, the teachers used to call him T.J. The only person who regu-larly called him Tyler was his grandmother—because he'd been named after her husband.

Abbie grinned. "I have a bad habit of remembering all sorts of useless information. What is it, Tyler John?"

"Tyler James," he corrected her as he cleared away her empty glass and sponged off the ring of moisture it had left on the bar. "I guess I named the place Tyler's as an inside joke—for you and the six other people in the world who know what the *T* stands for."

"You didn't want to keep calling it Mike's Place?"

"Hell, no," he answered spiritedly. "It was such a dive when I bought it—dirty and falling apart, infamous as a hangout for bikers and punks. I had to change the name. And—" he set the sponge aside and shrugged again "—I've got enough of an ego to figure that if I was going to buy the place and fix it up and run it, I might as well go the distance and name it after myself."

"I never would have figured you for an entrepreneur, T.J.," Abbie said, her smile becoming tenuous. He could reasonably guess what she was thinking: that he hadn't fulfilled his destiny, that he'd wound up far differently than anyone could have predicted. He only hoped Abbie didn't see that as something negative. It was a fact, after all, nothing he could alter.

She unhooked her feet from the lower rung of the stool and stood. The realization that she was about to leave saddened him, but he forced his grin wider in compensation. "How long are you planning to be in town?" he asked her.

"I suppose I'll stay until it's time to leave," she answered cryptically. "Good seeing you, T.J. And thanks again for the beer."

His gaze remained on her as she pivoted on the heel of her shoe and strolled out of the bar. One part of his mind focused on her hips—trim, sleek-looking hips that earned an appreciative smile from him—while another part of his mind remained on thoughts of her visit to Wheeler, and of her vagueness about when the visit would end. Would she be able to leave once she found out about her father's situation? Would she want to?

It was a question of loyalty, not to Wheeler but to her father. T.J. wondered how loyal she actually was. He wondered whether she would choose to stick around and offer her father the moral support he was going to need, or run back to New York and put as many miles between herself and her father's problems as she could.

T.J. hoped she would stay. Roy Jarvis would never ask her to, but T.J. knew Roy would want her with him throughout the ordeal he was bound to face.

Roy would want her around—and so would T.J., for a very different reason. Damn, but she'd turned into one fine-looking lady.

THE FLATNESS TOOK SOME getting used to. Drive a few miles east and you'd find yourself in the foothills of the Sierra, on hairpin-twisting roads that cut through the rocky buttes and swept on up into the pine- and red-wood-forested mountains. But Wheeler was centered within the Sacramento River Valley, and it was monotonously flat. Abbie recalled thinking as a child that Wheeler was the best place in the world for riding a bicycle. Two or three pumps on the pedals and you'd coast forever.

She steered her father's van slowly down Palmer Street, scanning the well-maintained modest houses that lined the road and experiencing twinges of déjà vu. Peggy Robinson had lived there, she recalled as she cruised past a driveway framed by two elm trees. And Mrs. Rapple had lived in the old blue house—you would never trick-or-treat at her house because she was reputed to be a witch—and the home ec teacher, whatever her name was, lived over there. Abbie's worst subject in high school had been home economics.

Faye Hinkel lived in a small bungalow-style house a few blocks farther down on Palmer, if she hadn't moved. Abbie knew it was safe to assume she hadn't. People didn't often change addresses in Wheeler—and if for some reason Faye had moved, T.J. probably would have mentioned it to Abbie when she'd asked him about Faye last night. Her more realistic concern was whether the woman would be home when Abbie rang the doorbell. She was anxious to talk to someone who might be able to provide her with a lucid explanation for what was going on at Jarvis's Hardware. In fact, Abbie was so anxious she hadn't bothered to call Faye in advance.

She had finally gotten into the back office at the store that morning. Her father had gone out for brunch with a salesman, and she had meandered up and down the aisles, pretending to be fascinated by the racks of tools and garden supplies and carpentry doodads while surreptitiously making sure that Joe Dunbar and Stan DeCinto were too occupied to notice her. Then she had slipped behind the counter, filched the key to the back office from the drawer beneath the cash register, and let herself in.

It was a small, windowless room, crammed with several file cabinets and an old metal desk. When Abbie's mother had been alive, this office had been her bailiwick. She had been a whiz at bookkeeping, and she'd kept the store's financial records in impeccable order. Monthly bills, long-term loans and customer credit lines had all been recorded precisely. Accounts Payable and Accounts Receivable had been entered in a daily log and totaled one against the other, so the store had an accurate tally of its bottom line at the end of every day. Abbie's mother had even preserved the tapes from the adding machine so she could double-check her entries.

That Jarvis's Hardware still relied on an antediluvian adding machine instead of having updated its bookkeeping system with a microchip calculator was all the proof Abbie needed that something was out of whack. But the adding machine was the least of her worries as she entered the room and switched on the light. What she discovered in the back office were not the neatly arranged files of bills, monthly outlays and inventory lists she had expected, but rather a few open boxes filled with loose paper, a dozen dog-eared file folders leaking more paper across the desk, a stack of computer printout letters from the I.R.S., and several letters from the bank thumb-tacked to the bulletin board above the desk.

The state of the office was worse than merely a mess. It was a mess implying that the store's finances were in serious disarray.

Abbie felt a bit uncomfortable about snooping through her father's papers. But as an assistant district attorney, she frequently had to do sleuthing, sorting through evidence to build a case. If there was a problem with the store, Abbie owed it to her father—and herself—to find out what it was.

She leaned over the desk and read the first bank letter:

Dear Mr. Jarvis:
Third Notice. Payments on Loan #37450 are presently three months in arrears...

She turned to the second bank letter:

Dear Mr. Jarvis:
I invite you to come in and discuss with me the refinancing of Loan #37450 in order to avoid having the bank take legal steps...

Wincing, she lowered her gaze to the top I.R.S. computerized letter on the desk.

Dear Mr. Jarvis:
Regarding Schedule C payments on small-business

income for Tax Years 1986, 1985, 1984: Our calculations indicate an underpayment for all three years as follows . . .

She cursed. Flipping through some of the scattered papers, skimming the dunning letters from suppliers, the phone company and Pacific Gas and Electric, she cursed again. And then Joe Dunbar called in through the open doorway, "Abbie? I don't know that your dad wants you in here."

"Joe," she said hastily, spinning around and presenting him with a sheepish smile. Given how long he'd been with the store, she knew him well enough to comprehend the fear hardening his usually benign gray eyes, the tension tugging at the corners of his mouth. She understood at once that there was no point in fabricating a lie to explain her presence in the back office. "What's going on here, Joe? Why is this place in such a state?"

"Don't ask," he said, rubbing his fingers nervously over the bald spot at the crown of his head and then shoving his hands into the deep pockets of his striped denim overalls.

"Too late. I already did."

"Ask your dad."

"He's having brunch with a salesman," she pointed out, not bothering to add that if her father had felt comfortable discussing the problem—whatever it was—with her, he would have mentioned something about it already. Over dinner last night and a cup of coffee this morning, he had talked animatedly about local politics, the births of his friends' grandchildren, the drought conditions that continued to plague the Sacramento Valley. He'd had plenty of opportunity to tell her about the chaos in the back office—if he'd wanted to. Obviously, he didn't.

She met Joe's beseeching gaze, and they scrutinized each other in silence for a moment. "Has he gone to the bank to discuss refinancing?" she asked.

"A couple times."

"And?"

"And he comes back smiling, says he thinks they worked it out . . . and then he gets another letter."

Abbie closed her eyes. She adored her father, and she respected his expertise regarding the merchandise he sold. He knew everything there was to know about hardware. Blindfolded, he could identify the size, weight and composition of a nail placed in the palm of his hand. He was thoroughly versed in the strengths and weaknesses of each wrench he stocked, each screwdriver, each cotter pin and brand of glue. Roy Jarvis knew the goods in which he dealt; he would spend hours explaining to a customer how a certain tool was used, how a certain putty was applied, and he would never sell the customer a product the customer didn't need.

But when it came to keeping accounts, he was totally inept.

"I'm not sure I understand," Abbie said cautiously. "The store's been in existence for half a century. I could accept misplacing a few zeros here and there, Joe, but . . . why can't he make his loan payments?"

Joe shrugged. "It's none of my business, Abbie."

"It *is* your business," she retorted. "If the store goes under, you're going to be out of a job."

"Don't think I don't know it," he muttered. She could see his fingers fisting in his pockets. "Rent's been doubled, I can tell you that much."

"Doubled? Why?"

"I'm not sure. I guess the landlord thinks he can get it. Rumor has it one of the chains wants to open an outlet around here—Ace or Tru-Value or one of those. So the landlord gave your father a two-year lease last time, and he doubled the rent."

Abbie clamped her jaws shut to keep herself from indulging in any more swearing. She could curse in private, but not in front of a mild-mannered man like Joe Dunbar, who had known her since she was a toddler. "All right," she said, crossing briskly to the door. "I'll talk to my dad. Thanks, Joe." She handed him the key to the office and hurried outside, resolved that she would pay Faye Hinkel a call. Faye had kept the store's books for a while; she might be able to enlighten Abbie about the situation.

Driving was an activity she rarely performed in Manhattan, and driving her father's van, which he'd insisted that she use while she was in town, felt stranger yet. The vehicle was wider than most cars, the seat high above the road, and she was keenly aware of the bright green letters painted across the white sides of the van: Jarvis's Hardware—Working For Wheeler. Fifty Years of Know-how. Not exactly sparkling with memorable wit, but Abbie's father wasn't about to hire the talents of Madison Avenue to come up with a new slogan for his store. Even if he wanted to, he couldn't afford it.

She spotted Faye's familiar-looking bungalow and pulled to the unpaved edge of the road. Noticing the tricycle parked on the front walk, Abbie hesitated. Then she drew in her breath and marched up the walk, figuring that if a young family had bought the house from Faye, they might know where she had moved. She climbed the step to the veranda and tapped on the screen door.

"Coming," a woman's voice emerged through the screen from the shadowy interior of the house. Within a minute, Faye appeared on the other side of the door. "Abbie Jarvis?" she shrieked. "My word—is that you?"

"It's me, all right," Abbie said, examining the sturdy-looking middle-aged woman on the other side of the screen. "How are you, Faye?"

"I'm fine, just fine! Look at you, Abbie! You look fabulous! Come on in—and watch your step, honey. There's toys everywhere."

"Whose baby?" Abbie asked, glancing over her shoulder at the tricycle in the front yard before she entered the house.

"Sherry Alcott's. Sherry Mullin before she got married. I don't know if you remember her—she was a few years behind you in school. She just got a job doing data processing up at the state university in Chico, and I'm doing child-care for her. It's a living, you know?"

Child care. Abbie vaguely remembered Sherry Mullin. Mostly, what she remembered—what she didn't need to remember—was that Sherry was younger than Abbie. And she had a child. Abbie would probably never have a child; time and biology were working against her. Simply seeing the clutter of playthings strewn across Faye's living room floor caused a deep sadness to well up inside Abbie.

Doing her best to ignore it, she followed Faye to the kitchen, where a freckle-faced little boy was seated at the table, munching on a banana. "Daniel Alcott, Abigail Jarvis," Faye introduced them with comical formality. The little boy greeted Abbie by jamming the banana into his clenched teeth and mushing it over his lips.

Abbie tried not to laugh; it might encourage him. "Faye," she said, turning away, "can we talk for a minute?"

"Longer than that, if you'd like," Faye said generously. "How about something to drink?"

"No, thanks. I see you've got your hands full right now." An ominous noise caused Abbie to turn in time to see Daniel hurling chunks of banana across the table, and she welcomed the sight as evidence that perhaps children weren't so wonderful. "But I've been curious about why you're no longer keeping my father's books at the store. I know he hired you after my mother died. What happened, Faye? Do you know what's going on there?"

Faye's eyes narrowed slightly. "What has he told you?"

"Nothing," Abbie admitted. "Which makes me think he *can't* talk to me about it. And all I got from Joe Dunbar was that the landlord doubled the rent on their most recent lease."

"He did?" Faye snorted. "The bastard. Well, I hate to say it, but that may be the straw that breaks it, Abbie. Jarvis's Hardware has been having its troubles for a long time now."

For some reason, Abbie wasn't shocked. Faye's revelation upset her, but after viewing the havoc in the back office, she couldn't say it took her by surprise.

"Can you tell me anything about it?" she asked with impressive poise. She had always believed that there was no point in becoming hysterical, at least not until you had solid grounds.

Faye crossed to the sink to get a sponge. "It might take longer than a minute," she warned, returning to the table and wiping the smears of banana from its Formica top.

"Would you rather I come back when you aren't busy?" Abbie offered.

"I'm always busy," Faye said with a chuckle. She carried Daniel to the sink and rinsed off his gooey fingers, then set him down on his feet. He hurtled through the living room to the front door and outside to his tricycle. "Come on," Faye invited Abbie, chasing after Daniel.

Abbie settled on the veranda step beside Faye, from where they could watch Faye's young charge as he pedaled his trike up and down the front walk. "When did things start going bad at the store?" Abbie asked.

"I regret to say it was while I was working there," Faye admitted, coiling her index finger through a cropped lock of blond hair and keeping her gaze fixed on Daniel. "Your mother used to advise your father on things—you know, like how much stock to order, when to pay the bills, when to revise the budget and all. He'd listen to her, Abbie, but . . . he wouldn't listen to me, not the same way."

Abbie recognized that Faye's discontent over that fact extended beyond her simply wanting to help Roy in his business. Roy had listened to his wife because he'd loved her. No matter how fond he was of Faye, he didn't love her as he'd loved his wife.

"Then a couple of farms started having difficulties," Faye continued. "You know how it's been—not as bad as the Midwest, but the smaller farms are facing some hardships these days. I told Roy he'd have to do something about all the credit he'd extended to those folks, and he said, 'What can I do? They're my neighbors.' Lots of people started owing him lots of money, and he just didn't have the heart to make them pay their bills. He said it would force them over the brink. Now he's facing the brink himself."

"Why did he fire you?" Abbie asked.

"He didn't. I quit," Faye informed her, keeping her gaze riveted to Daniel so she wouldn't have to look at

Abbie. The older woman's profile was stern, her eyelids lowered against the midday sun. "He couldn't afford my salary," she went on, "and I asked him to let me work part-time for free. He wouldn't hear of it. The only way I could keep him from paying me was to stop working for him." Faye sighed. "He's a good man, your father. I like him, Abbie, I...I like him," she concluded, disguising with her bland words what was obvious in her poignant smile: she was smitten with Abbie's father. "I hate to see his store go under, but the man hasn't got any sense when it comes to finances."

"I know, Faye," Abbie confirmed.

Daniel cut too tight a turn, and his tricycle flipped onto its side on the grass. The little boy let out a howl. Faye sprang from the veranda and dashed to his side, Abbie at her heels. They pulled Daniel off the tricycle, inspected him for damage, found none and wiped his tears. Faye gave him a big hug, which he returned, wrapping his small arms around her hips. "I can't say this job is easier than working for your father," she remarked once she'd gotten Daniel back on the seat of the upright tricycle, "but at least I'm appreciated."

"I'm sure my father appreciated you, too," Abbie insisted.

Faye exchanged a meaningful look with her. They both knew that that was exactly what was wrong about Faye's relationship with Abbie's father: she yearned for his love, and what she got was his appreciation.

Faye wasn't tearful as Daniel had been, and a hug wouldn't mend her as easily as it had mended the frantic little boy. But Abbie hugged her, anyway.

MAYBE IF HE JOGGED in the early morning, when the air hadn't already been roasted for hours by the hot valley sun, T.J. might do better than a nine-minute mile. But given how late at night he had to stay up running Tyler's, there was no way he was going to haul himself out of bed at the crack of dawn just to jog. Besides, he wasn't out to set any records. All that mattered was covering a few miles, strengthening the muscles that surrounded his bum knee and keeping the joint loose.

The disadvantage of jogging in the midafternoon was the heat, and its adverse effect on his speed. The advantage was that he didn't have to deal with other joggers. He didn't have to smile and wave at anyone ten or twenty years his senior, sporting a potbelly and jiggly thighs, who sped past him without any effort. Objectively, T.J. was proud of himself for having recovered as much as he had, but subjectively...subjectively, he still remembered what it had been like to have a body that responded like a fine-tuned engine, that did what he demanded of it and then some. Jogging—if that was the right term for the uneven glorified limp T.J. managed—had a way of reminding him of his limitations.

But at least when he went out for his exercise in the middle of the afternoon, he had the dirt path running alongside the railroad track to himself. Nobody—other than the engineer of the freight train that lumbered through Wheeler every day at around two-thirty—saw T.J. Nobody had to view his braced knee and his pained expression as he pushed himself along the path; nobody had to pity him.

It was nearly two-thirty now, and he heard the rumble of the train chugging south out of Red Bluff, a huge engine puffing as hard as T.J. and dragging numerous boxcars and flatcars behind it. Several different engineers ran the route; today it was the cigar-chomping fellow with the red beard. He waved his unlit cigar at T.J. through the open window, then creaked the slow-moving engine past him. T.J. blinked the sweat out of his eyes, waved back, and distracted himself from his fatigue by counting the cars.

He stopped counting somewhere after the twenty-fifth car, shoved his perspiration-soaked hair off his brow, and lowered his eyes to the hard-packed soil of the gully paralleling the tracks. He watched the extension of one foot in front of him and then the other, the imprint his jogging shoes left in the dust, the clenching and stretching of the muscles in his thighs. He thought about the delay in the shipment of cocktail peanuts he was expecting for the bar. He thought about whether he should tell Meagan to tone down her flirtatiousness with the customers. Maybe it led to bigger tips, but T.J. didn't like his waitresses coming on to his customers, no matter how playfully they went about it.

He thought about Abbie. He thought about the mugging incident she'd described so matter-of-factly to him, and about the strange legal cases she had to contend with . . . and about her eyes, bright and clear even in the subdued light of Tyler's, and about her thick, dark lashes, and her delicate cheekbones. Friday was Roy's usual night to drop by Tyler's for a drink; T.J. wondered whether Abbie would accompany her father tonight. If not, T.J. wondered when he would see her again.

Glancing up, he spotted the caboose coming slowly around the curve of the track, rolling closer to him. Just for the hell of it, he set himself the challenge of reaching the ancient oak tree a few hundred feet up ahead of him before the caboose reached it from the other direction. T.J. accelerated his pace, immediately feeling the strain in the tendons of his left leg.

Gasping and grimacing, he beat the caboose by a few seconds. He slapped his hand against the trunk, as if to prove to himself that he'd succeeded in his modest goal, and watched the caboose rattle past him, heading south. Then he drew in a wheezy breath, pushed away from the tree, and stumbled over a pair of outstretched legs.

If he hadn't been so worried about remaining upright, he would have recognized right away that they were a woman's legs—a very attractive pair of long, smoothly shaven woman's legs. But his primary objective was to prevent himself from falling; a fall might twist his knee and lay him up for weeks. He grabbed on to one of the low-hanging limbs of the tree and used it to regain his balance. Once he was certain that his bad leg wouldn't collapse under him, he turned to discover Abbie Jarvis rising to her feet on the shady side of the tree.

Her eyes were downcast as she wiped from her shins the layer of loose dirt T.J. had kicked up onto her. "Sorry," she mumbled, straightening up and smacking the dust from her rear end. Then she raised her face to T.J.'s and her mouth fell open. "T.J.? What on earth are you doing here?"

"What do you mean, what on earth am I doing here? This happens to be the part of the earth I live on," he said, grinning. He ordinarily didn't like encountering other joggers—but there wasn't anything ordinary about encountering Abbie. She was wearing a pair of loose-fitting cotton shorts, a baggy sweatshirt with the sleeves cut off, and a terry cloth headband. She looked sweaty and dirty and tired. And fantastic. "Don't tell me you're another maniac who likes running when the temperature hits three-digits Fahrenheit," he joked.

"I don't," she informed him, wiping her hands off on the edge of her sweatshirt. "That's why I was sitting in the shade and trying to catch my breath. It's ghastly out here."

"Then why are you jogging now?"

"Because I..." Her voice drifted off as she studied him, shifting her gaze from his glistening face to the broad, bony shoulders protruding from the large armholes of his tank top, lowering her eyes further to his chest, the lean contours of which were revealed by the damp, clinging fabric of his shirt, to the waistband of his shorts, to his hips. He realized that she was ogling him, and he didn't mind it in the least—until she latched on to the wide elastic brace wrapped around his knee. She opened her mouth to speak.

"Don't say it," he cut her off.

She jerked her head up, and her gaze latched on to his. "Don't say what?"

"How it's too bad, what happened to my leg."

"I wasn't going to say that."

He should have been skeptical, but she sounded so earnest he believed her. "What were you going to say?" he asked.

"That I think you're pretty amazing."

"Don't say that, either," he retorted, conscious that he sounded belligerent yet unable to stop himself. He'd had over a dozen years of dealing with the sort of attitude he detected in Abbie now, and he couldn't stand it, especially coming from her. "I'm not out here because I want to be amazing, Abbie. I hate jogging. But it keeps me mobile and builds strength. I do it because if I don't I'll wind up in a wheelchair. All right?"

She sized him up with an unreadable stare. "You're even more defensive than you are amazing," she observed. "Learn how to take a compliment, T.J."

He accepted her criticism with a small, reluctant nod. "Sure. Thanks for the compliment," he said gruffly, wishing he could stifle his irritability. Maybe in time, in another dozen years or so, none of it would bother him. Maybe by then nobody would remember that he was once a fantastic athlete. They'd see him simply as a middle-aged guy with a web of scars crisscrossing his knee, and they'd figure he'd hurt himself falling off a ladder or taking an unfortunate spill on a ski slope, not reaching for the sun and coming up short. "So what are you doing out here, running in this heat?" he asked in a low, ameliorating tone.

Abbie continued to stare up at him. She was at least half a foot shorter than he, and she had to crane her neck to see him. Sunlight slammed into her face, causing her to squint, lifting the red highlights from the depths of her auburn hair and making her skin shimmer with beads of sweat. "I don't know," she confessed. "Next time, I'll jog at night."

He didn't believe her. Abbie wasn't the sort of woman who did things for no good reason. "Do you jog during the day at home?"

"In New York, you mean?" She raised her hand to shield her eyes from the sun's glare. "No. I work during the day. I jog in the evenings, on a track at a health club."

"Yeah?" His gaze traveled down her trim, well-toned body. He liked what he saw, but he thought she'd be put off if he said so, so he kept his opinion to himself. "I'm having trouble taking you for a jogger, Abbie. You weren't much of a jock in high school."

"I didn't have to cope with so much pressure in high school," she pointed out.

He hadn't expected her to reveal anything so personal about herself. She evidently hadn't expected to reveal it, either. She looked suddenly abashed, and she turned to study the oak tree, running her fingertips nervously over its peeling bark.

He longed to reassure her. He longed to swear that her secret—whatever it was—was safe with him, that he wouldn't compound the pressure she was under by prying into her private affairs. He longed to tell her that it was all right, everything was all right and she could jog whenever she wanted to, without answering to him or anyone else.

All of which wouldn't be nearly as reassuring as leaving her alone, he concluded. "Well..." he murmured. "I guess I ought to do the rest of my run before I stiffen up."

"Are you fast?" she asked, shooting him a brief glance.

"Fast?" He laughed caustically. "Compared to what?"

"Compared to me. I'm really slow, T.J., but I've got to get back to my dad's van, and it's about two miles south, down by First Street."

If she were anybody else, he'd refuse the company. He'd claim that he still had another mile north to go before he made his U-turn and headed back to civilization. But to abandon Abbie Jarvis would be crazy, and T.J. wasn't crazy. "I'm probably slower than you," he said, "but I'll do my best to keep up."

She flashed him a hesitant smile, then pushed away from the tree and joined him on the dirt path. They adopted a leisurely tempo. T.J.'s legs were longer than Abbie's, and she took three steps to his every two, but her pace was just about right for him.

Neither of them spoke for a while. T.J. resisted the temptation to keep his eyes fixed on the slender woman beside him, but he permitted himself occasional glimpses of her. She kept her face forward, displaying her small, straight nose and determined chin in profile, and she held

her fingers curled into her palms as she pumped her arms.
He tried to picture the torso hidden beneath the nubby
fabric of her sweatshirt. No jiggly thighs or potbelly here,
he mused. Whatever pressures drove her to jog, the re-
sults were fine with him.

"You know, don't you," she said abruptly.

He peered down at her. For the first time since they'd
started their side-by-side run, she was looking directly at
him. Her cheeks shone and her eyebrows seemed to spar-
kle from the drops of sweat trapped in them. Her lips were
quirked into a bittersweet smile.

"I know what?" he asked, unable to decipher the
question in her eyes.

"About the fact that my father's store is on the verge
of bankruptcy."

"Oh." He let out a long breath and took the space of a
few strides to formulate his response. "I . . . uh . . . I know
he's having some problems," he said discreetly.

"How did you find out?" she asked.

"He . . ." T.J. paused, searching her face. Her smile was
more bitter than bittersweet, he noticed, and the question in her bright eyes was almost an accusation. Yet T.J.
couldn't lie to her. "He told me."

"Great," she muttered, looking away. "He didn't tell
me, but he told you."

"I'm a bartender," T.J. reminded her. "People tell me
things. I hear more confessions than a priest, Abbie."

"Of course. He can tell a bartender things he won't
even tell his own daughter, the person closest to him in the
whole wide world."

"Abbie—"

"I'm his daughter, his own daughter, and I had to find
out about it from Faye Hinkel and Joe Dunbar today. My
own father . . ." Her voice began to waver, and she swal-

lowed to steady it. "Why?" she demanded. "Why wouldn't he tell me?"

"Because you're his daughter, probably," T.J. replied gently. He had owned Tyler's long enough to know that people could bare their souls to bartenders a lot more easily than they could to their nearest and dearest. "Maybe he didn't want to trouble you. Maybe he figured there wasn't much you could do about it—you're in New York, living your own life, dealing with your own problems. Maybe he wanted to protect you."

She inhaled shakily and tilted her face up to T.J.'s. He could tell that she was fighting tears, and he saw no reason for her to. If jogging was therapeutic when it came to easing pressure, so was a good cry.

He touched her shoulder, arching his long fingers around the narrow ridge of it and pulling her to a halt. As if on cue, she covered her face with her hands and surrendered to a quiet sob.

Chapter Three

The last thing Abbie had expected to do was burst into tears.

Crying was an activity she rarely indulged in—and when she did, she usually chose the time and place with extreme caution. To cry at work would be professional suicide; even though it had recently been decreed that women in the business world could wear feminine attire instead of pinstriped suits and severe blouses, if those women revealed the merest hint of feminine sentimentality they could kiss their careers goodbye. Women on Wall Street or Madison Avenue or the Manhattan District Attorney's Office were required to be twice as tough as their male counterparts if they wanted to survive.

Abbie was tough. She had never been the sort to fall apart in times of crisis. Despite the agony of losing her mother, Abbie had taken care of the many things her father had been too bereft to cope with: funeral arrangements, settling the hospital bills, contacting the insurance company, satisfying the terms of her mother's simple will, which left a few pieces of jewelry to Abbie and everything else to Roy. As grief stricken as Abbie had been, she hadn't broken down in front of her father.

She hadn't broken down in front of Bob, either. No matter that she had loved him, that she'd been ready to get married, that she desperately wanted to have a child—whenever she and Bob had entered into discussions concerning those thorny subjects, Abbie had never resorted to histrionics. It simply wasn't in her to make a spectacle of herself.

She occasionally shed a few tears when she was with Suzanne or Jaime or Marielle. But they were her close friends—and they were women. They understood, as men seldom did, that crying wasn't a sign of weakness or immaturity.

T.J. was neither a close friend nor a woman, and he probably didn't understand. Abbie fought to maintain her composure, but it was impossible not to lean on him when he was holding her so tenderly, when his large, powerful hands were molded to her trembling shoulders and her body nestled so comfortably against his, so naturally.

"I'm sorry," she whispered, her lips pressed against the sweat-damp skin of his upper chest, exposed above the rounded neckline of his shirt. A few soft curls of his chest hair brushed her chin and she jerked her head away, startled by the intimacy of their position.

T.J. refused to release her. His hands slid from her shoulders so he could circle his arms loosely around her waist. "Don't be sorry, Abbie," he said consolingly. "I don't mind."

"*I* do." She wanted him to let go of her, yet she was secretly glad that he didn't. His arms were strong and secure around her, protective. And his eyes, gazing down at her, looked so dark and tender, so resonant with sympathy. Abbie wasn't used to depending on men to prop her up—it was the sort of dependency she'd never wanted to get used to—but right now, it felt good.

"You're entitled to be upset," T.J. assured her. "No matter how you found out, learning that your father's facing some serious problems is a real downer, Abbie. You don't have to apologize for crying."

"It isn't just that," she insisted, inhaling deeply and sniffling away the last of her tears. She rolled her shoulders in a slight shrug, which T.J. correctly interpreted to mean she didn't want him holding her anymore. He obediently let his arms drop to his sides, and she took a step away, then nervously paced up the grassy embankment to the steel rail of the track and prodded it with the rounded tip of her running shoe. "I could hardly sleep last night," she confessed. It was easier to talk to T.J. when he wasn't hugging her, when his firm, leanly muscled torso wasn't pressed to hers, when she didn't have to angle her head way back just to view his face.

He regarded her from the path below, his lips curving into a puzzled smile. "I thought you said you found out about the store only today."

"It's not just the store," Abbie explained, pulling off her headband and using the terry cloth fabric to wipe the lingering drops of moisture from her cheeks. "Sleeping in the house after all this time, after my mother..." She sighed, unable to express in words how peculiar she'd felt last night in her narrow childhood bed, in a bedroom that, despite the changes it had undergone in decor and function since Abbie had moved out, was still hers, still the room where as a young, optimistic girl she used to lie awake plotting her flight from Wheeler, dreaming of the spectacular life she would lead once she escaped from this dull, dreary town. In those dreams she was going to be the next Clarence Darrow, the next William Kunstler—how she'd ended up as a prosecutor instead of a defense attorney was still a mystery to her—and she was also going to be the mother of a brood of darling youngsters fathered by her perfect husband, who was going to be sweet and liberated, and who was going to be as gorgeous as... well, T. J. Hillyard.

She gazed at his ruggedly chiseled face, at his dazzling eyes, at the tiny lines fanning from their outer corners, visible even though he wasn't quite smiling, at his attractively large nose and thick, silky mustache. She had always known he was a handsome man, but she'd never been one of the countless high school girls who had scribbled valentines on the locker room walls, with their own initials and "T.J.H." inside. While other girls were fantasizing about what it would be like to kiss T. J. Hillyard, Abbie had been fantasizing about what it would be like to live in New York City, to shop in Bloomingdale's and go to the theater whenever she felt like it, to sip white wine on a blanket in Central Park with a man who was both sensitive and a hunk and was madly in love with her, to boot. And yet... in her imagination, the role of the sensitive, adoring hunk could easily have been played by T.J.

Rattled by the thought, she descended from the railroad track to rejoin T.J. on the path. "We ought to get back in gear," she said, addressing the dirt at her feet. "Haven't you got a business to run?"

"Lina's got a key," he answered. "If she gets to Tyler's before me, she'll unlock the place. We don't open for business until four, anyway." Abbie felt his eyes on her even though she kept her face averted. "But you're right, we should get back to running. If I stand still too long my leg'll stiffen up."

He commenced jogging at a leisurely pace, one Abbie had no trouble matching. The air hadn't cooled down much since she'd begun her jog a half hour ago, and she

smoothed her headband around her forehead, lifting her
bangs up over it. As hot as it was in Wheeler, she found
this workout more pleasurable than the tedious workouts
she had at the gym in New York. Running laps on an oval
track was monotonous and sounds were distorted by the
vaulted ceiling, echoing the shouts and sneaker squeaks of
the men playing basketball on the court below the track.
Even the air-conditioning annoyed her—she'd rather smell
the tangy aroma of almond and citrus trees than the scent
of nothing at all, even if it was a cool nothing.

Most of all, the scenery at the gym was boring. Here,
the scenery included a rustic railroad track, a ragged
hedge of manzanita and honeysuckle, a row of unassuming houses beyond it, an occasional shade tree, and a man
who happened to look a lot better than most of the ag-
gressive, compulsive men who shared the track with Abbie in New York.

"You know what I'm thinking?" he said after several
minutes. "I'm thinking, sure, it must be rough on you,
coming back to Wheeler and all, but...you just can't
spend your entire time here missing your mother and
worrying about your father."

Abbie cast him a suspicious look. It was one thing to be
comforted by T.J., and quite another to be psychoana-
lyzed by him. "I take it you're going to offer me some
unsolicited advice," she muttered.

His lips spread into a crooked grin. "Not advice, Abbie—just dinner."

"Huh?"

"Dinner. Tyler's is closed on Sunday. Maybe we could
drive up to Chico. With the university there, they've got
some pretty decent restaurants."

"You mean, just us?"

His smile expanded. "You want a class reunion? Yeah, just us."

"Like a date?"

Although he was still smiling, his eyes narrowed on her. "What's with you, Abbie? Haven't you ever been asked out for dinner before?"

"Of course I have," she mumbled, scrambling to make sense of his invitation. Granted, he was a friend, and as of that afternoon he was a jogging partner, but even so... This was Wheeler, not New York. She was just visiting for a short while. She hadn't traveled all this way to go out on a dinner date with an old high school acquaintance.

"What's the hang-up?" he inquired. "I'm thinking it would do you some good to put your problems out of your mind for a few hours. We'll have a nice meal, and you can tell me more about life in the Big Apple, and I can tell you that, other than your so-called 'lucky' mugging, the city seems to be agreeing with you."

"New York City disagrees with me over just about everything," Abbie complained. Then she returned T.J.'s friendly smile. "I appreciate the invitation, T.J., but no."

He contemplated her, his expression mildly quizzical. "I know your father, Abbie, and I don't think he's going to mind if you spend one night away from him."

"It isn't that."

"Then what? Is it me? I know I must smell pretty awful at the moment, but I promise I'll shower before I pick you up."

"It isn't that, either," Abbie said, allowing a small laugh to slip out. "It has nothing to do with you, T.J. You really don't smell that bad at all."

"Coming from a sweatball like you, that's some compliment," he snorted.

Abbie laughed again, not at all insulted. The fact was, T.J. was remarkably attractive even now, as sweaty and dirty and out of breath as he was. "Sweet talk will get you nowhere," she teased.

"I don't want to get anywhere," he swore, although his eyes were sparkling with lusty humor. "Of course, I'm always open to suggestions."

Abbie shook her head. "I'm very flattered, T.J. I mean it. But..." She concentrated for a moment on her jogging, hoping that it would help her to sort her thoughts. One half of her brain struggled with the astonishing notion that T. J. Hillyard, high school hero, Wheeler idol and star of the daydreams of countless local girls, was actually making a pass at Abigail Jarvis, the ambitious egghead of their graduating class. The other half of her brain absorbed the incontestable truth that, seventeen years after graduation, T.J. was a charming man with a delightful sense of humor, and she was truly pleased by the genuine friendship that was developing between them.

But beyond that, the reason she'd come to Wheeler in the first place—long before she'd had an inkling of the dire financial condition of Jarvis's Hardware—was that she was fed up with the way things had been going in New York. She was fed up with her cases, with having to prosecute a woman for trying to sell her baby when the woman should have been in jail ages ago. More than that, she was fed up with romance, with a man who had vowed that he loved Abbie, yet had been unable to make her happy. Six months after she'd ended her relationship with Bob, she was still angry about what had happened between them, still bitter about it.

One thing she didn't need in her life right now was a dinner date with an extremely desirable man while she happened to be passing through town. She was here to recover, not to reinfect the wounds.

"Just tell me this," T.J. questioned her. "Are you turning me down because of your father, your mother or me?"

"None of the above," she admitted wistfully. If she was going to reject T.J.'s invitation, the least she owed him was an honest explanation. "I'm recovering from a bad relationship," she said, unconsciously accelerating her pace slightly, as if by running faster she could burn off her fury over Bob.

"Oh." T.J. digested this information, mulled it over, smiled compassionately. "Back in New York?"

"Back in New York."

He nodded. "How bad is 'bad'?"

"Four years bad." She raised her eyes to his. "I need some time off, T.J. I need to give my emotions a break."

He eyed her dubiously. "Who said anything about emotions? I thought we were talking about dinner."

Abbie suffered a twinge of embarrassment at having read too much into T.J.'s invitation. But she'd opted for candor with him, and she wasn't about to change her strategy now. "You were talking about dinner. I was talking about how I'm a little bit wary around men these days."

"Uh-oh," T.J. intoned, feigning profound concern. "Sending your resume out to all the convents, are you?"

She grinned. T.J.'s amiable attitude was almost as rejuvenating as the fresh air and isolation she'd come to Wheeler to enjoy. "I'm planning on a full recovery," she assured him. "It's just ... I'm not quite there yet."

He perused her for a minute. "Four years, huh," he pondered aloud. "Were you married to the guy?"

She wondered whether she truly wanted to go into the dismal details of her relationship with Bob, then decided that she did. T.J. was divorced; he'd survived the demise of a love affair. Maybe he would understand. "No, we weren't married," she told him. "I wanted to make it legal, but he didn't."

"It took him four years to figure out he didn't want to marry you?" T.J. asked, his expression both incredulous and scornful. "What was the guy's problem?"

"Have you got a couple of hours?" Abbie said caustically. Then her temper subsided, and she continued in an even tone. "His problem was that he loved me but he was afraid of commitments. My problem was that I thought if he loved me enough, I could convince him that commitments weren't so terrible."

T.J. jogged in silence for a minute. "You're probably better off without him."

"Thanks," she scoffed. "In times like these, nothing fits like a cliché."

"All I said was—"

"You're right, T.J., of course you're right. It's just that I feel like an idiot, you know? Four years I wasted on Bob. Four years I spent waiting for him to grow up."

T.J. glanced down at her. "Would you like to cry some more?" he asked, patting his shoulder in invitation. "You're more than welcome."

"No," Abbie said firmly. She'd squandered enough sorrow on Bob back in New York. "My dad's money troubles are worth crying over, and my mother. Not this." She ran a bit, meditating on nothing more complicated than her respiration, her slow, steady strides, the sun-baked path stretching ahead of her and T.J. "How long did it take you to get over your divorce?" she asked.

"I don't remember, exactly," he said. "A while." He ruminated for a couple of minutes. "I think I started getting over it before it actually happened. I knew Mary-Jane and I weren't going to make it, long before we started talking to lawyers. We both knew it."

"Why? What broke you up?"

"What broke us up?" He frowned and gestured toward his brace. "This did."

"Your knee?" Abbie wondered whether his injury had affected his ability to function as a husband...and she discarded the idea as soon as it took shape. One good look at T.J. was all it took for a sane woman to realize that, however extensive the damage to his leg, it hadn't affected any other parts of his anatomy.

He reminisced for a minute, then elaborated. "Mary-Jane and I dated all through college, and we got married right after graduation. The man she married—the man she wanted to be married to—was a football star. It wasn't *me*, Abbie—it was T. J. Hillyard the football star. Don't get me wrong," he hastened to add. "It's not like Mary-Jane was heartless or anything. Neither of us realized at the time that what she loved about me was actually only one part of me. I *was* T. J. Hillyard the football star back then, so it was an easy mistake to make."

"And when you weren't a football star anymore...?"

"That's when we started having problems. But I don't want to speak ill of her. She was good to me. She stuck by me through the worst of it, even after we knew the marriage was over. She was by my side through all the surgeries, all the rehab. She went through a lot with me, Abbie. She might not have been much of a wife anymore, but she was a good nurse, and she was tolerant of my black moods, and she refused to leave until she was sure I'd be able to make it on my own."

Abbie had never before heard a divorced person describe a former spouse in such benevolent terms. She
wondered whether T.J. still loved his ex-wife, but she
wouldn't ask. It might hurt him too much to have to answer.

Bright green letters declaring "Fifty Years of Know-
how" loomed into view beyond a clump of dusty under-
growth as Abbie and T.J. neared the First Street crossing
where she'd left her father's van. "This is where I get off,
I guess," Abbie said, disappointed that the jog was over.
Usually she couldn't wait to be done with her workout,
but usually she wasn't working out in such delightful
company. "Would you like a lift home?" she asked.

T.J. shook his head. "I'll run it—I could use the extra
mile." He slowed to a walk when Abbie did, tramping
with her through the shrubs to the parked van. Before she
could open the driver's side door, he flattened his hand
against it, holding it shut. "I'm sorry the guy gave you a
rough time," he said, "but think about Sunday night a
little more, okay? You're not going to be able to solve
your father's problems then. You may as well hit me up
for a free feed."

Abbie gazed at T.J., absorbing all over again how good-
looking he was, how cheering, how downright nice...and
remembering how wonderful his arms had felt around her
when she'd broken into sobs on the jogging path. She also
thought about his words—*"hit me up for a free feed"*—
as if he were deliberately discussing their date in the least
romantic terms he could think of.

She appreciated that. The truth was, she appreciated a
lot about T.J. Too much, maybe. "I don't think so," she
said ruefully.

"If you can't say yes right now, say maybe," he urged
her, sliding his arm around her shoulders and giving her

a friendly squeeze. "And in the meantime, why don't you stop by Tyler's later tonight for a drink?"

"I can't," she said, this time speaking decisively. "Tonight I'm going to sit down with my father and find out what's going on in his life—and in his store."

"Friday night's your dad's regular night at Tyler's," T.J. alerted her. "You could sit down with him there—in fact, it might be better to talk to him if it's not just the two of you squaring off in his house, one-on-one. Judging by my experience, he'll probably open up a lot more if he's nursing a shot of Jim Beam."

"All right," Abbie said, conceding privately that she might need T.J. and his bar's supply of liquor to help her through what was certain to be a difficult conversation with her father. Conceding, as well, that she might be better able to face whatever horrible news her father might ultimately disclose if she knew T.J. was near, ready to offer his strong shoulder if she needed someone to lean on.

THEY CAME IN AROUND eight o'clock. Tyler's was already jam-packed with customers, but T.J. spotted Abbie the instant she entered the crowded tavern. She wore a stylish pair of pleated trousers and a loose-fitting blouse that emphasized her slim build. She had obviously washed her hair since her jog that afternoon; it hung straight and silky, glimmering with red highlights beneath the overhead amber lamps.

Roy was also dressed neatly, in a pair of clean blue jeans and a checkered shirt. He had sprouted a slight paunch within the last few years, and his chin wasn't as cleanly defined as it used to be, but despite those symptoms of late middle age, Roy Jarvis was a handsome man. As he entered the bar with Abbie, he held his hand at the small of her back in an almost possessive manner, as if defying anyone to make a pass at his precious daughter.

Nobody would; T.J. would see to that. He knew what she and Roy would be talking about tonight, and he was determined to make sure they wouldn't have to endure any interruptions. The crush of patrons notwithstanding, T.J. had reserved a private table for the Jarvises as far as possible from the rowdy atmosphere surrounding the pool table and the jukebox.

Abbie glanced toward the bar, and when her gaze intersected with T.J.'s he smiled and nodded in a silent greeting. "Lina," he called to his senior waitress, "give Roy the corner table, okay?"

"Okay."

"And take their order right away."

Lina eyed him, her dark blond braid drooping against her shoulder as she tilted her head inquisitively. "Hey, T.J., Roy Jarvis is a regular. How come the red carpet treatment?"

"I'm operating on a hunch that he'll need it tonight," T.J. said, not bothering to elaborate. Just as he frequently took confessions like a priest, T.J. made it a practice not to betray the confidences of those who confessed to him.

Shrugging, Lina picked up her tray and wove through the crowd to usher Roy and Abbie to the corner table. In less than a minute she was back at the bar, requesting a Jim Beam and an Olympia for them. Her face registered no surprise when, placing the two orders and a bowl of pretzels on her tray, T.J. told her to let the Jarvises know that their drinks were complimentary.

He tried to keep an eye on them as he hustled from one end of the bar to the other, mixing drinks, stuffing bills into the cash register, laughing indulgently at the wisecracks of the customers seated across from him on the barstools. He wanted to slip away for a moment and eavesdrop on Abbie and her father, just long enough to be sure they were all right. He wished he could pop a quarter into the jukebox and provide them with the Beatles classic, "We Can Work It Out" as background music. But there were too many farmhands in Tyler's tonight, and they tended to favor songs that dwelled in the border region between country-western and rock. Bonnie Raitt had already crooned "Love Has No Pride" three times through the jukebox's speakers. If it weren't such a great song, T.J. might have been tempted to unplug the damned machine.

About a half hour after the Jarvises arrived, when the population inside the bar seemed to have doubled, Lina appeared at the bar with a tray loaded with empty glasses and bottles. "Joint's hopping tonight," she remarked wearily.

"I noticed," T.J. said with a grin, pouring a margarita from the blender into a salt-rimmed glass. "Do you think we should turn on the air-conditioning?" he asked when Lina grabbed a cocktail napkin from the nearest stack and used it to mop her brow.

"Nah. I just told Meagan to open the windows. It's cool outside."

"How's she doing tonight?" T.J. asked. Lina had been with him nearly since he'd opened Tyler's, and he relied on her to help him keep Jackie and Meagan in line. Meagan was the newest addition to his staff. She'd recently moved to Wheeler to live with her boyfriend, who was supposedly working on a master's degree in agriculture at the university in Chico. T.J. couldn't comprehend why anybody would want a master's degree in agriculture—he assumed a person would get a bachelor's degree if he wanted to farm and a doctorate if he wanted to teach. But whatever Meagan's boyfriend was up to, Meagan herself had a tendency to behave coquettishly around the customers. She was a good waitress and T.J. wasn't about to let her go. But he liked Lina to keep an eye on her.

"Pretty toned down," Lina reported. "Roy Jarvis wants another Jim Beam. Is it on the house?"

"Yes." T.J. filled a fresh shot glass with the bourbon. "Do you need another Oly, too?"

"No. His date's just sipping."

"That's not his date," T.J. corrected Lina. For some reason, it rankled to hear Abbie referred to as someone's date, even if T.J. was far from certain she would be his own date on Sunday night.

"I thought she looked too young for him," Lina commented. "Roy's not bad looking for an old guy, but—"

"She's his daughter," T.J. said.

"His daughter?" Lina tilted her head, peering around a cluster of people to spy on the Jarvises. "The fancy New York lawyer he's always bragging about?"

"The one and only."

"She doesn't look much like him, does she," Lina mused, lifting her tray and sashaying through the crowd to deliver Roy's drink.

T.J. followed Lina to the Jarvises' table with his gaze. She was right—Abbie didn't look much like her father. She resembled her mother much more strongly.

He hadn't gotten to know Roy's wife too well. In fact, he'd only just begun to develop a friendship with Roy when Grace had been killed in that terrible car accident. A month earlier, T.J. had bought Mike's Place with some of the insurance money he'd received from the Chicago Bears, and he'd been spending time in Jarvis's Hardware, trying to figure out what equipment he would need to refurbish Mike's Place and how much it was going to cost. He'd talked to a couple of contractors, but he had wanted to do at least some of the work himself. It had been a part of his therapy, a way to prove to himself that he was no longer helpless. He'd had to prove it, for both his own sake and Mary-Jane's.

Returning to Wheeler had been a tough decision. During the previous few years, T.J. had chosen his places of residence based mainly on how close they were to the hospitals where his orthopedic surgeons were affiliated, or to the assorted rehabilitation centers where he'd spent time learning how to use his leg again. The apartments he and Mary-Jane had inhabited were way stations, not homes. When the collective medical profession had finally decided to discharge T.J. from their care, the only place he could think of as home was Wheeler.

Mary-Jane hadn't been pleased, but she'd seen the logic in moving there. T.J.'s parents had still been living in town then, and his younger sister had been attending the university in Chico as a day student. Even with their other obligations, his parents and sister had been available to give Mary-Jane a reprieve from constantly having to ferry T.J. around and assist him with his exercises.

The first year back in Wheeler had been grim—T.J. and Mary-Jane had had plenty of money but not much else. Gradually, however, he'd become more independent, more able. Wielding first crutches, then two canes, then one, he'd begun to move around on his own, to get a feel for living again, and a feel for Wheeler.

He had spent many years with the goal of becoming a professional football player. After he'd reached that goal only to have it snatched away from him, he had spent many more years with the goal of being able to walk again. That goal achieved, he found himself in need of yet another goal. So he bought Mike's Place.

Even the physical toil of converting the bar turned out to be relatively easy, with the help of one of the contractors and the dependable advice of Roy Jarvis from Jarvis's Hardware. Roy was unbelievably generous with his time and knowledge. Refusing to charge T.J. for his services, he visited the ramshackle bar on the outskirts of town with T.J. and the contractor and counseled them on the paneling, the lighting fixtures, the best wholesalers from whom to purchase furnishings.

Grace Jarvis had been a quiet, resolute presence at Jarvis's Hardware. Frequently posted near the cash register when T.J. came in, she would nod at him, say, "You're looking well today," and then busy herself totaling receipts. T.J. remembered thinking that she was extremely pretty. She didn't look younger than her age—to her great credit, she didn't try to—but her skin was smooth and supple in spite of her years, her figure trim, her large hazel eyes expressive and her hair soft and lustrous, mostly auburn with just a few sprays of silver shot through it. More than once, T.J. recalled, he'd found himself wondering whether Grace's feisty daughter would wind up taking after her, looking better as a woman than she had as an adolescent.

He had attended Grace's funeral out of respect to Roy. T.J. felt that Roy's loss was unreasonable, unfair, totally without logic. He hadn't felt so indignant about his own catastrophe. Taking chances with his physical condition had been a deliberate choice on his part; he'd known the risks going in. Football players got hurt, sometimes disastrously. If you got lucky, if you weren't injured, you could make a terrific career for yourself. T.J. had tried, he'd aimed high...and he'd gotten unlucky. But it had been his choice to make.

What choice had Grace Jarvis had? Some idiot blinded her with his headlights while she was driving at night, and she lost track of the road for a split second. That was all it took—a split second.

Abbie had come home for the funeral, of course. She'd looked pale and shaken, essentially in shock. Her hair had been longer then, T.J. recalled, and she'd worn it pulled back into a ponytail with a black velvet ribbon. She'd had on a fashionably tailored gray wool suit, but she had been too bewildered and mournful to appear particularly chic. T.J. had introduced her to Mary-Jane, and he'd told Abbie he was sorry, and she'd mentioned that she was sorry about his aborted football career, and that had been that.

Even if he hadn't still been married then, it would never have occurred to him that seven years later he would find himself wondering what Abbie looked like under her jogging outfit.

Was she crying? Through the forest of bodies milling around the bar, T.J. glimpsed her dabbing her eyes with a handkerchief. It took all of his willpower not to vault over the bar and sprint to the table to comfort her.

Crying or not, she didn't need him right now. Her attention belonged totally to her father; her free hand clutched his across the tiny table. It looked to T.J. as if Roy might be crying, too. His eyes looked unnaturally damp, belying his brave smile. He belted down his bourbon, then leaned toward Abbie and said something. Her grin was a poignant reflection of his.

"Two rye-and-gingers and a pack of Camels," Meagan demanded, offering T.J. a cute smile as she shoved her tray across the bar to him. "Have you ever considered creating a no-smoking section here, T.J.?"

He forced his attention away from the corner table to the pert young waitress, with her head of thick black curls and her coy, dimpled grin. "No," he said laconically, reaching for two tumblers and filling them with ice. "Never have."

"From a health standpoint—"

"From a health standpoint you're absolutely right, Meagan," he confirmed. "But that's not what Tyler's is all about. Nobody rubs anybody's nose in anything here. If people want to be healthy, they can go to a gym."

"Doesn't the smoke bother you?" Meagan persisted, drumming her fingers on the edge of the bar as T.J. sloshed rye into the two glasses. "Being an ex-athlete and all..."

"My comfort is irrelevant," he said, then let it rest. Meagan was self-absorbed and self-righteous. He couldn't expect her to understand the philosophy behind a place like Tyler's. She wasn't an authentic Wheelerite. She hadn't grown up inhaling the delicate fragrance of the almond trees in bloom, or basking in the dusty desert heat of a Wheeler August. She hadn't ever floated down the Sacramento River on an inner tube or skinny-dipped in any of the smaller creeks, late at night. She hadn't ever swung by her legs from the lower limbs of the oak tree standing guard over the old Chapman farm, or peeked through the windows of Mrs. Rapple's house after dark, spying on the old lady to see if she performed black magic rites within the confines of her gloomy parlor. She hadn't ever raced through a field of sunflowers at night when the sky was ablaze with heat lightning.

She could never begin to understand why Tyler's couldn't have a no-smoking section.

"Well," she said, "it was just an idea."

"A good idea, too," T.J. reassured her. "But not for Tyler's."

Meagan tossed him her kittenish smile and vanished from the bar with her tray. As soon as she was gone, T.J. glanced toward Abbie again. She and her father were standing, talking to Lina. Then Roy strolled to the front door and Abbie moved in the opposite direction, heading toward the rest rooms off a hallway at the rear of the barroom. In a trice, their tiny table was overtaken by a cheerfully noisy foursome demanding a pitcher of Budweiser. T.J. could hear them ordering all the way across the room, and he had the pitcher and mugs ready for Lina by the time she returned to the bar.

"After you deliver this, could you cover me for a minute?" he asked her. She'd been with him long enough to have learned a sufficient number of bartending skills.

She nodded and went to deliver the pitcher of beer. T.J. kept his gaze fixed on the back hallway, watching for Abbie. She hadn't appeared by the time Lina returned to the bar, and he slipped out and crossed to the hallway.

It was dimly lit, and two women were waiting in line outside the restroom door. When Abbie emerged, she eyed the other women and then turned to T.J. Her smile indicated that she wasn't terribly astonished to find him waiting for her.

"Have you got a minute?" he asked in a whisper, motioning toward a fire door at the end of the hall.

Without speaking, Abbie accompanied him down the hall and outside. A few cars and pickups were parked in the unpaved lot at the rear of the building, and a brilliant silver three-quarter moon illuminated the earth through the windless night air. T.J. took Abbie's hand and turned her to face him.

Her skin shimmered in the moon's glow, and it smelled faintly sweet. It took him a second to place the familiar scent: the liquid soap in the bathroom dispensers. She must have just washed her face. She must have washed it because she'd been crying.

"How are you?" he asked quietly.

Abbie's fingers curled around his, and she lifted her gaze to his. However much she might have wept, her eyes were now clear and dry, steady with resolve. "I'm all right, T.J."

"How's your dad?"

"A little bit shaken," Abbie admitted. "And relieved, I think. Trying to keep the truth from me had put a strain on him. It's been rough for him—but now at least he and I can share the problem."

Her hand was so small compared to his, he felt as if he were holding a child's hand instead of a woman's. Her fingers were slender, her palm soft and velvety. He let his thumb stroke hers, and then wander to the skin of her inner wrist and trace a circle there. "What are you going to do now?" he asked.

If she was unnerved by his gentle caress, she did nothing to stop him. "We're going to go through the books together this weekend," she replied. "It'll take us at least that long just to sort out the records. Then, on Monday, we'll go back to the bank and see if we can refinance the store's debts."

"That sounds like a good idea," T.J. said, eager to offer her any support he could.

She laughed sadly. "The bank's probably going to shoot us down," she predicted. "I'm no economics genius, T.J. I can't just sweep in from New York and snap my fingers and make everything better." She sighed and forced a weak smile. "But we'll try," she went on, "and if that doesn't work, we'll try something else. I'm not going to leave Wheeler until we've run out of things to try. My father has already lost my mother, T.J. If he loses his store, too..." Her voice cracked and she looked away.

T.J. slid his thumb under her chin and steered her face back to his. Her eyes were disturbingly large and bright, shimmering in the silver light of the moon. He wondered if she was at all aware of how lovely she looked. "You still need to eat Sunday night," he reminded her.

"I have the feeling that by the time I finish going through my father's records, I'm not going to have much of an appetite," she muttered, a feeble joke.

Her answer angered him in some unreasonable way, but he reined in his emotions. Frustration wasn't fatal; he'd get over it. "Okay," he said, releasing her hand and shaping a mechanical smile. "Just thought I'd give it one more try."

"I wish..." Her eyes met his, her long lashes shimmering as the moonlight caught them. "I really wish I could say yes, T.J. But I can't, not now." She reached for his shoulder and gripped it, as if trying to draw strength from him, then turned and hurried around the building and out of sight. After a minute, the crunching sounds of her footsteps against the gravel receded into silence.

Chapter Four

Another restless night.

Abbie lay on her side, staring at the window across the room. She'd left the drapes open as well as the window itself; not only did this permit a refreshingly cool night breeze to enter the room, but it also let in a sloping shaft of moonlight which landed in a rectangle on the rug just inches from her bed.

Abbie didn't mind the light. Nor did she mind the nocturnal sounds of the valley: the incessant chirping of the crickets and the baying of a coyote up in the buttes. Even if her bedroom had been sealed in darkness and silence, she knew she would be unable to fall asleep.

Last night, memories of her mother were what had caused Abbie's insomnia. She had lain under the lightweight blanket, the pillow a misshapen lump of down beneath her head, and relived the last time she'd been in this bed. During that long-ago visit to Wheeler, she had managed to spend the bulk of her time attending to business: sorting through her mother's clothing and packing it up for delivery to the Methodist church in town; contacting the Social Security Administration and arranging for her father to receive survivor's benefits; writing responses to the countless condolence cards and notes that filled the mailbox daily. Every evening at dinner time, she and her father would sit in the kitchen, their food scarcely touched, and they would sip bourbon or beer and talk about Abbie's mother. "Remember the time she decided to redecorate the entire house?" Abbie's father had said. "She redid the bathroom and then decided the whole project was silly."

"She never got into the domestic arts in a big way," Abbie had recollected. "Like mother, like daughter, unfortunately."

"Remember the year she volunteered to organize the town's canned food drive?"

"In our house," Abbie had chimed in. "She was so damned organized, by the end of the first week she had hundreds of dollars' worth of canned food stacked up all over the living room."

"We couldn't watch TV. All those soup cans were in the way."

"It was like being trapped inside an Andy Warhol painting." Abbie had chuckled. "By the end of the second week, I was finding containers of Spam under my bed."

"A whole year later, I found a dented can of beets in the tool shed. Beets! I hate beets!"

Abbie and Roy had dissolved in laughter. In spite of their melancholia—or perhaps because of it—they couldn't keep themselves from laughing. And they couldn't keep themselves from talking that way, with the sort of intimacy and familiarity that blossomed from love and trust.

Someday, Abbie hoped, she and her father would be able to laugh about their current heartache. It was *theirs*, no longer Roy's problem alone. Abbie was a Jarvis, too, and she had accepted the task of rescuing Jarvis's Hardware as her responsibility no less than her father's.

He hadn't wanted her to accept it. "The reason I didn't discuss it with you is because you've got enough problems of your own," he'd explained, cupping his hands around his glass of bourbon at the dimly lit table at the rear of Tyler's. At first, Abbie had been afraid she and her father wouldn't be able to hear each other, let alone discuss something important, in the smoky, crowded barroom. But they'd heard each other well. After a few false starts, they'd managed to communicate as well as they had to. "You didn't need me bothering you about the store when you had your own miseries. That fellow of yours, stringing you along for so long—"

"Bob's behavior was my fault as much as his," Abbie had protested.

"Like hell. You like to think everything's within your control, Abbie, that if things go right it's because you did them right, and if things go wrong you're to blame. Nothing's that simple, sweetheart. The guy was a louse. He told you he loved you and then he didn't follow through. You were upset about it, and then you were upset about that friend of yours whose husband had a heart attack—"

"Of course I was upset," Abbie had snapped. "He was younger than me, and suddenly, without any warning…" She'd cut herself off. The issue hadn't been worth going into. "All of this is irrelevant, Dad. Granted, it's been a rough spring for me, but you should have told me about the store. You should have let me know."

"It's my situation, Abbie, not yours."

"It's not just your situation, Dad," Abbie had argued. "We're a family, you and I. If you're having money trouble, I'm the one you're supposed to come to."

"And what are you supposed to do? You earn a nice living, Abbie, but you aren't one of those corporate lawyers in the high-priced firms. You're supporting yourself, you pay a steep rent for your apartment, and look at what food costs in that crazy city! Last year when I visited you, you were laying out close to two dollars for a melon. A dollar a pound for tomatoes, and they didn't even taste like tomatoes. You took me out for dinner at that seafood restaurant—fifty bucks for the two of us, and that was without drinks. You've got expenses in New York, Abbie. I can't take money from you."

"I'm not asking you to take money from me," Abbie had maintained. "I'm asking you to let me give it to you."

"Give what? You want to wipe out your savings? I won't let you do that."

Her father had had a valid point. For all the ostensible glamour of her job, Abbie was a city employee, earning less than half what she could make as a partner in a major law firm. But she didn't want to be a partner in a major law firm. She had always been content to receive an adequate enough income to live on without having to scrimp. She had no urge to be excessively wealthy.

Until now. If she were rich now, she could pay off all the store's debts.

She laughed sadly. Not only couldn't she wipe out her father's debts with a single stroke of her pen, but she had serious doubts about whether she could convince the bank to extend her father's loans or assist him in refinancing. "A fellow named Ed Garcia is the head of the loan department," her father had told her over a second glass of bourbon. "Sweet kid, moved to Wheeler from Vacaville about two years ago with his wife and the cutest little baby girl. He's doing a good job for the bank—maybe too good a job. It's no picnic being a loan officer in a farming community these days, Abbie. Garcia tries not to tighten the screws on you, but what can he do? It's his job. Remember Vin and Pearl Ambrose, they worked a small spread just north of town? They had to sell acreage to pay off the bank. By the time they were done, all they had left was two acres and the house—and an early retirement neither of them wanted. They wound up selling whatever was left and moving into a mobile home near their son down in Modesto."

"You can't blame that on the loan officer, can you?" Abbie had said, chastened by the news that people she knew, the parents of a boy with whom she'd played clarinet in the school orchestra, had been wiped out by their debts.

"I'm not blaming anybody," her father had sworn. "I'm not even blaming this new landlord who's been buying up pieces of Main Street. I'm just saying, seems like they're trying to get water from a stone."

"We're just going to have to find a way to wring a few drops out of that stone," Abbie had said fervently.

"*I'm* going to have to. Not you, Abbie. It's not your problem."

"It is," she had claimed. "I'm not going to let you go through this alone, Dad. You've been alone too much since Mom died—and maybe that's my fault—"

"There you go again, Abbie. Don't be silly, it's not your fault."

"I'm not being silly. I've been alone too much, too. I thought I had Bob, but I never really did. I have a few close friends, but two of them moved away from the city this summer. I'm alone, too, Dad—and neither of us should be, because we've got each other. And we're going to see this thing through together."

Her father's eyes had begun to fill with tears then, and so had Abbie's. It wasn't simply resolving the store's difficulties that made her want to stay in Wheeler. It was her keen awareness that she'd been trying too hard, for too long, to establish her independence. She had achieved a great deal in her life, but in the process she'd cut herself off from her roots, her home. Now she was a lawyer, a career woman, self-sufficient and sophisticated, but the goals she had attained no longer seemed as lustrous as she'd once imagined them to be. She had striven to outgrow Wheeler, and she'd succeeded, but what did it mean if she couldn't be with her father when he needed her?

Through the open window she heard the plaintive howling of a cat. Tossing back the blanket, she sat up, then stood and walked to the window. The smooth enameled wood of the sill felt cool along her forearms as she leaned against it, gazing out at the moonlit backyard. Here in Wheeler, where the humidity was generally low and air pollution practically nonexistent, a partial moon seemed brighter and more vivid than even a full moon on a clear night in New York.

She could stay in Wheeler for a while, just to help her father. She had left things rather indefinite at the office; she could phone and let her associates know that a family crisis required her presence in California for longer than the week she'd originally anticipated. She could ask Marielle to check in on her apartment, to forward her mail and help herself to any food Abbie might have left in the refrigerator.

And she could tell T.J. that, although she wasn't in the proper frame of mind to have dinner with him this weekend, she wouldn't object to spending some time with him later. They could jog together, perhaps, or she could stop by at Tyler's for an Oly on an evening when business was slow, or they could meet for lunch. Nothing romantic, nothing remotely resembling a date, but they could nurture their budding friendship. T.J. was so easy to talk to— it was no wonder his customers liked to confide in him. He was so open, so nonjudgmental, and his hypnotically dark eyes and gentle smile demanded trust.

Yes, Abbie could see staying in Wheeler for a while.

BY NOON ON SATURDAY, she was desperate to get outdoors. She wondered how her mother had been able to tolerate working in that gloomy windowless office at the rear of the store. The window in Abbie's New York office overlooked a grimy air shaft, but if she stooped down next to the radiator and craned her neck to just the right angle, she could glimpse a few square inches of sky. As offices went, her niche within the district attorney's headquarters was fairly dingy, but at least it didn't seem like a tomb.

What bothered her most about the back office at Jarvis's Hardware wasn't the absence of a window, she admitted as she emerged from the store, blinking like a mole in the midday sun. She was troubled not by what the office was lacking but by what it contained. She had spent the past three hours going through the mess of records, painstakingly sorting them into piles: rent and utility bills, bills from wholesalers, customer credit lines, letters pertaining to the bank loans Roy Jarvis had signed. Now that she'd gotten the files into a semblance of order, she intended to start calculating the income and the outgo. But not on that archaic adding machine.

Shopping for a calculator gave her an excuse to leave the store, to inhale some fresh air and feel the daytime sun against her cheeks and bare arms. As she was leaving the store, she saw Faye Hinkel strolling briskly around the corner where Palmer crossed Main Street. "Hello, there, Abbie," Faye greeted her, lifting her sunglasses up onto the tousled yellow tufts of hair at the crown of her head. "Don't tell me your dad's talked you into trading that wonderful New York City career of yours for a job in his store."

Abbie grinned. "He hasn't, but he might be able to,". she answered genially. "That 'wonderful' New York City career of mine isn't all it's cracked up to be."

"To hear your dad tell it—"

"My dad's a proud father," Abbie pointed out, holding the door open for Faye. "I've got an errand to run. I'll see you later."

Once Faye vanished into the store, Abbie headed down the sidewalk. In the past two days, she had observed many of the changes the downtown area had undergone, but as she walked up the block she took note of them again: the video rental store located in the storefront that used to belong to an appliance fix-it shop when Abbie was a child, the voguish clothing boutique where Annabelle's Dress Shop used to be, the placards advertising discounts on personal computer supplies in the window of the stationery store where Abbie used to buy notebooks and ballpoint pens for school. She wondered how many of the Main Street retailers had seen their rents doubled, and how many of them could afford the rent hikes. Were they all in as much trouble as Jarvis's Hardware, or was her father the only one in financial straits? And what about people like the Ambroses, hardworking folks who'd never hurt anybody in their lives but who had lost their land because of the changing economics of farming?

Rents were skyrocketing in New York City, too. Merchants were being forced out of their gentrified neighborhoods; apartment buildings like Yorktown Towers were going co-op and tenants who couldn't afford to buy in were finding themselves homeless. Abbie ought to be as worried about what was happening in the city as she was about Wheeler. New York was her home; Wheeler hadn't been her home in seventeen years.

Some home, New York. She had her apartment there— an overpriced apartment where the plumbing never worked quite right. And now that Jaime was no longer around to fix it, Abbie could expect the shower to change temperature on her in mid-shampoo and the toilet to back up on her at least once a month. She had her job—a job where she could spend weeks on a case, months, occasionally years, only to learn that the arresting officer had Mirandized the suspect in English instead of Spanish and the conviction had to be overturned. She had her social world—a world where, in a romantic partnership, if you weren't willing to do all the household chores and all the cooking, pay at least fifty percent of the expenses, buy the concert tickets and reserve the squash courts, kill cockroaches without behaving squeamishly and yet assure your lover that he's indispensable and that you couldn't possibly function without him, he would leave you for another woman.

Thinking about it that way, she was tempted to give serious consideration to Faye Hinkel's joke about trading her big-city career for the tranquil life of a clerk in a nearly insolvent hardware store on Wheeler's Main Street.

The notion provoked a grin, and Abbie entered the bookstore feeling more cheerful than she had a right to be. "Can I help you?" an energetic young salesman asked Abbie.

"I need a calculator," Abbie replied, curious about the identity of the salesman. The fact that she no longer knew everyone in town sobered her, reminding her all over again that Wheeler was no longer her home. "I'll take the cheapest one you've got," she added.

A few minutes later she left the store, a brand new calculator tucked into her purse. She honestly didn't want to race back to Jarvis's Hardware and bury herself in the rear office with the store's records, but she felt guilty dawdling. There was too much to be done.

The sunshine beat down upon her as she sauntered along the sidewalk. The relentless heat, so unlike the hazy mugginess of New York's dog days, fried her hair and her shoulders and caused the exposed skin of her sandaled feet to tingle. She ducked under the green-and-white-striped awning of Sparky's Luncheonette for a moment's reprieve from the searing midday glare.

Standing in the shade refreshed her, but she couldn't remain beneath the luncheonette's awning forever. Sighing, she stepped out into the sunlight again and then halted as she spotted two men leaving the jewelry store across the street. The shorter one wore a T-shirt, faded overalls and a duckbill cap which failed to conceal his long strawberry-blond hair. The taller one had his back to her, but Abbie easily recognized him.

The heat gnawing at Abbie seemed to have no effect on T.J. His thick, dark hair was slightly windblown, and his skin was dry. The sleeves of his navy-blue shirt had been rolled up only as far as his elbows. He was wearing leg-hugging blue jeans as well, and the uniform color of his outfit emphasized the masculine lines of his physique. Abbie was unexpectedly visited by a memory of how marvelous she had felt in his arms, how safe and sheltered and cared for—and the memory made her blush. She had spent her entire thirty-four years of existence trying to prove to herself and the world that she was strong, independent and indomitable. She shouldn't rel-

ish a man's protectiveness so much. She shouldn't have
found it to be such a turn-on.

Acknowledging how much she had been aroused by
T.J.'s embrace caused her blush to intensify, and she
quickly stepped deeper into the awning's shadows, waiting for her cheeks to cool off before she let T.J. see her.
She watched as he started toward one of the cars parked
at the curb near the jewelry store, then turned back to his
companion to talk some more. He interrupted himself
when an attractive young woman, evidently someone he
knew, exited from a store a few doors down the block. He
and the man in the overalls exchanged a few neighborly
words with the woman, then resumed their own conversation, then paused again to holler a friendly salutation to
someone who cruised past them in a car with the windows open.

How unlike the streets of New York City, Abbie mused.
She tried to remember the last time she had run into an
acquaintance on Eighty-sixth Street or Third Avenue.
Even if she did wind up on the same block with someone
she knew, she probably wouldn't have been conscious of
the encounter, for the simple reason that pedestrians
generally strove not to look at each other as they hurried
along the bustling sidewalks. A sensible woman wouldn't
risk making eye contact with a stranger in New York. The
proper technique was to gaze at the chin of someone
walking toward you, or to stare just beyond his shoulder.
If you looked directly at him, he might assume you were
challenging him.

This wasn't New York, though, and T.J. would never
think that by saying hello to him Abbie was issuing a dare.
She stepped out from beneath the awning and called
across the street to him, "Hi, T.J."

He spun around and broke into a grin. "Hey, Abbie! How's it going?"

"All right," she shouted, but her words were drowned out by the rumble of a pickup revving its engine at the corner stop sign. T.J. waved for her to join him. She glanced both ways and darted across the street, dodging another noisy truck that rattled to a stop at the corner.

"Hey, Abbie," T.J. repeated in a normal voice once she'd reached his side. He slung his arm casually around her shoulders and gave her an amiable hug, then let his hand fall to his side. "Do you know my brother-in-law?" he asked, presenting the man in the overalls. "Mark Beloit, this is Abbie Jarvis, an old classmate of mine. Abbie, Linda's husband Mark."

Abbie shouldn't have been dumbfounded by the news that T.J. had a brother-in-law. She vaguely recalled that there had been a younger Hillyard a couple of years behind her and T.J. in school, a popular girl with absolutely no athletic aspirations. As Mark Beloit pumped Abbie's hand in an enthusiastic handshake, Abbie felt swamped by the understanding that even though she'd left Wheeler, other people had stayed and other families had remained intact. Brothers-in-law actually lived in the same town and ran errands together. It all seemed so charming and wholesome . . . and alien.

"Nice to meet you," she remembered to say as Mark released her hand.

"Is this lady trustworthy?" Mark asked, tossing T.J. a sly smile.

T.J. pretended to inspect Abbie, sizing her up with a long, lingering gaze that made her inexplicably uneasy. "More or less," he allowed. "Why?"

"Maybe we ought to get a female perspective on this diamond stuff," Mark explained. "I don't feel like blowing all those bucks and then Linda up and says the damned thing's ugly or something.''

"Sure,'' T.J. agreed, turning fully to Abbie. "Linda's and Mark's tenth anniversary is coming up, and Linda's been making loud noises about how the appropriate gift for a tenth anniversary is diamonds.''

"Diamonds?'' Abbie laughed. "I thought you didn't give diamonds until the fiftieth or the seventy-fifth anniversary.''

"That was before inflation,'' T.J. said, lightly touching her elbow and steering her to the jewelry on display in the store's window. "I say Linda would prefer a pendant—that necklace over there, or something like it. Mark thinks he ought to give her earrings.''

"The earrings are more expensive,'' Mark noted, sidling up to Abbie and scrutinizing them through the window. "If I go with the pendant, Linda might think I'm cheap.''

"You are cheap,'' T.J. teased. Mark reached behind Abbie and poked his brother-in-law in the ribs.

Abbie tried to concentrate on the jewels before her, but it was hard to concentrate on anything other than T.J.'s closeness, the clean male scent emanating from him, the warmth of his large hand taking her arm and ushering her to the window. Yesterday, when he'd asked her out for dinner, she'd had no hesitation about turning him down. Today, however, when he was behaving as if she were just another passerby on the street—which, she supposed, was what she was—she was vexed by his impersonal friendliness.

"The pendant,'' she mumbled, edging away from him. "It's more visible. I imagine she'll want everyone to see the lovely gift you gave her, Mark. Why give her something that's going to be hidden by her hair?''

"Linda's hair is short," Mark pointed out.

"I think Abbie's right," T.J. argued. "I've known Linda longer than you, Mark. She's ostentatious, she likes showing off. Go with the pendant."

"Yeah, and then when she shows it off, everybody's going to be getting up close and personal with her chest," Mark muttered.

"Buy her the pendant and tell her she should wear it around the house," T.J. advised. "With nothing else."

Mark grinned lecherously as he pictured the sight. "Mmm...I see your point, Tyler James. After the kids are asleep, of course..."

"You guys are awful," Abbie protested, although she suspected that their lewd comments were intended solely to rile her. "Why don't you just ask her what kind of jewelry she wants?"

"And spoil the surprise?" T.J. gave her a reproachful look. "Where's your sense of romance, Abbie?"

Good question, she responded privately. If she had a sense of romance, she would have accepted his dinner invitation yesterday. She would have agreed to sit across a candlelit table from T.J. and gaze into those soulful eyes of his and forget all about Bob and her father and everything else. She would have been able to enjoy an elegant dinner with a handsome man, and afterward...

Mark broke into what was undoubtedly a perilous train of thought by saying, "I suppose I don't have to make up my mind today. Thanks for the input, T.J. I gotta get back to work. Catch you later."

"Tell the kids I'll be by tomorrow."

"Yeah. Thanks again, T.J. Nice meeting you, Abbie." Mark nodded a farewell to them both, then turned and strode to a bright red pickup parked a few car lengths down the block.

Abbie watched until the red truck had driven away. Then she turned back to T.J. He was studying her, his gaze dark and penetrating, his lips half hidden by his mustache. "So, you're an uncle," she said brightly.

"That's right."

"I sort of remember your sister," she remarked, eager to keep talking so she wouldn't revert to dwelling on how attractive T.J. was. "I can't believe she's been married ten years."

"Why can't you believe it?" T.J. asked, the corners of his mouth twitching upward.

"I don't know anyone who's been married that long," she confessed, sharing his smile. "At least not from our generation."

"Well, Linda and Mark seem to be in it for the long haul—and more power to them. They tied the knot a few months after they graduated from Chico State," T.J. told her. "Marrying straight out of school seems to run in my family. Fortunately, Linda's done a much better job of it than I did."

"Is Mark from around here?" Abbie asked. She couldn't recall having known any Wheelerites named Beloit.

T.J. confirmed her supposition by saying, "No, he's from Yuba City. He met Linda in school, majored in ag, and now he's managing his grandfather's farm up in Princeton. So," he continued, his smile flagging, "how come you were standing around in the shadows across the way for so long? Why didn't you come on over and say hello as soon as you saw us?"

Abbie pressed her lips together and gazed over her shoulder at the luncheonette, hoping she wouldn't start blushing again. She resented T.J.'s ability to fluster her. "I wasn't standing around," she protested. "I was reminiscing how good the hot-fudge sundaes used to be at Sparky's."

"They're still pretty good. Can I treat you to one?"

"No," Abbie said automatically, then turned back to T.J. and smiled sheepishly. "If you want to know the truth, I was thinking about more than Sparky's sundaes while I was standing there. I was watching you say hello to everybody who walked past, and thinking about how you know so many people in Wheeler you can't even leave a store without running into friends. And in New York, where the population is about a thousand times as big, I don't have half the number of friends you've got here."

T.J. appeared surprised. "New York may be bigger than Wheeler," he commented, his smile becoming sympathetic, "but when you take into account all those muggers and fruitcakes on the subways and all the thugs you're busy putting into jail, maybe there aren't that many potential friends left." He angled his head toward the luncheonette. "How about a cup of coffee? I could sure use one."

"All right," Abbie accepted.

They crossed the street and entered the luncheonette. As soon as they did, T.J. announced to the slim gray-haired waitress posted behind the counter, "Hey, Thelma, look who I've got here—Abbie Jarvis!"

"Hey yourself, T.J.," Thelma rejoined placidly. "Good to see you, Abbie. Joe Dunbar was in earlier today, he told me you were in town. You're looking well, honey. How you been?"

"Fine, thanks," Abbie answered. "And you?"

"As well as can be expected, for an old broad. A touch of arthur-itis, but I ain't complaining. Coffee, T.J.?"

"Two," T.J. requested, escorting Abbie to an empty booth just beyond the counter.

"No ice-cream sundae?" Thelma ribbed Abbie, her clarion voice carrying across the nearly empty luncheonette. "I remember when you weighed ten pounds less and stuffed your face with sweets. Not that you're fat now, of course, but you've filled out a bit. Joe was just telling me this morning, you've turned into a real woman."

"Did he?" Abbie muttered faintly. She was beginning to remember the downside to knowing everybody in town: not only did you know everybody, but everybody knew you—and made your business their own. She was nonplussed to think that Joe and Thelma had taken it upon themselves to analyze her physical maturation.

T.J., on the other hand, seemed vastly amused. "Good God, is that what happened to you?" he whispered, sliding into the booth facing her once she was seated. "You've filled out into a real woman."

"Shut up," Abbie retorted, though she couldn't suppress a begrudging grin.

Thelma arrived at the table carrying two large porcelain cups full of coffee. "You take it black, hon?" she asked Abbie. "I don't remember. You, I know," she said to T.J.

"Black is fine," Abbie answered.

"I like your hairdo," Thelma went on, inspecting Abbie. "Roy's been telling me for years that you look real stylish and all—well, of course, I figured you were stylish but I couldn't really picture it. It looks good, Abbie. I'd love to look more stylish but Jerry'd have a fit if I so much as colored my hair. Do you color yours, Abbie?"

She had to laugh. "No, I don't."

"All those red highlights," Thelma said with an envious sigh. "Me, I started going gray the minute Jerry retired. The man drives me nuts, he's always around now, always underfoot. It's no wonder I'm always working my tail off here. Better'n being home with Jerry breathing down my back all the time, you know?''

"Thanks for the coffee, Thelma," T.J. said pleasantly but firmly.

"Sure. You need anything else, just give a yell." Thelma pivoted on her heel and bounced back to her post behind the counter in time to greet the two uniformed patrolmen who'd entered the luncheonette. Within a minute, she was fetching them Danish and coffee and griping about her retired husband to them.

Abbie stirred a packet of sugar into her coffee and chuckled. "I just remembered why I left Wheeler," she confessed.

T.J. nodded knowingly. "Plenty of friends, and not enough privacy," he summed up before lifting his cup to his mouth. Before taking a sip, he paused and studied her intently. "Am I keeping you from anything important?"

Abbie thought about the calculator in her purse and the heaps of files awaiting her attention in the back office of her father's store. "No," she said, deciding that, while the monetary health of Jarvis's Hardware was important, so was having this cup of coffee with T.J. "I've been working at the store all morning. I need a break."

"How has it been?" T.J. asked. "Do you want to talk about it?"

"Not really." The truth was, until she added up the numbers, she didn't have much to say on that subject.

T.J. accepted her answer with a nod. "Then let's talk about why you feel like you don't have enough friends in New York."

"I never said I didn't have *enough* friends," she corrected him. "I don't have many, but the ones I have are close. They're so different from the people we grew up with, T.J."

"Oh? In what way?"

Abbie tasted her coffee and smiled. For some reason, the coffee tasted better here than it did in any of the coffee shops she frequented in New York. Maybe it was the clean water, or the fresh air.... She took another sip, then settled against the vinyl cushions of the banquette and thought about her friends back east. "They come from much different backgrounds than ours, T.J. Some of the lawyers in my office grew up in elite, high-powered families where everyone who isn't a lawyer is married to one. One of my colleagues claims he's the rebel of his family simply because he's chosen the D.A.'s office instead of a Wall Street firm."

"Yuppies are alive and well in the Big Apple," said T.J.

"They aren't all yuppies," Abbie defended her acquaintances. "But...they've got a different dimension to them. It's hard to explain, T.J., and it doesn't have to do with money per se, but...they're cultured."

"Unlike us hicks from the sticks," T.J. concluded with a mocking laugh.

"I'm not saying people in Wheeler are hicks," Abbie elaborated. "But...well, take Jaime, for instance. She's one of my closest friends. She used to live in Yorktown Towers—that's my apartment building—but she moved to New Orleans this summer. She's a social worker, very young and dedicated...and her mother is Leona Faber."

T.J. gave Abbie a blank stare. "Who's Leona Faber?"

"A famous artist," Abbie told him. "She's a big success, very famous in the avant-garde movement."

If she was coming across as condescending, T.J. clearly wasn't offended. "Oh, of course, the famous artist," he murmured, his cheeks dimpling as he laughed. "Avant-garde art is all the rage in Wheeler these days. When we aren't talking about how nicely Abbie Jarvis has filled out, we're usually talking about Leona Faber and the avant-garde movement.''

Abbie scowled, but T.J.'s laughter was contagious, and soon she was laughing, as well. "I know it sounds pretentious, T.J. I'm just trying to explain to you that you meet different kinds of people in the city. Before I became friends with Jaime, I didn't know much about the contemporary American art scene, either. And Jaime didn't know that northern California was a primary source of brown rice.''

"You learned a lot from each other," T.J. commented, his eyes still glinting with humor.

Abbie conceded with a shrug. She *had* learned a lot from Jaime—not only about contemporary art but about what it was like to grow up without roots, without a sense of hometown or home. The very aspects of her youth that Abbie had found smothering were what Jaime had yearned for in her own youth.

"Tell me about your other friends," T.J. urged Abbie.

She took another sip of coffee. "Suzanne's a television star," she revealed.

T.J. perked up. "Suzanne who? That ditzy blond woman?''

"Suzanne Allman. She was one of the stars of *Reach for the Sky*. It's a soap opera. Or, as the people in the industry prefer, a daytime drama.''

T.J. arched his eyebrows and nodded. "You travel with a pretty classy crowd," he said.

"They're not classy at all," Abbie asserted. "Suzanne's gorgeous, I'll grant you that, but . . . she's a terrific woman. She's only four years older than me, and she's already got a daughter in college." Abbie sighed. Thinking about her friends' children always made her wistful. "Marielle has two children, too—Emily's five and

Christopher is still so little. I spoil those kids rotten, T.J.," she admitted wistfully. "I never really got to spoil Suzanne's daughter—she was too old—but the babies..."

"Yeah, I know how it is," T.J. said. "I spoil Linda's kids, too. That's what uncles are for. I guess you're kind of an honorary aunt to your friends' kids."

"More than that, I think. They lived right down the hall from me. Marielle's husband died of a heart attack last spring, and we all pitched in to help her. Whenever I had the chance, I took the children. I even took Emily to the office with me one day when Marielle had a meeting with her lawyer. Even in those miserable circumstances, Emily and I had a lot of fun together. I love kids so much...." Realizing she was rambling, Abbie stopped the flow of words by drinking some more coffee.

T.J. scrutinized her thoughtfully. He seemed on the verge of questioning her, then thought better of it and signaled Thelma. "Brace yourself," he whispered to Abbie as the loquacious waitress neared their table with a glass decanter of steaming coffee.

His warning was well heeded. "So, tell me, Abbie—" Thelma chattered as she refilled their cups "—what brings you to town?"

"Just a visit," Abbie said discreetly.

"How long you staying?"

"A while."

"Good. I'm sure your dad loves having you around. That man's crazy about you, Abbie, you know? To hear him talk, you're the light of his life."

"Thanks, Thelma," T.J. said again, a clear hint. Thelma grinned and waltzed back to the counter. Once they were alone, T.J.'s gaze tightened on Abbie. "How long is a while?" he asked.

Her eyes locked with his and she smiled. "Longer than I originally intended. I hardly think I'm the light of my father's life, but I'm not going to abandon him when he's facing such a disaster with the store."

T.J. appeared oddly satisfied by her statement. "Are you going to have trouble with your boss back east if you stay here for the duration?"

Abbie hoped she wouldn't. She had requested a personal leave from the office only once before, when her mother had passed away, and that year she'd compensated by taking fewer vacation days than she was entitled to. She considered this leave just as necessary as that one had been, and if her superiors didn't view it that way...

"I don't care," she heard herself say. "Right now, this is where I belong."

"Why don't you quit your job in New York and hang out a shingle here?" T.J. joked. "This town could use another lawyer."

"Oh, really? Don't tell me Wheeler's caught the litigation bug."

T.J.'s smile faded. He muttered something unintelligible and swallowed a long drink of coffee. When he lowered his cup, he was frowning. "As of nine o'clock this morning, I'd have to answer yes."

Abbie had little trouble deciphering his mood. "Oh, Lord. Who's suing you, T.J.?"

"Forget it," he grunted, shaking his head. "Last night you got an earful of your father's problems. You don't want me to lay mine on you, too."

"If I didn't I wouldn't have asked," Abbie said, sincerely concerned. "What happened, T.J.? Are you really being sued?"

"Tyler's is. I haven't seen the suit yet, but I'm probably named in it, too. That's the way these things are done, isn't it? They name everybody they can think of in the suit, and figure somebody'll have to come up with the money to settle." He shook his head again. "Look, Abbie, I really don't want to trouble you with this. It'll take care of itself."

She wanted him to trouble her. He had been so sympathetic yesterday when she'd burst into tears over her father's travails. She wished to give him as much support and comfort as he'd given her. "Tell me," she said sternly.

T.J. eyed her dubiously, then conceded with a shrug. "Some kid staggered into Tyler's about a year ago, obviously a teenager, obviously drunk. He asked for a beer, and I poured him a cup of coffee. He got kind of obstreperous, told me he wasn't drunk, and demanded some booze. I tried to get him to drink the coffee. Instead, he threw the cup at me, left the bar and got behind the wheel of his father's Cherokee."

Abbie shut her eyes, overcome by a sudden wave of nausea. She didn't want to hear any more. She didn't want to hear that this boy, no matter how drunk and foolish he might have been, had driven down a county road, flipped his car, and wound up dead like her mother.

"The kid's okay," T.J. said quickly, plainly able to comprehend her distress. He reached across the table and gathered her clammy hands in his large, strong ones. "He's as okay as I am, Abbie," he said soothingly. "Meaning, on a bad day he limps."

She opened her eyes slowly, cautiously. T.J. was staring at her, his gaze unwavering, hypnotically sweet. His hands closed around hers, holding them just tightly enough to still the slight trembling in her fingers. "I'm sorry for overreacting like that," she whispered hoarsely.

"No, *I'm* sorry. I should have listened to myself and skipped telling you. I should have realized it would shake you up."

"After all this time," she mumbled, "I ought to be able to hear about an auto accident without going to pieces."

"There's no time limit on these things," T.J. reassured her.

"Tell me more about the suit." She inhaled deeply, willing herself to listen impartially, like the lawyer she was.

"It's a garbage suit. The police didn't charge me with serving liquor to a minor. But the kid's family wants a handout and they know Tyler's has insurance, so they're ramming a suit through the civil courts. They served the papers yesterday afternoon but I was already at work, so my thoughtful lawyer sat on the news until this morning. He has a tendency to forget that when you work until 2:00 a.m., you sure as hell aren't in any condition to get a bad-news phone call at nine o'clock that same morning."

"Who's your lawyer?" Abbie asked him.

"Who else is there?"

"Not John Thorpe," she groaned. John Thorpe had been Wheeler's only lawyer since before Abbie was born. By now, she had assumed that he would have been retired or at least sharing his small practice with another lawyer. Abbie estimated Thorpe to be in his seventies, at least. As a younger man, he'd never proven to be much of a go-getter. He'd been adequate at handling wills and deeds—just about the only legal business people in Wheeler had—but by no means had he been a firebrand. These days, he was probably dreaming about little besides golf and fishing—if he wasn't traveling a doddering path toward senility.

"John Thorpe," T.J. confirmed.

"What has he advised?"

"He wants me to settle." His brow furrowed and his mouth skewed into a grimace. "The insurance will cover it."

"You don't want to settle," Abbie guessed without any difficulty.

T.J. laughed grimly. "Forget it, Abbie. I shouldn't have even told you."

"Well, if you think you have a case, you ought to fight it with everything you've got."

He continued to laugh, more gently. "Did anyone ever tell you, Abbie, that you're beautiful when you're being self-righteous?"

Abbie struggled to digest his combined insult and compliment. She hadn't felt this self-righteous in a long time. She was good at her job, she won more cases than she lost—but too often, lately, she felt as if she was just going through the motions, not fighting for the principles that had attracted her to the law so many years ago. Back in New York, if someone had presented her with the case T.J. had just described, she too would have counseled the client to settle out of court.

But she wasn't in New York now. She was in Wheeler, where certain values were supposed to endure, where the coffee tasted uncommonly good and the sky was clear and the moon illuminated the night more vibrantly than the sun illuminated a Manhattan summer day. This was Wheeler, where you could leave for seventeen years and then come home, and find that the people you left behind still remembered you.

This was Wheeler, where nobody ought to settle for anything less than what was right. "If I were you," Abbie said grittily, "I'd fight it. I'd fight it, and I'd damned well make sure I won."

Chapter Five

As soon as he'd heard T.J.'s hoarse grumble over the phone, John Thorpe had realized that he'd called his client too early. "Sorry I woke you up, T.J.," Thorpe had apologized. "Why don't you stop by my office later today and we'll talk." Such an open-ended appointment entailed no inconvenience on the part of Wheeler's one and only lawyer; his office happened to be located in his house.

Despite his drowsy condition during the brief telephone conversation with Thorpe, T.J. had understood that he would have to visit his attorney before opening time at Tyler's. But he'd had to wake up first—a process that had seemed to take longer than usual that morning—and he'd had a long-standing date to meet Mark at the jeweler's on Main Street at twelve o'clock to look at diamonds for Linda, and then he'd run into Abbie... and frankly, he couldn't think of anywhere he'd rather be right now than sitting at a table in Sparky's having a cup of coffee with her.

He had already noticed more than a few times how pretty she'd become in the years since she'd departed from Wheeler. But the instant he started describing his minor legal hassle to her, her appearance underwent a magnifi-

cent transformation. Her eyes began to glow, their gold
flecks gleaming, ablaze with conviction. She straightened
her spine, raised her chin and spoke with a forcefulness
that astonished him.

Had he actually believed that Abbie was suffering from
professional burnout? Not this lady, not this gloriously
defiant soul. She looked and sounded as if she was prepared to conquer the world—or willing to die trying. Her
vehemence reminded T.J. of the way he used to feel on the
football field—ready to take on all comers, ready to make
his point, unwilling to accept anything short of victory.

Sure, he'd nearly died trying. But he didn't regret having made the effort. And he could tell, from the steel in
Abbie's voice, from her gritty words and resolute attitude, that for all her frustration with her job in New York,
she also didn't regret making the effort, aiming again and
again for victory. Something told T.J. that, if the circumstances were right, being represented in a legal contest by
Abbie would be a whole lot different from being represented by John Thorpe.

Abbie wasn't T.J.'s attorney, though. That she had decided to stay in Wheeler longer than she'd originally
planned didn't mean she had any interest in opening an
office in town and signing on as the head of T.J.'s defense team.

And anyway, a nuisance suit was just that—a nuisance, not a cause. Tyler's had been named in nuisance
suits twice before, once by a fanatical woman from Artois
who blamed the purveyors of demon alcohol for the demise of her marriage—T.J. had joined forces with the
other three bar owners she'd sued and they'd easily won
the case—and once by a local fellow named Steve Haw-
kins who had sprained his ankle when he'd tripped on a
pothole in the parking lot outside Tyler's. T.J. had set-

tled that one out of court, paying Steve a hundred dollars and leaving his insurance company out of it. In truth, T.J. had been happy to give Steve some money. At the time, the poor sap had been laid off from his janitor's job at the primary school and as a result, had lost his medical coverage. T.J. wouldn't begrudge a neighbor the opportunity to receive financial assistance without losing his dignity.

But the case Thorpe had phoned T.J. about that morning was different. T.J. recalled the incident well. At the time, he had done everything he could do to protect both the bar and the boy, short of stealing the kid's car keys. The suit made false a claim about the way T.J. ran his business. His integrity was under attack.

Settling would be easier than fighting the suit, of course. "It's always better to avoid a protracted court battle," Thorpe had reminded T.J. in his wispy, perpetually tired voice. "You know how it is in cases like these— even when you win you wind up losing. We can't contact your insurance company until Monday morning. But I say that if they're willing to pay the plaintiff off, let 'em. You'll save yourself a lot of grief."

T.J. wasn't sure of that. Thorpe's argument had sounded reasonable, but T.J. just wasn't sure.

"I've got to get back to my father's store," Abbie said, finishing her coffee. "And you probably have to hit the jogging path before you open Tyler's."

Jogging. Maybe he could delay his trip to Thorpe's office a little longer by taking a run along the railroad track. "Are you going jogging this afternoon?" he asked Abbie. "We could work out together."

She shook her head. "I'm afraid not."

"No pressure today?"

"No time." She slid out of the booth. T.J. stood as well, reached into his hip pocket for his wallet, and left a couple of dollars on the table for Thelma. "I didn't even have time for this coffee break," Abbie added, flashing T.J. a timid smile, "but somehow, you managed to talk me into it."

"Yeah, I really twisted your arm," he played along, pleased to think that a woman who spoke so militantly about fighting for legal justice could be susceptible to his powers of persuasion.

"I'm glad you did," she admitted.

"I'll walk you back to Jarvis's," he said determinedly—not that he expected her to decline his offer, but he didn't want to provide her with a chance to bid him farewell. He wasn't ready to leave Abbie yet. As much as he'd enjoyed her company the previous few times they'd been together, he liked her even more now, when she was all fired up, intense and committed and eager to storm the barricades.

After saying goodbye to Thelma—a task that took twice as long as necessary because Thelma had to expound upon the red highlights in Abbie's hair one last time before they left—T.J. and Abbie started down the street to Jarvis's Hardware. "I don't know why she went on so much about my hair," Abbie commented. "It's always had a reddish cast to it. Wasn't it this color in high school?"

T.J. honestly didn't remember; he simply hadn't been that aware of Abbie's appearance seventeen years ago. He was acutely aware of it now, aware of the narrow line of her nose and the arch of her cheeks, the inherently stubborn angle of her chin and the iridescence of her eyes, the neat proportions of her figure. And now that they were outdoors, he was definitely aware of the way the sunlight seemed to permeate her hair and imbue it with fiery streaks.

When he'd asked her for a dinner date yesterday, he had done so as a neighborly gesture. He had assumed they'd have fun talking about the old days, and he'd figured Abbie would probably want to be distracted from her father's problems for an hour or two. But maybe, T.J. conceded silently, he had also asked her out because—as he'd joked the first time she had been to Tyler's—everybody knew everybody in Wheeler. He was already well acquainted with just about every single woman in town. Few as they were, it wasn't terribly difficult to get to know all of them. He and Doreen Gallagher had had a good thing going for a while a couple of years back, but before T.J. could make up his mind whether to consider establishing something permanent with her, she had abruptly succumbed to wanderlust and moved to San Francisco. And although he'd been interested in pursuing a serious relationship with Marilyn Macy, her obnoxious children had interfered, whining to their mother that they despised him and making him feel so ill at ease whenever he visited the Macy home that he gave up on Marilyn.

He might initially have asked Abbie to join him for dinner out of boredom, or simply because she was a novelty in these parts. But if he asked her out today, it would be for a much better reason: because she intrigued him. Because, despite how jaded and acerbic she seemed whenever she described her work and her life back in New York, she had a passion inside her, hot and dazzlingly bright, just waiting to be fanned into flame. He'd glimpsed it in the luncheonette, and it excited him in a way he hadn't been excited since...probably since the first time he'd met Mary-Jane, fifteen years ago.

He wasn't going to ask Abbie out for dinner again, though. She had already turned him down several times, and he didn't believe in pushing himself where he wasn't wanted. Besides, even if Abbie was going to remain in Wheeler longer than she'd anticipated when she'd first arrived, she wasn't going to stay forever. It didn't take a genius to recognize that Abbie wasn't the type to indulge in a quick fling while she happened to be passing through town. T.J. wouldn't mind having a brief affair with her, no question about that. But Abbie was still recovering from a messy split with some jerk in New York. And even if she hadn't been recuperating from that painful breakup, she simply wasn't the kind of woman who'd fool around for the fun of it.

"Well," she said softly as they reached the hardware store. The glass-paned front door was propped open on a narrow wooden wedge, and sale items were displayed along the sidewalk on either side of the doorway: a row of rakes leaning against the front window, a stack of bushel baskets, a pyramid of cinder block bricks.

Abbie made no move to enter the store. Her gaze came to rest on one of the rakes, and she stroked her fingers over its painted handle. Her mood flagged noticeably; her smile became brittle.

It bothered T.J. that she could be so spirited about his problems and so demoralized about her father's. "You know, Abbie, it doesn't hurt to be optimistic," he pointed out in a gentle voice.

She glanced sharply up at him. "What's that supposed to mean?"

"It means..." He had no right to sound off about the hardware store's financial difficulties—except that Abbie had sounded off about Tyler's legal difficulties. She and T.J. were friends, and friends were allowed to speak their minds. "You look so glum, Abbie, like you're ready to throw in the towel—and you've just barely started to tackle the problem."

Abbie's lips relaxed into a grin. "What is this, some sort of locker room speech?"

T.J. laughed. "No, Abbie. Locker room speech is something I wouldn't repeat in the presence of a lady."

"Sexism is more offensive than dirty words," Abbie chided, although she was chuckling. "Believe me, T.J., I've heard it all."

"On the New York City subway?"

"I wish. Usually it's at work—in interrogation. Thugs tend to have the most colorful ways of expressing themselves," she muttered.

"I'm sure you bring out the best in them," T.J. teased as he ushered her into the store.

Stepping inside Jarvis's Hardware always invigorated T.J., the way candy stores invigorated youngsters or record shops invigorated teenagers. Like a candy store or a record shop, Jarvis's had ambience. The floors were constructed of unvarnished pine boards and smelled of sawdust. The shelves were packed with tools and carpentry items, garden and plumbing supplies, clearly labeled bins of nails, screws, tacks, and bolts of various shapes, paint brushes, chicken wire, fish wire, tape measures, folding aluminum ladders... The overhead fluorescent lighting was bright, and several long-armed ceiling fans revolved, silently churning the air.

"Hey, T.J., how's tricks?" Stan DeCinto bellowed, descending from a ladder with a ratchet set, which he'd retrieved from an upper shelf for a customer. Stan had played football with T.J. back in school, even though he stood only about five foot nine or so. The regional high school's population had been small enough that any guy able to make sense of the playbook was all but guaranteed a place on the team.

"Hey, yourself," T.J. returned the greeting. Before he could run through the standard questions regarding Stan's family, Roy Jarvis came bustling down the aisle toward them, his eyes wide with alarm.

"Abbie!" he accosted his daughter, slightly out of breath. He acknowledged T.J. with a quick, edgy smile, then turned back to Abbie. "Where've you been, honey?"

Abbie's face went pale. "What's wrong, Dad? I told you I was going out to buy a calculator, and then T.J. and I—"

"Abbie," Roy cut her off, "Faye Hinkel was in a little while ago. Right after you left—you just missed her."

T.J. couldn't imagine why Roy Jarvis should be so keyed up over a visit to the store by Faye Hinkel. As far as T.J. knew, Faye had worked at Jarvis's for a while after Roy's wife had died, and although she no longer worked there, Faye and Roy were reputed to be friends. T.J. wondered whether something horrible had happened to Faye, whether her house had collapsed or her pipes had rusted through and she was desperate for Roy's professional assistance.

"Faye and I saw each other outside," Abbie told her father, looking nearly as panicked as Roy. "Why? What happened? She didn't mention anything to me."

"She's leaving," Roy blurted out, obviously distraught. "She said she's moving away."

"From Wheeler? Faye Hinkel's leaving Wheeler?" Abbie shook her head in disbelief. "Why?"

"Well, I don't know that it's definite, but... It was the darnedest thing, Abbie. Faye didn't come to the store to buy anything. It was like—like she came in just to tell me this news. She marched right over to me, said hello, and without any further ado she announced that she was thinking maybe it was time for a change in her life, that Wheeler just didn't have much of a hold on her anymore, and she was considering moving down to Sacramento. Her sister has a condo there.''

T.J.'s gaze shuttled between Roy and Abbie. She seemed to be waiting for her father to elaborate, and when he didn't, her expression registered impatience. ''That's it? That's the whole story?''

''That's what she told me, Abbie, more or less. She said her sister told her there are lots of single men in Sacramento. Now why she thought she had to come all the way to the store to tell me about the population of single men in Sacramento, I can't begin to figure out . . .''

Abbie stared at her father for a minute longer, then burst into laughter. ''Dad, you are the densest human being I've ever met.''

T.J. scowled. He must be as dense as Roy, since he had no idea what Abbie found so humorous—let alone what Faye Hinkel's abrupt decision to move to Sacramento had to do with the Jarvises.

''What?'' Roy asked testily. ''What's so funny?''

''Dad, why do you think she'd come to you, of all people, to mention that she might be moving somewhere where there are lots of single men?''

''I don't know,'' Roy answered, obviously puzzled. ''I thought maybe she'd like my help getting her things packed into boxes. Maybe she needs a screwdriver to take apart her stereo or something . . .''

''Dad,'' Abbie emphatically cut him off, ''she wanted you to talk her into staying.''

''She did?''

''She likes you,'' Abbie said. Her tone had softened in a soothing, womanly way that T.J. found peculiarly moving, even though she was addressing not him but her father. "She *likes* you."

"Faye Hinkel?" Roy exclaimed in astonishment. "Faye Hinkel *likes* me?"

"Of course. You're a single man, too, Dad. Why else would she threaten to leave? She's trying to catch your attention."

Roy mulled Abbie's words over, then shook his head. "I'm just an old widower, Abbie—"

"You're a handsome middle-aged widower. And Faye's a charming middle-aged widow. Wake up, Dad. She's been sweet on you for years. Tell him," Abbie demanded, turning to T.J. "Tell him I'm right."

T.J. held his hands up in surrender. "Don't ask me, Roy," he protested. As appealing as he found the notion of Roy Jarvis and Faye Hinkel pairing up—particularly with Abbie serving as their matchmaker—he sure as hell wasn't stupid enough to express an opinion either way. Let Abbie and Roy work this one out themselves.

Roy appeared bemused. "Faye? Sweet on me? Where's the evidence, Abbie? You're a lawyer—I'd like to see some evidence to support this notion of yours."

"You want evidence?" Abbie said, her eyes lighting up again, her face animated as she organized her thoughts. "Here's some evidence: how often did Faye visit you after Mom died and I went back to New York?"

Roy meditated for a minute, then yielded with a reluctant shrug. "Okay, she was over to the house a lot. But she was just being neighborly," he argued lamely.

"Right. Neighborly. Did Margaret Schaller bring you as many casseroles as Faye did? Margaret's your next-door neighbor, Dad."

"Margaret's married."

"My point exactly. And who offered her services as a bookkeeper?" Abbie forged ahead. "The very job Mom used to do here at the store. Faye knew how much you needed a new bookkeeper, and she took the job. Even when you couldn't afford a salary, she volunteered to stay on."

"She's a generous soul," Roy granted.

"She's a generous *woman*," Abbie stressed, "and it's about time you noticed. Why do you think she mentioned the number of single men in Sacramento, for heaven's sake? She wants you to notice that she's a desirable woman. She wants to make you jealous."

"Jealous!" Roy guffawed, then grew sober. He shifted his skeptical gaze to T.J. "Does any of this make sense to you?" he asked.

It made a lot of sense to T.J. Even if it hadn't made sense, even if Faye Hinkel hadn't done anything to indicate an interest in Roy, that shouldn't stop him from courting her. T.J. didn't know Faye that well, but she seemed like a nice lady, unattached, well-groomed and pleasant company. Hell, if she were younger, T.J. would have asked her out himself. "Go for it, Roy," he urged Abbie's father, giving him a knowing nod.

"Go for what?" Roy questioned him, his smile touchingly artless and his eyes round with bewilderment. "What do I do?"

"Call her up and ask her out for dinner," T.J. recommended. "The worst that'll happen is, she'll say no." He peered down at Abbie when he said that, wondering if she regretted having said no to him yesterday, wondering whether he ought to ask her one more time. After all, if he did, the worst that would happen was, she'd say no—again.

Coming from Abbie, though, another rejection would really disturb T.J. More than having Doreen fly off to San Francisco, more than hearing Marilyn Macy's brats whining about how they wanted their estranged parents to get back together again, more than sitting face-to-face with Mary-Jane and saying, "This thing isn't going to work, honey, we just aren't going to make it..." He could think of no good explanation for why being turned down by Abbie would bother him so much. When she'd declined his invitation last night outside Tyler's, he had been annoyed but not demolished. Today, for some reason, he felt differently. Today he recognized that Abbie had the power to demolish him.

"Call her up and ask her out," Roy mused, breaking into T.J.'s troublesome thoughts. "I think I'll just do that." Abbie's father pulled himself to his full height and thrust back his shoulders in a posture of proud courage. "I'll just go and call up that fine woman and ask her if she would do me the honor of joining me for dinner." He turned and strode resolutely to the rear of the store.

Abbie watched him disappear into the back office, then spun around to T.J. and smiled gratefully. "Thanks for supporting me, T.J.," she said.

He shrugged good-naturedly. "I just hope the lady doesn't cut him down, now that we've got him so pumped up."

"Faye won't cut him down," Abbie predicted with a certainty bordering on smugness. "She's had her eye on Dad for a long time."

"You think so, huh." T.J. was tickled by Abbie's confidence, and a bit disconcerted by it. He remembered how positive she'd always sounded in Mr. Daniels's social studies class when she was expounding on the immorality of the Vietnam War. T.J. wasn't so sure that the war had been immoral—and he wasn't so sure that Faye Hinkel had her eye on Roy Jarvis. But when Abbie got this way, when her eyes started glowing and she set her chin at a certain combative angle, T.J. knew better than to cross her.

"Stick around for a minute," Abbie invited him. "You'll see."

He checked his wristwatch. It was already well past two o'clock, which meant that jogging was definitely out for today—unless he skipped a visit to John Thorpe's office. T.J. was tempted to call Thorpe and tell him that he'd decided to hire Abbie because she wasn't too lethargic to fight his case for him the way it ought to be fought. But the idea of hiring Abbie as his attorney was merely a fantasy. By the time his case came to trial—if it ever reached that stage—she would be back in New York City, prosecuting her foul-mouthed thugs.

A couple of foul words passed through his brain. Why, all of a sudden, did he want Abbie professionally, romantically, sexually and every which way? How had this old classmate of his managed to tie his emotions into such knots? "One minute," he granted her, his indulgent grin revealing nothing of his tangled thoughts.

It took less than that for Roy Jarvis to emerge through the back office door and work his way down the aisle to Abbie and T.J. He appeared slightly dazed. "I asked her to have dinner with me tonight, Abbie, and she said no," he reported. Abbie's smile slipped, but it came back fuller than before when Roy continued, "What she said was, she'll have dinner with me tomorrow."

"That sounds reasonable. She deserves twenty-four hours' notice," Abbie asserted, beaming triumphantly.

"I reckon I'll need twenty-four hours, too," Roy mumbled. He looked as if he wasn't sure what he'd gotten himself into. "The last time I went out on a date, was...Lord, Abbie, it was right after I got back from Korea and your mom decided to sink her hooks into me. She did the asking, Abbie, not me. Of course, I had the good sense to say yes..." He drifted for a minute, focusing on a memory. When his eyes sharpened again, he directed his gaze to T.J. "You're pretty experienced at this dating business, T.J. Can you share any words of wisdom with a rookie?"

T.J. shot Abbie a quick look and found her smiling hopefully at him. He wasn't sure he wanted to get involved in what he considered a private family matter—except that he was already involved with the Jarvis family. He'd been in on their bad news; he ought to leap at the opportunity to participate in their good news. Especially for Abbie's sake, he pondered, absorbing her enchanting smile, her strangely imploring gaze.

He slung his arm around Roy's shoulders, adopting a man-to-man pose. "First of all, let's talk after-shave," he said sagely, guiding Roy down the aisle away from Abbie, although he deliberately spoke loud enough for her to overhear. "What's at issue is, do you want to impress Faye or do you want to get her into bed?"

"T.J.!" Abbie roared, chasing him and Roy through the narrow aisle.

T.J. laughed. Abbie had dragged him into this—she was going to get what she paid for. "If you want to get Faye into bed, Roy," he went on in a stage whisper, "I would recommend—"

"T.J.!" Abbie snarled through clenched teeth.

He glanced over his shoulder and discovered her standing just a couple of feet behind him and Roy, her hands on her hips and her eyes burning with condemnation. He couldn't resist saying, "Forgive me for repeating myself, Abbie, but you sure are beautiful when you're angry."

"Last time, you told me I was self-righteous," she reminded him peevishly.

He winked. "If the shoe fits, sweetheart..." Turning his back on her, he deftly steered Roy out of Abbie's range of hearing before filling him in on the restaurants up in Chico. Deep in his heart T.J. might well be a teddy bear, but Abbie didn't have to know that.

SHE FELT MORE OR LESS SAFE in assuming that T.J. had only been teasing her. She didn't begrudge her father a sex life; indeed, she didn't believe that he'd been totally without female companionship in the seven and a half years since her mother's passing. But there was no tactful way for Abbie to broach that particular subject with her father—and it really wasn't her business.

Punching numbers into her calculator and jotting figures onto a yellow legal pad, Abbie ruminated on her father's impending date. Maybe he *would* wind up in bed with Faye Hinkel—but if he did, it would be because destiny led them there, not because he had contrived some after-shave-drenched strategy under the tutelage of Wheeler's most eligible bachelor.

But why had T.J. taunted Abbie that way? What, besides mischief, had she discerned in his eyes when he tossed her that final, branding grin and said, "If the shoe fits, sweetheart..."? Why had his offhand remark about her alleged beauty stirred something inside her, something deeper and more complex than a simple acknowledgment that she'd been complimented? Why was she still acting like a run-of-the-mill high school girl smitten with the town hero and taking his every utterance to heart? He had been kidding about Roy's after-shave; surely he'd also been kidding about Abbie's beauty.

Cautioning herself not to take any of it too seriously, she forced her attention to what she *did* have to take seriously: the store's unbalanced budget. Even at the current doubled cost, the rent her father paid was absurdly low compared to what stores rented for in Manhattan. Judging by Wheeler standards, however—or, more significantly, judging by what the store could afford—Abbie easily predicted major problems in getting the numbers to line up. She hadn't gone through all of the charge accounts yet, but much of the money owed to Jarvis's Hardware by customers was probably uncollectable. The Ambroses were never going to pay the store the three hundred seventy dollars plus interest they owed; other customers were undoubtedly in similar positions. Faced with the choice of feeding her family or paying off a hardware store bill, Abbie would buy groceries. Any normal person would.

And in the meantime . . . in the meantime, any normal man, after years of solitude, would pay for dinner on a date with a lovely woman like Faye before he'd pay his store's Pacific Gas and Electric bill, wouldn't he? Abbie's father might well be reeling toward bankruptcy, but she wasn't going to allow that to spoil his date with Faye tomorrow night. Let him take Faye someplace elegant, let him order the most expensive entree on the menu. Let him spruce himself up, even invest in a new after-shave if he felt it was necessary. Let him spend money like a sport for one night. He could file for bankruptcy after he and Abbie met with Ed Garcia at the bank on Monday.

Monday was two days away. Until then, her father deserved to live as if he were a king and Faye was his queen. There would be plenty of time afterward for reality to set in.

Chapter Six

The clamorous jangle of the ringing telephone startled Abbie so much she jumped.

If the office at the rear of Jarvis's Hardware had been dismal on Saturday, it was even more depressing on Sunday, when the store was closed and Abbie was alone in the dark, nearly silent building. Her father had wanted to accompany her when she returned to the store to finish tallying up the budget figures, but she had insisted that he use the afternoon to prepare for his upcoming dinner date. Not that he had so very much to take care of: a quick jaunt to the automatic teller machine outside the bank for some cash, a touch-up on his dress shirt and wool-blend slacks with the iron, a trip over to the tiny meadow abutting the Covingtons' walnut orchard on the southern end of town to pick a bouquet of wildflowers for Faye. All told, his errands wouldn't take more than an hour or two. But he was so jittery about his impending date, Abbie knew he would drive her crazy if he came to the store with her. He would fret and worry and alternately congratulate and belittle himself, as he'd done all the previous evening and that morning, and Abbie wouldn't be able to get any work accomplished.

So she had insisted on coming to the store by herself. And there she was, trying not to be daunted by the looming shadows created by the daylight filtering dimly through the windows that faced Main Street and skimming over the shelves of merchandise, the creaking of the floorboards and walls, the reverberations of every small sound Abbie made, from the rattling of a sheet of paper to the scraping of her chair's legs against the floor. The eerie echoes unnerved her enough that she found herself making a major effort not to create any noise at all. She was thankful for the new calculator she'd bought; she didn't think she could have borne the clicks and clanks of the old adding machine.

The unexpected pealing of the telephone jolted her. In the distance, she heard the extension by the cashier counter at the front of the store resounding in a spooky harmony with the blaring extension on the desk just inches from her ear. The shrill suddenness of it didn't alarm her as much as the knowledge that the caller had to be her father; nobody else knew she was at the store today. She assumed that the only reason he would phone her at the store was to report a disaster, real or imagined. Had Faye decided to back out on him at the last minute? Had he been unable to find the chamois cloth he used to buff his shoes? Was he embarrassed about having to ferry Faye to dinner in a van that said Fifty Years of Know-how in vivid green letters across the side?

Abbie lifted the receiver, effectively putting an end to the head-splitting noise. Finding herself once again in tranquil surroundings, she inhaled a steadying breath, braced herself for whatever catastrophe had befallen her father, and with admirable serenity said, "Hello, Dad."

As soon as she spoke, she realized that whoever was on the other end of the line wasn't her father—unless her father's house had been invaded by children. Through the receiver she heard a jumbled cacophony of television noises and giggling, along with a plaintive high-pitched oration on the subject of promises made…and then T.J.'s voice, clear and crisp and tinged with laughter. "Wrong, Abbie. But I'm such a nice guy I'll give you another guess."

"T.J.?" How had he found her here?

He answered her unspoken question. "I tried you at home, Abbie, and your father told me you were at the store. Tell me, was it just my imagination or is your old man nervous about tonight? He sounded kind of jumpy and jittery when I talked to him."

Abbie grinned and relaxed in her chair. She was pleased that T.J. had called, so pleased she wasn't even bothered by the ominous squeak the chair made when she leaned back in it. "He's *very* nervous," she confirmed. "But he'll get over it, once the date is underway and he realizes how much Faye adores him."

"You sound awfully sure of that," T.J. noted, then excused himself and addressed someone on his end: "Well, go ahead and turn it on, Josh. I know it's almost time— I'll be in, in a minute." Back into the phone, he explained, "I'm calling from my sister's house. I came here to visit, and somehow I got roped into baby-sitting for a couple of hours so Mark and Linda could help Mark's grandfather repaper his kitchen walls—oh, excuse me again…" Abbie heard a muffled exchange between T.J. and a child, and then T.J. returned to her. "I promised the kids I'd make them popcorn to eat while we watch a football game on TV. Kickoff's in a couple of minutes."

"Uh-huh." Abbie wasn't quite sure why, when he was obviously well occupied by his niece and nephew, he had

bothered to call her. Now didn't seem to be a particularly
good time for them to indulge in a leisurely chat.

T.J. finally got to the point. "I was thinking, Abbie—
why should you be stuck having to eat supper all alone
tonight while your father and Faye are out painting the
town red? You're more than welcome to come over to the
farm here in Princeton, catch the game on the tube with
us, and then stay on for dinner. It won't be anything
fancy, but Linda always cooks enough to feed an army.
What do you say?"

Abbie said nothing. For a long, speechless minute, she
thought about how kind T.J.'s invitation was, and T.J.
himself . . . and how good-looking he was. She thought
about how comfortable she had felt with him yesterday
when they'd shared a cup of coffee, and then afterward
when she had enlisted his aid in getting her father to invite Faye out for dinner. She thought about how easy it
would be to say yes to T.J.'s invitation, how easy to become dependent on his friendship.

Her failure to respond immediately prompted him to
add, "This isn't a date or anything, Abbie."

Ironically, what he'd intended as a reassuring remark
compelled her to run for cover. "I appreciate your asking, T.J.," she said quietly, "but I'm afraid I'll have to
pass." It pained her to refuse him. Dinner with his sister's family would probably be a delightful event; Mark
had seemed quite pleasant, and Abbie loved children. But
as soon as she'd heard T.J. utter the word *date*, she'd
suddenly felt edgy, self-protective, anxious.

She *was* becoming dependent on T.J.'s friendship—too
dependent. She was growing to like too much the attention he lavished on her, the way he watched her and listened to her, the strength and warmth in his smile
whenever she opened up to him. She'd had difficulty fall-

ing asleep her first night in Wheeler because of memories of her mother, and the second night because she was upset about her father's financial plight. What had kept her awake last night were thoughts of T.J., of his sense of humor and his unflappability in the face of a legal challenge, of his dark, piercing eyes and windswept brown hair, his strong chin and his lanky, male physique and the way his large, able hands had felt on her the few times he had touched her.

She didn't want to be entertaining such thoughts about him, or such feelings. She didn't want to desire any man—particularly not T. J. Hillyard. He made his home in Wheeler, and Abbie made her home in New York City, and that put three thousand miles between them. No matter how long she planned to remain in Wheeler, she would ultimately leave and he would stay. Anything that might blossom between them was already doomed.

"Well, it was an idea," he was saying, his tone strangely heavy with resignation. "If you can't make it, you can't. I just thought I'd ask."

Her fingers tightened around the telephone receiver, as if by clinging to it she could hold onto T.J. himself. Despite his benign acceptance of her decision, he had to be disappointed. Her father had asked Faye for dinner only once and received a yes. T.J. had asked Abbie three times and received three rejections from her. He was a human being; he was probably frustrated or hurt, maybe frustrated and hurt enough to want to steer clear of Abbie for the remainder of her stay in Wheeler.

As attracted as she was to him, she couldn't permit a romance to develop between them. But she didn't want to lose his friendship. In fact, she couldn't shake the subliminal comprehension that at least one reason she'd elected to stay on in Wheeler was to nurture that friendship, to enjoy it and give it a chance to develop. To let it slip away would be a terrible waste.

"Here's a better idea," she said hastily, hoping to cure him of any resentment he might be harboring toward her. "I've got a lot more work to do here at the store this afternoon, but I plan to get home by five, in time to wave my father off on his great adventure. Maybe you could come to his house, instead, and we'll rustle up something to eat there."

It occurred to her, as soon as she verbalized the invitation, that what she was suggesting was far more risky than the invitation T.J. had originally extended her. After all, they would be all alone at her father's house, without T.J.'s relatives to chaperone them.

On the other hand, T.J. himself had declared that this was not a date. He struck Abbie as being straightforward enough that if he had any romantic designs on her, he wouldn't have made such a statement. All he had in mind was a meal shared by two friends while one of them recovered from an afternoon of baby-sitting and the other waited up for her social-butterfly father.

T.J. embraced Abbie's suggestion at once. "Sounds great. I can get there by five or so. Would you like me to pick up some hoagies at the 7-Eleven on my way?"

"No, T.J. I'll fix something for us."

"Are you sure you don't mind? After knocking yourself out at the store all afternoon—"

"It sounds as if you're knocking yourself out a lot more than I am," Abbie observed with a chuckle. She had to shout to be heard; on his end, T.J. was once again being besieged by melodramatic reminders about the popcorn he'd promised to make for his niece and nephew.

"All right, I'll skip the hoagies. How about wine? Should I bring a red or a white?"

"You're a bartender—surprise me."

He started to respond to Abbie, then wound up addressing his nephew. "I know I missed the kickoff, Josh. Believe it or not, pal, there are actually a few things in life more important than football." To Abbie, he said, "I've gotta go. I'll see you this evening."

With that, he hung up.

Abbie stared at the dead phone in her hand, a shy, astounded smile teasing her lips. She had no intention of falling for T.J., but still...it thrilled her in an immeasurable way to realize that her friendship was evidently one of those things in life that T. J. Hillyard, All-American out of U.S.C. and first-round draft pick by the Chicago Bears, considered more important than football.

HE BROUGHT A SIX-PACK of Olympia beer. For one thing, he knew Abbie liked Oly, and for another, he was expecting her to serve the sort of food one "rustled up," the kind of meal you'd equate with hoagies from 7-Eleven. He would feel like an idiot decanting a bottle of Château Whatever while she was busy slapping together some ham-and-cheese sandwiches.

He'd feel like an idiot decanting Château Whatever under any circumstances. Few customers at Tyler's requested wine, but on those rare occasions when somebody did order a glass, T.J. kept in stock a good Napa Valley burgundy for those who liked their wine to have a flavor, a decent California chablis for those who didn't care whether they could taste the stuff or not, and a rosé for anyone with affectations. But Tyler's wasn't a yuppie watering hole. If you cared more about the vintage of your booze than the company you were in, you might as well head north to one of the fern bars near the university in Chico.

He arrived at the Jarvis house around five-fifteen and tapped his knuckles on the screen doorframe. "It's open," Abbie sang out from somewhere inside the house. "Come on in—I'm in the kitchen." After raking his fingers through his hair once or twice to smooth out the tangles, he swung open the door and entered the house.

He had never been in Roy Jarvis's home, and he took a moment to examine the living room before setting off in search of the kitchen. It was larger than the living room in his parents' house when he'd been growing up, but smaller than the living room of the house he owned now. The furnishings were old and lived-in, the floral pattern on the sofa faded to a dull blue green, the carpet worn in spots, the coffee table scuffed. One part of T.J.'s brain grasped that this was the sort of house a man could be really comfortable in; for no good reason, another part of his brain calculated the value of the furnishings and concluded that, if he truly did go under, Roy Jarvis wouldn't pocket much money from a sheriff's auction of his property.

An extension off the living room held a dining table and four chairs that looked too clean and devoid of scratches to have been subjected to frequent use. T.J. strolled into the dining area and located an arched doorway leading to the kitchen. From where he was standing, he had a fantastic view through the doorway of Abbie's rear end as she bent to slide something into the oven. She was wearing a pair of off-white slacks that weren't too tight, just snug enough for T.J. to notice how slim her hips and thighs were.

So this evening's dinner wasn't a date. So Abbie, in turning down his requests for a *real* date, had made it perfectly clear that she wasn't interested in exploring anything hot and heavy with him. That didn't mean he couldn't appreciate the scenery, did it?

"Whatever it is, it smells better than what Linda was cooking," he said by way of greeting.

Abbie straightened up and spun around. Her cheeks darkened for a moment—perhaps she realized that the first thing he'd seen of her was her butt. Then she recovered with a smile and used the back of her hand to shove a stray lock of hair from her cheek. "It's just a bunch of ingredients I threw together," she said, her gaze shifting from T.J.'s face to the six-pack of Oly. "It's a bunch of ingredients that goes perfectly with beer," she added, smiling approvingly at his choice of beverage and gesturing him into the kitchen. "Come on in and have a seat. I'll put the beer in the fridge and make a salad."

He surveyed the kitchen as he entered. The pair of windows in the western wall allowed the late afternoon sunshine to spill in, lighting up the entire room. The appliances, while old, were immaculate, their white enamel surfaces sparkling, and the café curtains were fringed with little yellow pom-poms. A hackneyed still-life of a fruit bowl hung on a wall above the table in the corner, and on another wall a collection of copper molds had been arranged.

This was definitely a comfortable house. T.J. resolved, right then and there, that even after Abbie returned to New York he would make an effort to visit Roy at his house every now and then.

"What happened to you?" Abbie asked, breaking into his meditations.

He turned from the window to face her. "What do you mean, what happened to me?"

She was standing beside the refrigerator, a head of lettuce in one hand and a tomato in the other. "You're limping," she observed.

He glanced down at his jean-clad legs and then lifted his gaze to Abbie again. She looked petite, dwarfed by the refrigerator, her small palm scarcely able to balance the green sphere of lettuce. She was wearing a short-sleeved knit sweater of a muted orange shade, with a scooped neckline that highlighted her exposed collarbone and a patterned weave that drew his attention to her breasts.

He lifted his eyes from her chest and met her accusing frown. "Nothing happened," he said. "I always walk funny when I haven't gone jogging in a couple of days."

Abbie digested his explanation and a faint pink hue stained her cheeks again. She carried the salad fixings to the sink and said, "Why don't you sit down, T.J.? I'll get you one of those beers as soon as they've chilled."

Her voice sounded slightly breathless to him, and he allowed himself a private grin. He could figure out what she had been thinking: that the main reason he hadn't gone jogging in the past two days was that he'd been with her, instead. He wouldn't deny it—and, he wouldn't have lived the past two days any differently, even if he could. Killing an hour drinking coffee with Abbie yesterday and being her guest for dinner tonight were definitely worth having his knee stiffen up on him.

"Are you sure I can't help you with the dinner?" he asked, rolling up the sleeves of his shirt as the heat of the oven began to spread through the room.

She peeked over her shoulder at him, then handed him a couple of plates, silverware and napkins that she had stacked on the counter. "You can set the table if you want," she said in a clipped tone.

He puzzled over her apparent tension. It bothered him to think she could feel uneasy with him when he felt so relaxed with her. She'd been relaxed with him yesterday and the afternoon they had jogged together—relaxed enough to cry in his arms and tell him all about the creep who broke her heart back in New York. Carrying the plates to the table and arranging two place settings, T.J. tried to come up with a tactful way to question her on her edginess.

He hadn't by the time he was done setting the table, so he jettisoned tact and tried candor instead. "Are you tense or something, Abbie?"

She twisted around to glimpse him, then smiled and turned back to the sink, where she shook the tomato dry. "Not really. Maybe a little."

He was gratified that she was willing to meet him on the honest level he had established. "Not because of me, I hope," he said.

She laughed. "I think some of my father's nervousness rubbed off on me. I'm glad you didn't get here until after he'd left the house. The poor man was bouncing off the ceiling, T.J. And no thanks to you, I might add," she accused, waving a knife toward him in a mock threat before she used it to slice the tomato.

"Me?" he exclaimed innocently. "What did I do?"

"All that nonsense about what kind of after-shave to use. He's always used the same brand, but he has about a dozen unopened bottles of other scents that he's received as Christmas presents from my Aunt Martha. He proceeded to open all of them and make me inhale them. By the time we'd reached the last bottle I was wheezing worse than an asthmatic. The only good thing to come out of all of this is that we threw out all the bottles, and now there's plenty of extra space on the shelf of the linen closet."

"So he opted for the tried-and-true on the fragrance front, huh," T.J. said with a chuckle.

"And he smelled just fine." Abbie returned to the refrigerator for a celery stalk and a carrot, and her gaze collided with T.J.'s as she started back toward the sink. Her eyes were glowing with amusement and something else—suspicion, perhaps. "Should I ask what kind of after-shave you're wearing, T.J.?" she inquired.

He shrugged. If she didn't want to trust him, that was her choice. He was perfectly willing to live up—or down—to her distrust. "Come on over and give me a sniff," he dared her with a sly grin.

This time her cheeks remained their usual creamy shade. "Save your strategies for someone who'll appreciate them, T.J.," she said tartly, although her smile remained big and bright. Obviously he wasn't making her nervous anymore.

That should have pleased him, but it didn't. He didn't want Abbie to be nervous in his presence, but he didn't want her to presume that she was perfectly safe with him, either. All afternoon, Josh and Shelley had been making him promise to do this and that: watch football, pop popcorn, teach them the rudiments of draw poker, read and assess their most recent book reports. T.J. didn't make promises he couldn't keep, and he wasn't going to make any promises when it came to Abbie—especially when she was wearing that alluring scoop-necked sweater.

Armed with a pair of quilted pot holders, she opened the oven door, this time standing to one side of it so she wouldn't present an unobstructed view of her bottom to T.J. She pulled out a casserole dish, balanced it on one of the stove's burners, and lifted the lid. "I guess this is done," she said vaguely, carrying it on a trivet to the table. T.J. crossed to the refrigerator to get a couple of beers for them, and Abbie brought over the salad. "There," she said. "Dig in."

T.J. took a heaping portion of the casserole. A mixture of noodles, chopped meat and tomato sauce, it bore a resemblance to a macaroni stew his mother used to call American chop suey and he and Linda used to call, rather ghoulishly, "train wreck." He didn't know what Abbie called her version of the dish, but he decided after one taste that it was superior to his mother's.

"This is delicious," he complimented her, lowering his fork and reaching for his beer.

Abbie, he realized, had taken a tiny helping of the stew, and she hadn't touched it. She watched him, smiling hesitantly. "Would you like some bread and butter?" she asked. "I forgot to put it out."

"No, thanks. This and the salad is plenty," he said, wondering why she was gaping at him.

Apparently, she sensed his bewilderment and chose to explain herself. "I'm not used to feeding big, athletic men," she said contritely, spearing a chunk of tomato with her fork, "I didn't know how much to make."

T.J. laughed and glanced into the casserole dish, which was over half-full of stew. "If you're expecting a visit from the U.S.C. football team, you'd better send out for pizza. If you aren't, you won't run out of food. I'm not a jock anymore, and I don't eat like one."

Abbie laughed, too. "If you want to know the truth, T.J., I think you look much better now than you did when you were a jock. You weigh a lot less, don't you?"

"About thirty pounds less," he told her. "You should have seen me put it away in those days. I used to eat the equivalent of about six meals in twenty-four hours. Steak, eggs, some yogurt, a few slices of bread with peanut but-

ter, a quart of milk, a couple of oranges—and that was
just for breakfast.''

"That's more than I eat in a whole day!"

"I believe it," he said, eyeing her slender body. "Pig-
ging out isn't much fun, though—at least not if you've got
to do it on a regular basis. Besides, I was eating for muscle and energy, not fat. It was almost all protein and
complex carbs—real healthy stuff, real boring."

Abbie leaned back in her chair, fingering her beer bottle and scrutinizing him. "You don't seem to miss it," she
commented.

"Miss what? Eating like a pig?"

"Playing football."

He shrugged. For a long time, he used to hate talking
about his aborted pro career—but that had been because
when he first came back to Wheeler everyone kept raising the subject, everyone kept pestering him about how
bad he must feel. He *had* felt bad for a while, but by now
the whole thing was too far in the past to bother him
much. Sometimes, when he thought about his athletic
glory, he almost felt as if he were thinking about someone else, some other lifetime.

"I don't miss it anymore," he answered Abbie. "I
mean, I miss it the way I miss being a kid, or the way I
miss the dog I had when I was growing up. Rusty was a
great dog, but he's history, and so are a lot of other things.
I'm thirty-five years old, Abbie. I've grown up."

She appeared on the verge of questioning him further,
then thought better of it and sipped her beer. He was relieved. He didn't mind discussing the past with Abbie, but
he preferred not to get too philosophical about it. There
were certain things you simply had to accept, and talking
them to death didn't do a lick of good.

"How did it go at your father's store today?" he asked. While no amount of analysis could change what had happened thirteen years ago, the future was still wide open—and that future included the fate of Jarvis's Hardware.

Abbie grimaced. "It was lousy," she said.

"How lousy?"

She raised her eyes and managed a lame smile. "Worse than I thought, but not as bad as I feared," she reported. "If it weren't for a humongous bank loan, I think the store could almost make ends meet. Even with the high rent my father's paying, his monthly take isn't all that much less than his expenses."

"Really? That's a promising sign," T.J. noted. "Any ideas about how he can close the gap?"

Abbie consumed a forkful of stew and shrugged. "I don't know anything about retailing, T.J. I can only guess."

"Go ahead, then," he urged her. "Guess."

"Well..." Poking her fork through her noodles, she ruminated for a minute. "He's got items in the store that have been sitting there forever. Nobody wants to buy them, so they just sit there collecting dust."

"For instance?"

"For instance, gasoline cans. You know, those bright red five-gallon cans everybody was buying fifteen years ago, during the oil crisis, so they could carry some spare gasoline in their cars? There hasn't been an oil crisis in a long time, but my father still has all these five-gallon cans in stock. I know he's stuck with them since they're already paid for, but he's never going to see a profit from them."

"Inventory management," T.J. summed up. "It's more than that he's not going to see a profit, Abbie—it's that the cans are taking up valuable shelf space that could be used for rapid turnover items. He ought to take a loss on the cans and free up the shelf space."

Abbie stared at him. "How did you know that?"

T.J. didn't think he had said anything so remarkable. "Abbie," he reminded her, "I run a business myself. If I kept my shelves stocked with so many bottles of Cointreau I had no room for the rye whisky, I'd go out of business in a week. This is elementary stuff, Abbie. First-year stuff."

"First-year stuff?" she asked, still bemused.

"Who do you think you're talking to, here?" he retorted with spurious indignation. "I majored in business at U.S.C."

"You did? I never knew that."

"Hey, even the football team had to major in something," he said, his tone self-mocking. "And, not that I want to toot my own horn or anything, but business wasn't the easiest major on campus."

"You can stop bragging now, T.J. I'm impressed."

"Good." His smile became genuine and he ate some of his dinner. "So, other than inventory management problems, where's the store falling short?"

"The bank loan," Abbie replied. "My father's had numerous loans over the years, and last year he decided to consolidate them all into one whopper of a loan." She issued a grim sigh. "And now he's months in arrears on it...."

"Is the bank willing to refinance?"

"I don't know. They've gone back and forth with my father several times now. We're hoping to meet with a loan officer there tomorrow—"

"Ed Garcia?" T.J. asked.

Abbie nodded.

T.J. lapsed into a meditative silence. He knew Ed Garcia well. The Garcias lived three doors down from T.J. on Quentin Street, and—laughable though it sometimes seemed to T.J.—Ed considered T.J. a force to be reckoned with in the Wheeler business community. As the owner of not only a successful bar but the building that housed it, T.J. was considered a solid commercial entrepreneur, and Ed frequently turned to him for advice on how things worked in Wheeler. While T.J. might have resisted joining the Rotary, he had been instrumental in helping Ed to connect with the kind of folks who did join—the kind of folks who brought the bank a lot of loan activity.

Aware that Abbie was waiting for him to speak, T.J. said, "I know Ed pretty well."

"Is he a nice guy?"

"Not as nice as I am," T.J. joked, "but then, nobody is."

"Sure." Abbie chuckled. "You're so nice you're about to get sued. Did you ever get over to see John Thorpe yesterday?"

This time it was T.J.'s turn to grimace. "I don't want to talk about it, Abbie," he said brusquely.

She gave him a skeptical look. He recalled that he'd said the same thing yesterday—and then proceeded to talk nonstop about it, to tell her the whole sorry story of the civil suit that teenager's family had brought against Tyler's.

Ever since T.J. had left Thorpe's office and headed for work the previous evening, he had been simmering about the situation. It didn't bother him so much that he was getting sued; what bothered him was that Thorpe kept counseling him to take the "easy" way out, and the "easy" way out—settling with the plaintiff—wasn't at all easy for T.J. to swallow.

He wanted to fight. He wanted a lawyer like Abbie to fight for him, a lawyer with fire in her eyes and in her gut. He wanted on his side a lawyer who believed that justice was more important than taking the easy way out. But Abbie was beyond his reach, at least in the context of his current legal skirmish. Wishing she were his attorney was as futile as wishing he'd been with the Chicago Bears when they'd won the Super Bowl a few years back.

He had just finished telling Abbie that he'd grown up. Growing up meant facing reality, and the reality here was that the attorney he had working for him didn't want to fight his case.

"He told you to keep it out of court, right?" Abbie hazarded.

T.J. smiled reluctantly. "How'd you guess?"

"John Thorpe," she said calmly, "is not in possession of the most imaginative legal mind in the world. Not that I'm in any position to second-guess him—"

"No, go ahead," T.J. invited her, resolving not to take Abbie's comments as anything more than what they were—and resolving not to take the blaze illuminating her eyes as anything other than the passion that burned within what she herself would call an imaginative legal mind.

"Well—" she nibbled on some salad "—there's more than one way to keep a case out of court, T.J."

"You're saying Thorpe's right?"

"In theory, yes. In approach, no. His way of keeping it out of court is to have your insurance company settle with the kid who brought the suit." She lowered her fork and got that look on her face again—almost offensively confident, her eyes as hard and glittering as precious gems, her chin thrust forward in determination. "Another way to keep the case out of court is to get the plaintiff to drop his suit."

What Abbie proposed was so obvious, T.J. wondered why it hadn't occurred to Thorpe—or to T.J. himself. He leaned forward intently. "And how do I do that?" he asked.

"Convince him he hasn't got a prayer of winning. Place the onus on him. Make him realize that it's not worth it to *him* to drag this thing through the courts."

"How?"

"Let him know how strong your case is," Abbie said simply, nudging the casserole dish toward him. "Please help yourself to seconds, T.J."

He was too stunned—both by the logic behind Abbie's remarks and by Abbie herself, by the way the confidence in her smile was tempered by something else, something that might have been wisdom or classiness or just plain beauty—to consider eating any more. "No, thanks," he mumbled. "I'm full."

"Are you sure?" She glimpsed the dish's contents and muttered, "Maybe I ought to invite the football team over, after all. Dad and I are going to be eating this stuff for the rest of the week." Despite her complaints, she accepted T.J.'s claim. Rising gracefully from her chair, she began to clear the table.

"How?" he persevered. "How do I make the plaintiff realize it's not worth his while to pursue the case?"

She shrugged. "I'm not your lawyer, T.J."

"I want you to be," he blurted out. It was too late to pretend he hadn't been dreaming about having Abbie represent him, so he didn't bother. "Let me hire you, Abbie. What do you charge? I'll pay it."

She laughed. Setting the dirty plates in the sink, she turned and leaned against the counter, facing T.J. "You seem to forget that I've got a job in New York," she chided him.

"You took a leave of absence," he shot back, standing and carrying the rest of the dishes to the sink. "You can extend your leave a little longer, can't you?"

"How long? A case like yours might drag on for months." She adjusted the water's temperature and squeezed some dish soap into the sink. "Anyway, I'm not licensed to practice law in California."

"What would you have to do to get a license?"

She laughed again. He knew he was coming on strong— much stronger than he'd come on when the subject hadn't been justice but, rather, after-shave lotion. Even so…she didn't have to laugh at him, did she?

She armed him with a dish towel and started to wash the dishes. He watched her rinse the suds from a plate, then took it from her and wiped it dry. "I'm not asking you to give up your job in New York," he said, hoping he sounded reasonable. "Some lawyers serve clients all over the country."

Abbie scrubbed another plate. "Sure. Either they work for a national firm that has offices around the country, or else they take on super-rich clients who can afford to pay the air fare and phone bills."

"I thought we were talking about a license to practice in another state," T.J. corrected her.

Abbie handed him the plate and met his unwavering stare. He wondered if she knew how much he wanted her, how much of her he wanted. At that moment he wanted her brain, her legal expertise, her energy, her full, soft lips and a chance to kiss the pale, delicate skin above her collarbone…. "Look, T.J.," she said in such an emotionless voice that T.J. quickly put his fantasies into deep storage. "John Thorpe is your advocate. You've hired him to do your bidding. If you don't want him to settle the suit, all you've got to do is say so. He works for you. He's supposed to do things the way you want them done, as long as you aren't asking him to break the law. Asking him to fight the suit—"

"I don't want him to fight the suit," T.J. argued. "I want *you* to fight it, Abbie."

"I can't," she insisted sadly. "You know I can't."

"Why not?"

She exhaled and turned away, busying herself by fishing the silverware out of the sink basin to avoid having to look at him. "I'm just visiting Wheeler, T.J.," she said in a muted voice. "This isn't my home anymore. You know that."

They finished the dishes without speaking. While he dried the plates and silverware, T.J. tried to come up with a ploy to persuade Abbie to help him with his case—although he was no longer convinced that winning the suit was his primary reason for wanting her assistance. He mentally replayed her words: "I'm just visiting Wheeler...this isn't my home..." and found them unbelievably mournful. She had sounded so melancholy when she'd said them, as if she truly wished things were different, as if she wished that Wheeler *was* her home.

But it wasn't. The best T.J. could hope for was her support and advice, and her occasional company for as long as she was in town. He couldn't ask for anything more from her. He wondered if he could even ask for that much.

"How about if we make a deal?" he posed.

She shook the water from her hands and pulled a sheet of paper towel from a roll hanging on the wall near the sink. Blotting her hands dry, she studied T.J. thoughtfully. "What sort of deal?"

"I'll help you with your father's store and you'll help me with my lawsuit."

She weighed his proposal. "That's not exactly a fair exchange," she pointed out, though she didn't seem all that put off by the notion. "There's something known as the legal fraternity, T.J. Lawyers aren't supposed to go behind each other's backs to help clients—it's not completely ethical. What you're asking me to do is step on Thorpe's toes."

"If ever anyone's toes deserved to be stepped on, it's Thorpe's," T.J. grumbled. The hell with ethics and the legal fraternity. He could scarcely accept that Abbie Jarvis and John Thorpe belonged to the same profession—they sure didn't belong in the same fraternity. "I'm not asking you to sneak around behind Thorpe's back and steal me away from him, Abbie, any more than I'm offering to ask Ed Garcia to unlock a bank vault and let your father help himself to what's inside. All I'm asking is for a little help, from one friend to another. We *are* friends, aren't we?"

She dropped the used paper towel into the trash can and turned back to T.J. Her eyes shimmered and her smile was constant, warm with trust and affection and maybe something more. In a motion that seemed almost instinctive, she reached for him and circled her arms around his waist. "Yes, T. J. Hillyard," she swore. "We're friends."

Chapter Seven

Hugging him was an impulsive act on her part, but T.J. seemed to welcome it. More than welcome it—he returned her embrace, closing his arms gently around her waist and placing a light kiss on her hair before he released her. His gaze remained on her, dark and constant, as she took a cautious step backward and tried to think of something safe with which to occupy herself. If she didn't get busy soon, she would be tempted to try to explain her hug, to justify it and insist that it hadn't meant anything.

Except that it *had* meant something, something important, something that extended well beyond friendship. And they both knew it.

Her vision latched onto the coffee maker. "Would you like some coffee?" she asked brusquely, hoping T.J. wouldn't notice the scratchy quality of her voice. "I didn't have time to make anything special for dessert, but we've probably got a package of cookies somewhere—"

"Coffee sounds great," T.J. cut her off, lounging against the counter while she rummaged through the cabinets in search of the box of filters for the coffee maker.

As she measured coffee grounds into the filter, she cast him a surreptitious glance. His position, with his hips resting against the edge of the counter and his long legs extended in front of him, made him appear very tall, extremely relaxed and casual. He had left the top two buttons of his shirt unfastened, and she could see a few curls of chest hair where the cotton fabric fell open. His tooled leather belt emphasized his flat stomach and slim hips, and the way his broken-in blue jeans molded to his thighs and calves was extraordinarily sexy. Abbie skimmed her gaze back up his body to his broad shoulders, shoulders that were sturdy enough to lean on and secure enough to make her want to give him another hug.

She wouldn't hug him again, though. When she had assured him that they were friends, part of her message had been that they would never be anything more than friends. And yet... his posture, that indolently sensuous smile of his and the smoky darkness of his eyes filled her with a deep, visceral consciousness of T.J., an awareness that couldn't be contained by the term "friendship."

A tapping sound at the front door jarred her from her disconcerting thoughts, and her eyes flew to the electric clock hanging on the wall above the stove. Not even seven o'clock. Why had her father returned home so early from his date? "Somebody's at the door," she said, switching on the coffee maker before she darted out of the kitchen.

In the entry hall she stopped. Through the screened upper half of the storm door she saw the empty front porch, and beyond it the equally empty paved path leading across the grassy yard to the street. Had her mind conjured the noise as a means of getting her out of the kitchen, away from T.J.?

If that was all it had been, her mental subterfuge failed. T.J. followed her into the entry hall, and as she stared through the screen he came close behind her and gazed outside as well. "A cat, probably," he guessed.

"You heard something, too?" she asked, relieved that she hadn't imagined the sound.

"Mmm-hmm." He leaned closer, his chest pressing slightly into her shoulder blades, and surveyed the front yard in the fading dusk light. "There he goes," he said, pointing toward the lilac hedge that bordered the Jarvis yard. A flicker of furry black tail was briefly visible through the lower branches before the animal vanished into the Schallers' yard next door.

"At least I know I'm not crazy," said Abbie, flipping the switch that turned on the porch lamp. The amber light seeped through the screen into the house, filling the entry hall with a muted golden glow. "I thought what I heard was my father coming home—but it's much too soon for that."

"Much too soon for what?" T.J. countered with a smile. "Maybe he and Faye will decide to skip dessert and move on to better things."

"Will you stop talking like that?" Abbie scolded, jabbing T.J. playfully in the belly. "Even if my father and Faye hit it off in a big way, I can assure you they aren't going to go to bed together tonight."

T.J. grabbed Abbie's wrists to keep her from poking him again. He gazed down at her, grinning mischievously. "How can you assure me they won't?" he inquired in a deceptively mild tone. "Does your father make a habit of discussing his sex life with you?"

"Of course not," Abbie retorted, slipping out of T.J.'s loose grip and stalking back to the kitchen, with T.J. in close pursuit. "However, he happens to be a gentleman."

"What makes you so sure Faye's a lady?"

Abbie knew T.J. was only needling her, yet she couldn't seem to keep herself from responding way out of proportion to his sly insinuations. Ever since she'd wrapped her arms around him and he'd returned her hug, the air in the house had seemed strangely charged, and even the most innocuous allusion to something erotic reverberated dangerously inside her. "Faye Hinkel," she said quietly, but with such intensity that she might as well have been defending not her father and his dinner companion but herself, "happens to be a very sweet, decent woman, and my father—"

"The hell with that," T.J. overrode her. "Who says a sweet, decent gentleman wouldn't do anything within his power to satisfy a lady, and vice versa?"

"Exactly what are we talking about here, T.J.?" Abbie asked tautly, yanking two ceramic mugs from a row of wooden pegs attached to the underside of the cabinet.

T.J. took the mugs from her. When his palms slid along her fingers she automatically turned to him, holding her breath in anxious anticipation. "*I'm* talking about sex," he said calmly, setting the mugs on the counter and then catching her hands with his. "What are you talking about?"

"Friendship," she answered, her fingers reflexively curling through his.

"Sex and friendship can be one terrific combination," he observed, running his thumbs over the skin of her inner wrists. "It sounds like your father and Faye have got a spectacular night ahead of them." His smile was perilously seductive.

"Don't make fun of me," Abbie implored him, unable to suppress the quiver of tension in her voice.

"You?" he exclaimed with feigned ingenuousness. "I thought we were talking about Roy and Faye."

She was beginning to get angry, not so much at T.J. for teasing her but at herself for reacting, for letting his teasing get to her. "T.J...." She swallowed to silence herself, realizing abruptly that what was making her voice so thick and husky had very little to do with anger.

"But now that you mention it, maybe we aren't talking about them," he murmured, bowing toward her. "Maybe we weren't talking about them at all."

Before she could pull her hands from his and ask him to back off—before she could even make up her mind whether that was what she wanted him to do—he was touching his mouth to hers, moving his lips on hers and gathering her fully into his arms. For a fraction of a second she considered demanding that he stop, and then she discarded the notion. She didn't want him to stop, ever. Kissing him felt much too good.

"I've been thinking about doing this all evening," he confessed in a whisper, brushing his mouth over hers again and then leaning back to study her.

She gazed for a moment into his dark, spellbinding eyes, and then lowered her vision to the mouth that had grazed hers, that had offered her a tantalizing hint of the sensuality lurking within him. She focused her senses on the feel of his hands as they came to rest on the flare of her hips, his thumbs against her waist. She listened to the slightly labored sound of his breathing and wondered whether the kiss had unhinged him as much as it had unhinged her.

No way was she going to get involved with T. J. Hillyard. No way was she going to enjoy a quick fling with an old high school buddy while she was passing through town. Her sentiments had nothing to do with the fact that she had come to Wheeler, in part, to recover from her ill-fated romance with Bob, or that she was supposedly down on men in general these days. She wasn't down on sex, at least not in theory. But she didn't have the emotional

constitution to indulge in something as superficial as a
one-night stand—especially not with T.J.

On the other hand, kissing him couldn't possibly cause
her that much harm, could it?

T.J.'s eyes met hers and she discerned a question in their
radiant depths. She knew what he was asking her, and
without bothering to contemplate the consequences, she
answered with a slight nod.

He lifted his hands to her shoulders and slid his thumbs
under her hair to the sides of her throat, and then up to
the edges of her jaw. His mouth made contact with hers
and he cupped her head, holding her still as he deepened
the kiss. Her fingers flexed against his shirt, discerning the
hard surface of his chest through the fabric. She tried to
picture how his torso would look unclothed, how his
craggy shoulders and strong back would respond to her
exploration. She tried to imagine what it would feel like
to lie next to him, caught in the grip of his powerful jogger's legs... As her imagination spun wildly out of control, an involuntary groan slipped past her lips.

He took advantage of the opportunity to slide his
tongue into her mouth. As soon as it found its mate he
groaned, too, his passion unleashed by the increasing intimacy of the kiss. He ran one hand down her back to her
waist and pulled her body more snugly to his, unknow-
ingly feeding her imagination as he rocked his hips to hers.
His other hand rose to the back of her head, holding it
steady against the demanding surges of his tongue. He
raveled his fingers deep into her hair and fused his mouth
to hers, denying her the chance to protest—or the chance
to breathe.

For a mindless minute, Abbie believed that she didn't
need to breathe. She could survive on T.J.'s kiss alone, on
the overwhelming force of it. She could take nourish-

ment from the warmth of him as her fingertips probed the exposed V of his chest, tracing the soft swirls of hair adorning his skin there. She could derive energy from the unshakable strength of his arms around her, the solidity of his body against hers. If she had to breathe, she would inhale him, his essence, his spirit, and it would sustain her forever.

Except that she didn't have forever. She had only a couple of weeks, a brief hiatus from the rigors and stress of New York City.

"No." The single word emerged on a broken gasp as she drew her mouth from T.J.'s. He didn't release her immediately, and she couldn't keep herself from resting her head on his shoulder, relishing for one final minute the glorious sensation of being this close to him. Then she willfully pulled away and shook her head. "No, T.J.," she said in a faint, tremulous voice.

Reluctantly, he unwound his arms from her.

She moved backward a step and bumped into the counter, knocking one of the mugs onto its side with her elbow. For an inane instant, all she could think of was how lucky it was that she hadn't poured the coffee yet, and then she acknowledged that whether she spilled coffee all over the kitchen counter wasn't terribly significant at the moment. It just seemed safer to think about coffee than about the shocking effect T.J.'s kiss had had on her.

She drew in a desperate breath to clear her brain and dared to look at T.J. His eyelids were lowered but his eyes smoldered beneath them, his irises a churning mixture of brown and black. He reached behind her to set the mug upright, then offered her a dazzling smile.

"I'm sorry," she mumbled, her tone raspy.

"It's okay. Nothing broke."

"No, I meant..." She wasn't sure what she meant, and she certainly wasn't going to be able to figure it out with T.J. standing less than an inch from her, looking so damned irresistible. She sidestepped him and paced anxiously to the windows overlooking the backyard. Through the screen she heard the chugging motor of a neighbor's swamp cooler. It was an unexpectedly soothing sound, familiar and uncomplicated and real.

"Abbie." T.J. was sensitive enough not to crowd her. He stayed where he was beside the counter, scrutinizing her and trying to measure her agitation. "It's *okay*," he said, stressing the word in such a manner that she understood he wasn't referring to the overturned coffee mug.

"I just don't think I can handle this," she explained apologetically. "I mean—I'm only going to be in Wheeler for a little while. You know that."

"A lot can happen in a little while," he pointed out. When she didn't relent and cross the room to him, he gave her a tender, utterly unthreatening smile and poured the coffee. "I'm not going to push you into anything you can't handle, Abbie," he promised as he opened drawers in search of a teaspoon. He found one, located a sugar bowl in an overhead cabinet, and turned back to Abbie. "Come on over here and fix your coffee," he requested. "I'm not going to bite you."

No, but he might kiss her again, she thought apprehensively. And if he didn't kiss her again, she might take it upon herself to kiss him. T.J. was without a doubt the most effective kisser she'd ever met.

"It's nothing against you, personally," she insisted, reluctantly returning to the counter, although she cautiously left as much distance as possible between them. "It's just..." She spooned some sugar into her coffee, stirred it, and used the time to sort her thoughts. "I can't get involved with someone when I know I'm going to be saying goodbye in a couple of weeks.''

"I take it you like to enter into these things with an eye to the future," he said grandly.

She shot him a swift look, wondering whether he was making fun of her again. She was trying to be frank with him, to state her feelings as honestly as possible. If T.J. so much as hinted that he found her prudishness comical, she would punch him in the stomach again.

Detecting no overt mockery in his attitude, she allowed herself to relax slightly. "I like to avoid situations with built-in conclusions," she clarified. "What's the point of starting something when you can see the stop sign just a few yards up ahead?"

T.J. shrugged. "They could be wonderful yards," he argued. "Why not cruise them for the fun of it?"

"Because," she replied, struggling to come up with an adequate reply. "Because if I'm going to commit to something, T.J., I'm going to stick with that commitment for the long haul. I'm afraid that's just the way I am. Maybe you see things differently—"

"I didn't say that, did I?" he objected, raising his mug to his lips and taking a sip. "Of course, it seems to me that whenever you make that kind of long-haul commitment, you might find yourself waiting for, oh, say, four years for things to work out. And then, if they don't work out, you've wasted four good years."

"My experience with Bob isn't the issue here," Abbie said heatedly.

T.J. assessed her with a piercing stare. "Fine," he declared. "I just wanted us both to be clear on that." Holding his mug in one hand, he slid the other around Abbie's shoulders. "Let's sit down."

"Over here?" She lifted her mug and angled her head toward the table in the corner of the kitchen.

"How about the couch in the living room?" he asked. "I'd really like to kick my feet up. My knee's beginning to send me warning signals." At her dubious glance, he added, "Trust me, Abbie. I'm not going to do anything to you. I happen to be a nice guy."

Sure, he happened to be a nice guy. He also happened to be unbelievably handsome and unbelievably manly, and unbelievably tempting... But Abbie did want to trust him—and deep in her heart, she understood that he was worthy of her trust. Managing a feeble smile, she preceded him through the dining area to the living room and put her mug on the coffee table.

He placed his mug beside hers, then sat and pulled her down onto the couch next to him. "There," he said contentedly, swinging his legs onto the table and leaning back into the cushions, sliding his arm around Abbie again and urging her head onto his shoulder. "Comfy?"

Other than the fact that her pulse raced out of control every time she inhaled his subtle scent, she supposed she was reasonably comfortable. "So tell me, T.J.," she said, her voice falsely hearty, "what brand of after-shave do you use?"

"Do you really think I'm going to reveal my trade secrets to you?"

"Trade secrets!" she roared.

He ran his fingers along her upper arm in a placating massage, and she subsided against him. "That was supposed to be a joke, Abbie," he commented wryly. "Didn't Bob have a sense of humor?"

"I thought we established that we weren't talking about him," Abbie muttered.

"We're not talking about him," T.J. swore. "I'm just wondering why you take everything so damned seriously."

"I don't take everything seriously," Abbie maintained. Then she allowed herself a private grin. "Actually, Bob didn't have a particularly good sense of humor at all. It was one of his major flaws."

"Maybe I'm way off base," T.J. mused aloud, "but from the way you describe it, New York City sounds like it's overrun with people who don't have a sense of humor. Muggers, thugs, mothers selling their babies . . ."

Abbie's instinct was to assert that T.J. couldn't be more wrong. Lots of people in New York had marvelous senses of humor; you needed a sense of humor to survive in such a city. But the more she thought about it, the more willing she was to concede that perhaps he wasn't so very wrong. Abbie didn't laugh or joke around as much as she used to, and when she did there was frequently a bitter edge to her wit. Only among her closest friends—her neighbors from Yorktown Towers—did she ever feel inspired to succumb to a belly laugh, to rejoice in a funny situation.

And now it looked as if the last of Abbie's close friends from the building was going to be giving up on New York, throwing in the towel and moving on. "I called Marielle yesterday," Abbie informed T.J.

He continued to stroke the length of her upper arm, a gesture that seemed determinedly friendly even though it spread a sinuous warmth down to her fingertips and up into her heart. "Who?"

"Marielle Brandt. One of my best friends back in New York. I told you about her."

"Right." T.J. nodded. "Set me straight again—which one was she, the TV star?"

"No, that's Suzanne," Abbie corrected. "Last I heard from her she had dropped off Mouse—that's her daughter—in Colorado and had gone to visit some cowboy in Wyoming." She shook her head and smiled. "Somehow I just can't picture Suzanne on a ranch.... But anyway, about Marielle—she's the widow."

"With the two kids you love to spoil."

"Bingo." She was starting to find his caress lulling; she nestled closer against him and lifted her legs onto the couch. "She's thinking of moving to Chicago for a while."

"Chicago," T.J. murmured. "Great city. Great football team."

"I don't think Marielle cares one way or the other about football," Abbie noted.

"And you call her a friend?" T.J. erupted indignantly. "Joke," he added in a whisper.

"You don't have to—"

"Shh." He bent to kiss the crown of her head. "Remember that day we met by the railroad track and you complained that I was too defensive?"

She contemplated his indirect criticism and nodded meekly. "You're right, T.J. I'm a little jumpy tonight. I can't imagine why," she added in an accusing tone. In spite of herself, her tension was gradually leaving, responding to the mesmeric pattern his fingers sketched against her skin and the cozy enclosure of his arm arching around her.

He seemed on the verge of answering her charge, but he checked himself and instead said, "Why is your friend leaving the Big Apple?"

"Her husband left her an apartment building in Chicago, and she's decided she wants to move there. She won't be moving for a while—she said she'd be happy to forward my mail and water my plants as long as she's still in New York. But ..." Abbie exhaled. "Sooner or later, she's going to be gone. I don't know for how long, but she'll be gone, just like Suzanne and Jaime are gone."

"What makes you so different from your friends?" T.J. asked. There was no challenge in his voice, no sense that he was passing judgment on her. He seemed genuinely curious. "How come you want to stay there when the people you're closest to are all leaving?"

"New York is my home," Abbie answered simply— even though she knew as soon as she uttered the words that nothing was as simple as that.

"Wheeler used to be your home for, what, seventeen years?" he reminded her. "You didn't seem to have much difficulty leaving it."

"That's because I spent most of those seventeen years plotting my escape," she rationalized.

Tucking herself deeper into the accommodating curve of his arm, she gazed across the room at the framed watercolor of an old New England barn. Abbie's mother had copied the scene from a magazine photo. It was trite, but Abbie adored it because her mother had created it.

Her mother had taken up painting, she'd attempted to redecorate the house, she'd run various charity functions in town, and she'd worked at the hardware store. Grace Jarvis had chafed at the constraints of being a small-town housewife, and she'd fomented her small rebellions. But mostly what she had done was to encourage Abbie to flee the confines of Wheeler. "There's nothing for a bright young woman in this town," her mother used to say. "Wheeler is so conventional, so narrow-minded and limiting. Break out, Abbie, sow your seeds in the wide world and reap something more interesting than rice and babies. You can be whatever you want—but you'll have to leave Wheeler to do it."

Abbie had adopted her mother's dreams as her own, and as soon as she was old enough, she'd left. She'd sown her seeds... and if her most recent harvests weren't as abundant as she might have hoped, well, she'd grown up in an agricultural community, and she knew how difficult it was to produce a good crop, especially if you cultivated the same land year after year.

"I'm sure you'll make new friends," T.J. remarked optimistically. "Somebody's got to move into all those empty apartments in your building."

He couldn't see her face, so she didn't bother attempting a smile. Making friends in New York, where everyone was wary and distrustful of each other, wasn't nearly as painless a process as making friends in Wheeler. For years, Suzanne had only been a glamorous blond woman in the Yorktown Towers elevator to Abbie, someone with whom she could exchange vacuous comments about the weather. It took quite a while for them to open up to each other, to let down their guards. And for a long time, Marielle had merely been the pampered pregnant housewife down the hall, a perpetually cheerful, homey creature who seemed to want nothing more than the chance to dote on her daughter—and her husband, on those rare occasions when he was around. The only reason Abbie had become friends with Jaime so quickly was that Abbie had been trying to prosecute Jaime's client for child abandonment. Jaime had been young and idealistic and full of self-righteous fervor... not so different from the way Abbie had been when she'd first arrived in New York City, armed with her Yale Law School degree and a lot of lofty principles.

T.J. was right—different tenants would move into Abbie's building. But it would take years for her to develop friendships with any of the newcomers, if friendships developed at all. Abbie was older now, more cynical, more tired. She'd been burned in love, and she'd grown disenchanted with her work. She hardly had the strength to exert herself making new friends.

So why did she still insist on thinking of New York as her home? Was it conditioning, or inertia, or was she hoping, however futilely, that even as she tilled the same soil over and over again, the harvest might miraculously improve?

The sound at the screen door this time wasn't a product of her imagination. At the click of the latch T.J. discreetly shifted his arm from her shoulders to the back of the couch, and she pulled herself upright and combed her fingers hastily through her hair. The door swung open and her father entered. Alone.

"Dad!" Abbie cried out. Even though she thought his arrival home was a bit on the early side, Abbie was glad to see her father. His presence would keep her from dwelling on thoughts of the friends she was losing in New York—and the friend seated beside her on the couch, whom she would lose when she left Wheeler. "Dad, how did it go?"

"Hello, T.J.," Roy said, nodding toward his daughter's guest. He pulled the screen door shut behind him and ventured a few steps into the living room. "Abbie mentioned you were going to be coming over for dinner tonight. I was sorry I missed you." He focused for a moment on the coffee mugs, and then on his daughter and her companion, positioned, however tamely, on the couch. "Don't let me interrupt anything," he said, backing toward the hallway.

"No, Dad, you aren't interrupting," Abbie insisted, examining her father's face and failing to find in it any clues about how his date had gone. "How was your dinner?"

"It was fine, Abbie, just fine," Roy said. He was smiling, but his smile contained a hint of sadness. She wondered whether the date hadn't gone as well as he'd hoped, or whether it had gone so well he was disappointed about not having gotten to spend the night with Faye. Abbie's protests notwithstanding, she had no serious objections to her father enjoying a physical relationship as well as an emotional one with Faye.

"Did Faye enjoy herself?" Abbie asked.

"Oh, yes," he said with greater enthusiasm. "She told me she had a lovely time."

Abbie suppressed the spate of questions she longed to ask, giving her father an opportunity to elaborate without prompting. When he didn't, she stood and marched across the room to kiss his cheek. "Are you going to see her again?"

"Of course I am," he answered, grinning. "Matter of fact, she'll probably be by the store tomorrow. She told me she needs a staple gun—she's redoing the seats of her kitchen chairs, new cushions and new fabric. Faye's a real do-it-yourselfer, you know." His gaze wandered to T.J., who had also risen to his feet. "So, I guess I'll let you kids finish your coffee or something...." With a farewell wink at T.J., he strode down the hall to his bedroom.

Abbie waited until she heard his door close before turning to T.J. "Well?" she asked in a hushed voice. "What do you think?"

T.J. shrugged. "I guess if she's willing to see him again it couldn't have been a total bust."

"Seeing him at the store isn't the same thing as seeing him on a date," Abbie pointed out.

T.J. glanced down the hall at the closed bedroom door, at the line of light underneath it, at the heavy silence emanating from it. Then he shrugged again. "Your father's a shy man, Abbie. Maybe he doesn't want to come on too strong with Faye. Maybe he needs to recover from his first date with her before he starts planning his second."

T.J.'s comments implied that he no longer viewed her father as Wheeler's Romeo—that he no longer wanted even to joke about her father's conquest of Faye. Abbie herself had never viewed her father as a red-hot lover. But she wasn't satisfied by his subdued, reflective attitude about the date he'd just returned from.

"Oh, well," she said with a dejected sigh. "However it went, it's over."

"He said it went fine," T.J. reminded her gently. "He probably had the time of his life, and he feels awkward talking about it with you."

"Do you think so?" Abbie asked hopefully.

"The guy winked at me, Abbie. That's got to mean something."

No argument there—it meant something. But Abbie couldn't dismiss the possibility that the wink had been her father's acknowledgement of T.J.'s potential for success with Abbie, not an indication of his own success with Faye.

She longed to believe T.J.'s interpretation of her father's mood, but she couldn't. Nor was she consoled by the fact that her father was a grown man who had survived disappointments far worse than any he might have encountered that night. As Abbie herself had said, however the date went, it was over. There was nothing anybody could do to change it.

Drifting back to the couch, she tried to ignore the worry that nibbled at her. She dropped onto the cushion, lifted her mug in both hands, took a sip of the tepid coffee and scowled. "Would you like a fresh cup?" she asked, assuming that T.J.'s coffee must have cooled off as well.

He walked to the couch, but instead of sitting he removed the mug from Abbie's hands and pulled her to her feet. "I think it's time for me to leave," he said.

She opened her mouth to object, then closed it. T.J. was right in sensing that she was too distracted to give him her full attention—and if she couldn't give him that, she wasn't going to be a very good hostess.

The truth was, she wanted T.J. to stay for selfish reasons. She wanted him with her because she wanted to talk out her concerns and know that, like the bartender he was, he would listen. She wanted to lean on him. She wanted him to hold her while she wept over her father's pensive disposition and over the news that the last of her close friends would soon be gone from New York. Most of all, she wanted T.J. to stay because she had felt more vibrantly alive when he had kissed her than she'd felt in a long, long time, and she wanted him to kiss her again, and she knew she couldn't let him. If he kissed her again, she would only desire him more, and then it would hurt too much to say goodbye to him. Merely thinking about it made her want to weep.

It was peculiar, this urge to cry on T.J.'s shoulder. She wasn't used to it. In New York, she was always so strong; she never leaned on anyone. But perhaps that was only because in New York she didn't know anyone strong enough to accept her weight, to accept her tears.

T.J. was strong enough...but she could see the stop sign just up the road, reminding her that any relationship she could build with T.J. had a foregone conclusion. "Okay," she said, accepting the wisdom of his decision to leave. She collected the mugs and brought them to the kitchen, doing her best to keep her knotted emotions from showing.

T.J. didn't follow her into the kitchen. She doubted he'd depart without saying goodbye to her, but she appreciated his willingness, once again, to give her some room, some space, a chance to clear her head. By the time she was done rinsing out the mugs she was feeling better, and after drying them and hanging them on their wooden pegs, she left the kitchen to find him.

He was standing outside on the front porch, staring at the moon that hung high in the sky and inhaling the clean fragrance of the night air. Abbie joined him outside, and he slipped his arm around her waist and gave her a consoling squeeze. "In another week or so it's going to smell like an inferno around here," he remarked.

Abbie was touched by his choice of topic—a harmless subject, totally devoid of emotional overtones. "It doesn't smell that bad when they burn the rice fields," she contradicted him.

"It doesn't smell that bad to you because you haven't smelled it recently," he noted. "I know that if you don't burn the fields you can't plant them with next year's crop and expect to get much out of the soil. But it's still unpleasant to have to breathe that stench."

"Such is life, T.J.," Abbie said with mock solemnity.

He eased her around so she was facing him and peered into her upturned face. For an insane moment she prayed that he would take the responsibility away from her and kiss her, but he didn't. "I've got to jog tomorrow," he said. "Would you like to cover a couple of miles with me?"

She forced her consciousness away from the light caress of his hand at the small of her back. His face was half-hidden by the shadows, but the affection, the downright caring she saw in his eyes, compelled her to answer, "I'd love to."

"Even if the afternoon's a scorcher?"

"Even if."

He deliberated for a minute. "When are you and your father going to see Ed Garcia at the bank?"

"In the morning, I think. We haven't got an appointment, but—"

"He'll see you," T.J. said confidently. "I'll give him a call first thing tomorrow to let him know you're coming. You and Roy get to the bank around ten or so—I'll make sure Ed's waiting for you. Then you can call me when you're done, and we'll go burn off all the pressure you'll be experiencing."

A narrow frown line creased Abbie's brow as she considered T.J.'s suggestion. "I have to admit, T.J., I've got some misgivings about having you interfere—"

"I'm not interfering, Abbie. I'm trying to help you save your father's store. If things are as bad as you say they are, you haven't got the luxury of refusing my help. Besides—" he cut her off before she could argue "—you're going to return the favor, right? You're going to help me keep that kid with the drinking-and-driving problem from suing the pants off me."

Abbie yielded with a grin. This, she supposed, was how things were done in Wheeler. If the waitress at Sparky's could make your hair color her business and make her arthritis your business, then friends could certainly make their professional dilemmas each other's business. "All right, T.J. We'll have a double strategy session down by the railroad track."

"Good." He did kiss her, then. He slid his index finger under her chin, tilted her face up, and touched his mouth to hers in a way that left her incredibly aroused, despite his restraint—or because of it, she wasn't sure. Straightening up, he smiled tentatively, turned and disappeared down the front walk in that slightly lopsided gait of his.

Abbie remained out on the porch for a long while, listening to the chirping crickets, the distorted rumble of a truck's engine in the distance, the raucous barking of Tom Callero's labrador retriever as Tom took the dog for his final walk of the night. Leaning against the porch railing, Abbie stared at the statuesque trees lining the street, noticing the way the moon's sheer light played across their bark...and thinking about her father inside the house, wrapped up in his own emotions, and T.J. in his own house somewhere on the other side of town.

If her father had asked her how her evening had gone, she wouldn't have said, "Fine," or "I had a lovely time." Her evening hadn't gone as she'd expected...and yet, in a way, it had. She had been aware of T.J.'s attractiveness, aware that he could make her want him. Claiming that they were friends didn't mean they weren't more than friends.

The evening hadn't gone "fine." But it had gone exactly as it had to, even if it left Abbie shaken and confused. The dinners she used to share with Bob—or with any other man back east—had never knocked her off balance this way, never concluded with her standing alone beneath a shimmering moon, asking unanswerable questions, wondering why she was no longer sure of what she wanted or needed. Yet, unanswerable though those questions might be, they were too important to dismiss. She would have to deal with them.

What was it T.J. had said about the rice fields? "If you don't burn them, you can't plant them with next year's crop and expect to get much out of the soil." And she had said "Such is life."

You had to keep asking those questions, unpleasant though they might be. You had to keep asking them.

And sometimes you had to burn the rubble in order to plant something new.

Chapter Eight

"You look like a lady in desperate need of a workout," T.J. observed as Abbie climbed into his car.

She was dressed in an outfit like the one she'd been wearing when he had stumbled into her during his jog last Friday: an oversize sweatshirt with the sleeves cropped off, a pair of short cotton shorts, white socks, running shoes and a terry cloth sweatband around her head. She'd pulled most of her hair into a ponytail, but several locks had slipped out of the barrette and fell in soft, waving wisps about her face.

It occurred to T.J., as he gazed at her hairdo, that the nape of a woman's neck was an incredibly vulnerable part of her body. At least, this seemed to be true in Abbie's case. Despite her obvious tension, every other part of her anatomy appeared strong and fit, all set to tackle the jogging path. But the nape of her neck, where a few delicate tendrils of loose hair curled over the smooth stretch of pale skin, seemed so exposed, so heartbreakingly defenseless.

He wanted to kiss her there. For that matter, he wanted to kiss her everywhere—on her magnificently exercised legs, on her hidden breasts, on her cheeks and lips and throat. But T.J. prided himself on being a man of his word, and last night he had given Abbie his word that he wouldn't push her into anything she couldn't handle. He was convinced that she could handle having sex with him, but until she was equally convinced of it, he would have to keep his urges under control.

"If you're telling me I look stressed out," Abbie muttered, "your eyes don't deceive you. I *am* stressed out."

T.J. restarted the car's engine and pulled away from the Jarvis house. Abbie had telephoned him a half hour ago to tell him she was ready to jog, and by the time he had put on his running clothes and driven to her father's house, she was waiting for him on the front porch. It was another balmy September afternoon, and T.J. considered turning on the car's air-conditioning. If he did, though, he and Abbie might feel twice as hot when they got out of the car, and twice as reluctant to exert themselves on the path. He decided to leave the air conditioner off and the windows open.

"I take it you paid a visit to the bank today," he half asked.

Abbie nodded and stared out the window. A summery breeze gusted into the car, tugging a few more strands of her hair free of the barrette.

"So, what did Ed say?" T.J. prodded her when she remained silent. Her sullen mood didn't bode well, but no matter how badly her meeting with Ed Garcia had gone, T.J. wanted an unabridged report on it.

She sighed and turned to look at T.J. "He said Jarvis's Hardware is in pitiful shape."

T.J. slowed the car and coasted over the railroad tracks at the First Street crossing. Then he pulled off the road, parking on the rutted dirt shoulder where Abbie had parked her father's van last Friday. Pocketing the key, he twisted in his seat to confront her. "Okay," he said, sensing that Abbie needed a vigorous pep talk. "The store is in pitiful shape. This isn't exactly news, Abbie."

"No, but it's not much fun having to hear it from the loan shark who's holding your notes."

T.J. laughed. Accusing a mild-mannered man like Ed Garcia of being a loan shark was as absurd as accusing Abbie Jarvis of selling babies on the black market—or accusing T. J. Hillyard of having conquered the four-minute mile. Opening the car door, he swung his legs around and adjusted the brace on his left knee before he attempted to put any weight on it. Even after downing a few aspirins the previous night and a few more when he got out of bed, his knee had been balky and sore all morning. T.J. was no Olympic sprinter—and Ed Garcia was no loan shark.

With a litheness T.J. envied, Abbie sprang out of the car on her side, shut the door and loped around the front bumper to meet T.J. "Do you want to stretch a little before we start?" she asked, noticing the stiff movement of his leg as he made his way through the scrub to the parched dirt path paralleling the train track.

"Believe it or not, I already did some warm-ups at home," T.J. informed her. "It'll loosen up once we start. So why don't we get going, and you can tell me all about what 'Bone-Cruncher' Garcia threatened to do to your father if the old man doesn't pay up."

Abbie smiled sourly, a reluctant acknowledgment that she had perhaps overstated the bank's position regarding the store's loan. In a chivalrous reversal, she let T.J. set their pace, falling into step beside him as he began a sluggish jog that was closer to walking than running. "He threatened foreclosure," Abbie belatedly answered T.J.

"Real bloodcurdling stuff, huh," T.J. commented.

"To Dad and me, yes, that's bloodcurdling," Abbie retorted. "The idea of losing Jarvis's Hardware—"

"Hey, take it easy, Abbie," T.J. cautioned her gently. "Foreclosure is a last resort for the bank. Let's face it—do you really think they want to take ownership of your father's store? Do you think they want to get into the business of selling screwdrivers?" He shook his head. "All they want is their money, Abbie."

Abbie shot a dubious glance up at T.J. She wasn't an idiot; she had to recognize that he was talking sense. "All I want is for them to get their money, too," she conceded grimly. "Unfortunately, there's this small problem that, for want of a better word, I'll call reality."

T.J. chuckled at her acerbic wit. It occurred to him that she would be dynamite in a courtroom, putting that wit to use skewering thugs in her cross-examinations of them. "Let's talk about reality, then," he agreed. "What did Ed Garcia really say?"

"That if my father wanted to renegotiate the terms of the loan, the first thing he would have to do would be to sit down and work out, on paper—"

"A viable business plan." T.J. completed her sentence.

Abbie lifted her eyes to him again. This time they were filled not with doubt but with awe. "Those were Mr. Garcia's exact words," she told T.J.

"Uh-huh." He concentrated for a moment on the pain in his knee. He could feel the tendons pulling, the bones aching and the muscles straining in response to the exercise he was forcing upon them. It hurt in a drearily normal way, and T.J. stopped worrying about whether he was pushing himself too hard after having skipped exercising the past couple of days. He turned his attention back to Abbie. "I promised I was going to call Ed this morning," he reminded her. "Well, I did, and we talked about your father's situation."

"Mr. Garcia told you he was going to require us to come up with this viable business plan?"

"On paper," T.J. stressed, grinning. During his conversation, Ed had mentioned several times that he needed something more concrete and tangible than the verbal promises he'd been getting so far from Roy Jarvis. "I vouched for your father, Abbie," said T.J.

"What do you mean, you vouched for him?" she asked, her eyes widening in shock, glistening with silvery flecks in the sunlight. "Are you going to cosign his loan?"

"No." He scrutinized Abbie for a moment, hoping his answer hadn't disappointed her. She looked crestfallen but not truly angry. It was more an expression of resignation, as if, deep down, she knew she couldn't have expected T.J. to stick his neck out that far on her father's behalf. "What I *will* do," he offered placatingly, "is help Roy work up a viable business plan for the store."

"On paper."

"I'd help your father carve it into stone, if that was what Ed Garcia wanted. He's holding the cards, Abbie. At this point, he's got every right to demand a rational budget and a schedule of payments your father and the bank can both live with."

"Are you sure you'll be able to work up a plan like that for a hardware store?" Abbie questioned T.J. "It can't be that similar to a bar."

"You'd be surprised how much alike they are, Abbie," he said. "They're both retail businesses, and they both depend on service and customer loyalty—and on bank loans. I had to take out loans when I was first getting Tyler's on its feet. I've paid off those loans, but then I took out a new loan to cover the cost of having the front parking lot repaved, and I'm still paying that one off. That's the way businesses are run, Abbie. You need loans, and you've got to write up business plans to prove to the bank that you'll be able to repay your loans."

"I'm sure some businesses manage to stay out of debt," she argued.

"Some do," T.J. allowed. "But it isn't necessarily a sign of trouble if a business has debts. It's often a sign of growth." She looked unpersuaded, and he shook off the vague impatience that had begun to take hold inside him. He was speaking from knowledge, from education and experience, and it bothered him that she appeared so skeptical. "I know what I'm talking about, Abbie," he insisted, annoyed that he had to defend himself. "I might be a dumb jock, but I did learn a thing or two in college."

"You mean, like inventory management."

"For starters."

"You aren't a dumb jock, T.J.," she said quietly, her smile burning away the last traces of doubt that had darkened her face. "I never thought you were, not even in high school."

He peered down at her. The grass covering the slope that rose from the dirt path to the railroad track had dried to a pale golden shade, and the color somehow seemed to complement the rich, tawny shades of Abbie's hair. In high school, T.J. had thought of Abbie as a "brain," which had been an accurate assessment of her, but obviously an incomplete one. Like Thelma, the waitress over at Sparky's, T.J. had never before noticed how beautiful Abbie's hair was. He supposed she must have been a brain with beautiful hair back then, and he'd been a blind fool for having failed to perceive that. "What did you think I was in high school?" he asked.

"Well, I knew you were a jock, of course," she granted. "But I never thought of you as dumb."

"I bet you didn't think of me as smart, either." He was testing her, but he figured his grin would keep her from taking his questions too seriously.

Her eyes briefly met his. Her lids were lowered against the glare as the afternoon sun washed over her face, but through her thick lashes he saw flashes of green and gold and gray. "I don't know, T.J.," she admitted. "I don't remember ever thinking of you in terms of academics at all."

"Well, thanks a heap," he grumbled, pretending to be insulted. "We were in the same social studies class in twelfth grade, you know."

"I know," Abbie said. Her gaze returned to him for another moment, her expression inscrutable, and then she faced forward, squinting slightly as she followed the curve of the railroad track with her eyes.

"But my utter brilliance never made an impression on you," he continued to goad her.

"Oh, T.J., who would have even noticed if you were brilliant?" She sounded almost vexed. "You were a star athlete and a handsome hunk, and you were incredibly confident without being the least bit conceited. You had a nice personality, what little I knew of you. If you'd been a genius, too, I for one wouldn't have been able to stand it." She smiled slightly, but T.J. sensed a genuine exasperation underlying her flattery.

Was that honestly how she'd viewed him back in school? Granted, he'd been a star athlete. But even when athletes are in their prime, even when nothing seems beyond their reach, they never lose sight of the fact that sooner or later their bodies are going to give out on them, that their gift belongs to them only on a temporary basis.

If a vicious tackle during his first pro game hadn't done T.J. in, some other tackle during some other game would have, or a leap that got fouled up when he landed, or an off-season injury. Or old age, which in football usually meant younger than the age he was right now.

The *real* gift, as far as T.J. could tell, was the gift a person could keep forever: intelligence. Intellect. Wisdom. "You were brilliant in that class," he remarked. "I noticed."

"Brilliant," she scoffed. "The only reason I did well in school was because I worked my tail off. I studied, and then in my spare time I studied some more. I was a bookworm, T.J. I was a grind. But you . . ." Her eyes focused on a memory. "When you were out there on the football field, you didn't seem to be trying at all," she recollected. "It just came naturally to you."

Now it was his turn to scoff. She thought it came naturally to him? He'd had to work damned hard to play as well as he did. "I didn't seem to be trying, huh," he muttered, slowing his pace as if he were still exhausted from how hard he had exerted himself in those high school football games. "Every day—we're talking *every* day, Abbie, even when it wasn't football season—I did sprints for speed, I did long-distance runs for endurance, I did weight training for strength, I did calisthenics and pass practices. . . ."

Abbie was dumbfounded by this revelation. "Really? I never knew—"

"And as far as being confident . . . come on, Abbie, I was a teenager. Have you ever met a teenager who wasn't suffering from a terminal case of insecurity at least three quarters of the time?"

She gaped at him. "As a matter of fact, I had always thought there was one teenager in the universe who never felt insecure: you."

He snorted. "Come on, Abbie. I was a basket case, just like every other kid in the school. I had zits, I got turned down for dates—"

"No!"

"Of course I did. I fought with Linda, I fought with my folks, I got grounded for breaking the rules.... I wasn't so special, Abbie. The only thing special about me was that I wanted a ticket out of Wheeler—just like you did. And just like you, I worked my tail off to get it."

Adjusting to his slower pace, she continued to study him, apparently amazed by what he had said even though it seemed pretty unremarkable to him. Sure, he had had his admirers in Wheeler. Sure, the local newspaper had written him up a few times. But that didn't mean he hadn't been mortified, as any guy would have been, when his kid sister caught him drooling over a *Playboy* centerfold when he was fourteen. It didn't mean he hadn't questioned, time and again, whether he was spoiling what were supposed to be the best years of his life by working out instead of cruising Main Street with his friends. And it didn't mean he hadn't been demolished the night he'd finally gotten Stephanie Cox to agree to park with him down by the Sacramento River and she told him he kissed funny.

"If you had asked me out for a date," Abbie commented, "I wouldn't have turned you down."

"Like hell," he refuted with an amiable smile. "When I asked you out on a dinner date you said no."

"That's now. I meant then."

"I'm not such a good catch anymore?"

"You're a much better catch now than you were then, T.J.," Abbie responded, her tone strangely muted. "And I'm a much more mature woman than I was then. I'm old enough to understand that adventures have consequences."

T.J. eyed her with curiosity. She willfully refused to look at him, keeping her gaze locked on the path ahead of them. Her sudden wariness told him everything he had to know about what she meant by "adventures" and "consequences." By "adventures," she wasn't referring to mountain climbing or white-water canoeing—she was referring to sex for the sheer fun of it. And by "consequences" she didn't mean unplanned pregnancies that could result from such adventures—she meant the emotional repercussions that came afterward.

It was possible that when he'd asked her out for dinner the other day, he had only been looking for an adventure. But it was just as possible that he'd been looking for something else, something more. Maybe he was willing to face the consequences when it came to Abbie. She wasn't the only one who had matured in the seventeen years since they'd left high school. Part of maturing, T.J. thought, was not just to recognize what the consequences might be but to accept them, even welcome them.

The ancient oak tree that he used to measure his progress while jogging loomed in the near distance, spreading its broad, arching boughs over the path. It cut a stately silhouette against the horizon. Beyond it the town thinned into farmland, and above it the sky spread blue and cloudless. "Let's get out of the sun for a little bit," he proposed, pointing toward the pool of shade beneath the tree. "What do you say? Isn't this tree your favorite cooling-off spot?"

She lifted her gaze briefly to his, then looked away again. "We can take a break if you'd like."

It wasn't that either of them was out of breath or sweating profusely. But T.J. wanted to sit beside her, just sit and put his arm around her and relish the closeness he felt toward her... and talk. He hadn't deliberately meant to introduce any touchy personal subjects when he saw her today, but it was too late to backtrack now—and even if he could backtrack, he didn't want to. He and Abbie were adults. They ought to be able to talk about adventures and consequences and T.J.'s fear that once Abbie returned to New York, he was going to find it awfully lonesome jogging this path without her.

I don't want you to leave. For a moment he thought he'd actually given voice to the words—that was how clear and true they seemed to him. But if he had spoken his feelings aloud, Abbie wouldn't be so calm right now, sitting cross-legged on the grassy earth beneath the tree and resting her elbows on her bent knees. She wouldn't be placidly yanking a long reed of grass out of the ground and twirling it between her thumb and index finger. If he actually told her how much he wanted her to stay in Wheeler, she wouldn't be watching him intently and smiling enigmatically. T.J. wasn't sure what her reaction would be, but he was sure she'd react somehow.

He himself was startled by the comprehension of how much he had come to like having her around. Lowering himself to the ground next to her in the tree's generous shadows, he leaned against the trunk, extended his left leg straight and bent his right to lessen the strain on his back. Then he beckoned Abbie closer. She shifted toward him, and he looped his arm with deceptive nonchalance around her narrow shoulders.

He couldn't say what he *did* want from her; he hadn't thought things through that far. All he knew was that he didn't want to have to say goodbye to her and watch her drive beyond the town's limits, down to the airport in Sacramento or San Francisco or Oakland—any airport that would get her back to New York. He didn't want her to leave.

Thinking about it, he understood something else: he could never, never ask her to stay. She had left Wheeler by choice and by design. She had geared her entire youth toward getting out—as she'd said, she had worked her tail off with that goal in mind. If anyone could understand such a desire, it was T.J. Circumstances had brought him back, and he had since discovered that he could be very happy here—but that was his discovery, not Abbie's. He appreciated her need to get out of their small, smothering hometown because he had once experienced that need in his life, too. If anyone back then had ever said to him, "Don't leave," he still would have left, but he would have left angrily instead of peacefully.

He wouldn't lay a trip like that on Abbie. He wouldn't try to manipulate her into staying, or make her feel bad about going. Her stubbornness and independence were part of what made her who she was, what made him admire her so much. He didn't want her to change—and that meant he couldn't beg her to stay.

But he could have her for a while this afternoon, as the sun drizzled through the web of branches and leaves to dapple her face with golden light. He could have her company and her friendship and maybe a kiss or two.

SHE MIGHT HAVE TOLD HIM to stop, but that would be hypocritical. The truth was, she wanted T.J. to kiss her.

Especially this way, gently, almost chastely, with his hand following the contour of her jaw and guiding her mouth to his. This kiss wasn't as heated as the ones he'd given her last night, but the passion was there, just out of reach as he moved his lips over hers, as he teased her upper lip with the silky brush of his mustache.

"Did you kiss this well in high school?" she asked dreamily when he drew back.

T.J. chuckled. Somehow during the course of their kiss she had wound up nearly on her side, sitting on one hip and leaning the upper half of her body against him for balance. She had to tilt her head back to see him, but the view was worth courting a stiff neck. As good-looking as T.J. was, he looked even better when he smiled, his face aglow with dimples and laugh lines and warmth.

"You want the truth? No, I didn't kiss this well."

"Hmm. In that case, maybe I wouldn't have gone out with you."

"Oh, so you were out for a good time then? Brainy Abigail Jarvis a party girl.... I never knew."

She shaped her hand into a fist, but T.J. had no difficulty deflecting her punch. He kept his fingers wrapped around her wrist as her arm landed ineffectually against his chest. Then he bowed and touched his mouth to hers again, still keeping his tongue tucked safely away from hers. She found these kisses frustratingly incomplete, yet their modesty aroused her in an inexplicable way. She closed her eyes and simply savored the texture and taste of his lips. Her hand pressed against his ribs and she felt the rapid pounding of his heart.

After a long, luscious minute he pulled away. "This is very nice," Abbie murmured, cuddling up to him.

"Mmm-hmm."

"We really ought to be jogging, don't you think?" she asked, without making any move to stand up and resume their exercise.

A sly smile tugged at the corners of T.J.'s mouth as he answered. "Some folks say that when it comes to diffusing pressure, sex works just as well as jogging. I believe it, too, Abbie. One kiss from you and I'm getting all the same physical effects—speeding pulse, racing breath, overheated organs—"

"Don't!" she cut him off with a laugh. She nestled her head into the hollow where his neck met his shoulder, in part because it was comfortable and in part because she didn't want him to see her blushing. "We weren't talking about sex," she reminded him. "We were talking about kissing."

"Is there that much of a difference?"

"There'd better be," she said, still laughing, although the seriousness of his observation lingered in her mind. If it felt this good to kiss T.J., she could imagine how marvelous it would feel to make love with him. Even the light, almost virtuous kisses he was giving her here in the shelter of an old oak tree were laden with erotic promise. Perhaps the distance between what they were doing and what they were both thinking about wasn't so great, after all.

In which case, she chided herself, she really should bring the kissing to a halt. Apparently, when it came to T.J., even a gentle closemouthed kiss wasn't safe. If he'd been speaking the truth about his skills, he had obviously learned a great deal since high school.

"Let's talk about your lawsuit," she suggested, trying to sound enthusiastic.

T.J. laughed again, but he was hugging her too closely to himself for her to see his face. "Let's not," he countered.

"But it's important."

"So is this," he said, lifting her headband off and then kissing her forehead. He relaxed his arm around her, allowing his hand to wander up her side under her arm. He stroked her ribs through the bulky fabric of her sweatshirt, and then drifted forward to explore her breast.

She moaned involuntarily as the muscles in her abdomen clenched. The throaty sound was all the encouragement he needed to continue. His caress narrowed on the small swell of her flesh until he found the already hardened tip of her nipple and rubbed it. "T.J.," she whispered shakily.

"You like this," he murmured, not quite a question and not quite a declaration. His mouth wandered to her temple, to the fine arch of her cheekbone and then downward, seeking her lips once more. This time they parted for him, luring him, drinking him in.

Yes, she liked this, of course she liked this. "Like" scarcely began to describe the way she felt as T.J.'s tongue filled her mouth, sliding deep, pulling back and then sliding deep again in a shocking simulation of the sex act. "Like" couldn't accommodate the sensations his hand provoked as he slid it down to her waist and under the edge of her sweatshirt. He strummed his fingers back upward, where they came upon the stretchy cotton of her running bra. He followed it to the clasp in back. "Let me do this," he implored, as if to preempt the protest he expected from her.

"No," she groaned, grateful to him for giving her the opportunity to stop him.

He didn't remove his hand. He let his fingers remain where they were, tracing the clasp and then the ridge of her spine above and below the back strap. He exhaled, then lapsed into thought. The only sound Abbie was aware of, other than her own ragged breathing, was the rumbling motor of a combine harvesting the rice in a distant field.

After a long while, he said, "This *is* like high school, isn't it."

She comprehended the unspoken complaint in his words, and also the amusement. "I wouldn't know," she said, swallowing to combat the passionate huskiness in her voice. "One thing I wasn't in high school was a party girl."

"I didn't really think you were."

"T.J...." She sighed and lifted herself far enough from him that he had no choice but to let his hand slide out from under her shirt. Her action allowed her eyes to meet his, but she couldn't bear to look at him. She was afraid she might see bitterness or hatred in his expression; she was equally afraid that he might see the implacable longing in hers. "I'm sorry," she said, primly straightening her sweatshirt. "I know I'm giving you mixed signals—"

"You're giving me very clear signals," he disputed, running his fingers down the side of her cheek to her chin and forcing her to face him. "You want to make love, but your brain keeps nagging at you to be sensible."

That certainly summed up Abbie's dilemma rather tidily. "Sensibleness has always been one of my major assets," she noted.

"I'm not so sure it's an asset—at least not at the moment."

"Oh, T.J." His sweet humor only aroused her even more. "I've got to be sensible," she explained contritely, "because if I'm not sensible, I'll wind up hurt. I know myself, and I know what will happen if we pursue this thing. I can already see the stop sign, T.J. We could have a great time now, and then I'd have to say goodbye, and pack up and head back to New York—"

He winced—a fleeting, immeasurably brief look of anguish, and then his gaze regained its affectionate warmth. For a moment Abbie believed she had imagined the sudden glint of pain flickering across his features—especially since she couldn't see any justification for it. Why should the mention of her imminent departure disturb T.J.? He knew as well as she did that it was a fact, not open to debate. Her home wasn't Wheeler anymore. It was New York.

"You know what you are, Abbie?" he asked, scrutinizing her, his dark eyes absorbing her.

She glanced away sheepishly. "Don't say it," she mumbled, certain that he was about to label her with some crass term for the sort of woman who heartlessly led men on and then pushed them away.

"You're a prude," T.J. declared, surprising her.

She glanced up and found him grinning. "You're right," she admitted. "I'm also a worrier, and I think we ought to get back on the path before your knee stiffens up."

He laughed roguishly. "If you're such a worrier, how come you weren't worried about the possibility of other parts of me stiffening up a few minutes ago?"

"Hush," she scolded him, pulling herself to her feet and then gripping his hands to help him up. "Keep your overheated organs to yourself."

"Now, that would be selfish," he objected, still laughing. At Abbie's disapproving scowl, he subsided and flexed his knee a few times to check its mobility.

They headed back to the path. Beyond the rise of the track, Abbie saw the harvesting combine laboring in the flat farmland to the west, reaping the rice crop. Through the acreage the irrigation canals formed a weave of brown lines, their surfaces arid and cracked. The rice required a veritable sea of water during the spring and summer, but the growing season was over now, and the water had been allowed to run off.

It unnerved Abbie to think that she and T.J. had engaged in such intimacy outdoors, in a public place. When she'd half sat, half lain within the protective enclosure of his arms, the tree's shadows had seemed to create a private haven for her and T.J., making them invisible to the rest of the earth. And in a way, she supposed, they had been, because no one had been near, no one had seen.

She used to think it was impossible to have any privacy in a small town like Wheeler—but perhaps she was wrong. Perhaps she had been confusing privacy with anonymity, or isolation. In New York she had all the anonymity and isolation she had ever wanted...if that was, in fact, what she had wanted.

But what she'd really wanted was privacy, and she had found it here today, beneath the open sky, with T.J.

TYLER'S WAS RELATIVELY EMPTY when Abbie entered the bar at around seven-thirty. Only one waitress was on duty, the stocky one who wore her long sandy-blond hair in a braid. A couple of young men in Oakland A baseball caps were taking turns cuing up at the pool table, and Bonnie Raitt was singing "Love Has No Pride" on the jukebox, just as she had been the last time Abbie had walked into the bar.

That time, she'd walked in with her father. Tonight she was alone. Over dinner, her father had told her that Faye

Hinkel had asked him to help her reupholster her kitchen chairs. "When she was down at the store this afternoon," he explained, "she said she had used a staple gun once before and the darned think bucked all over the place on her. So I'm going over to her house tonight to show her how to do it without stapling her fingers to the seats."

Abbie had refrained from peppering her father with questions. Faye had invited him to her house, and he had agreed to go. If Abbie needed to know anything more, her father would keep her posted.

It was just as well that he had plans for the evening. She had wanted to visit Tyler's tonight, anyway—and without him. This was a business trip.

She had tried to broach the subject of T.J.'s legal predicament during the last part of their jog that afternoon, but T.J. clearly hadn't wished to discuss it. For that matter, neither had she. In spite of her noble attempt to appear outwardly composed, she had been a frazzled mess of emotions, hardly able to put together a lucid sentence, let alone a lucid legal strategy for T.J.

Why had she let him kiss her again? She should have known what would happen the moment his lips covered hers: she would go insane desiring him, and then she'd compound her insanity by refusing to cave in to her desire. She had never felt so profoundly aroused by a man before, not even by Bob. The organic heat of T.J.'s smile, the smoky yearning in his eyes, the virile proportions of his physique... he didn't even have to touch her to make her want him. And when he *did* touch her, when he kissed her and held her and caressed her body...

Merely thinking about it aroused her all over again. She felt like a feverish adolescent, eager to tumble over the edge and down into a deep dark place from which she would never escape. She wanted to fall in love with T.J.

And that would be doubly stupid. Not only because she was going to have to go back to New York, but because T.J. had never made any pretense of wanting to fall in love with her.

Given the low level of business in Tyler's, T.J. was keeping himself occupied by taking notes on his stock of liquor. He had his back to the door as he inched along the bar, checking the labels and jotting down the names of those brands he was running low on. The waitress noticed Abbie, however, and ambled over to her.

"Hi," she said pleasantly.

Abbie returned her smile, although she pondered the possibility that the waitress's familiar greeting meant that Abbie was spending too much time hanging out in bars—in T.J.'s bar, in particular.

"You're Roy Jarvis's daughter," the woman identified her. "T.J. told me, the other night when you were in here with Roy. I've got to tell you, Abbie, I've heard an awful lot about you from your old man. My name's Lina Murray, by the way."

"How do you do," Abbie said politely. "I'm sorry if my father's bored you to tears talking about me."

"Oh, no, Roy isn't boring," Lina said, balancing her empty tray between her two index fingers and twirling it around. "Some of the guys here...well, if I told you, I'd be boring, myself. Sit wherever you want, Abbie. As you can see, you aren't going to have to fight the crowds for a seat. You want an Oly, or are you up for a change of pace tonight?"

"An Oly would be fine, thanks."

"Hey, T.J.," Lina shouted over to him. "Abbie Jarvis is here."

Abbie found herself briefly wondering whether Lina Murray and Thelma from Sparky's were friends, or whether nosiness was simply one of the aptitudes waitresses tended to develop in practicing their trade. But the moment T.J. straightened up and spun around, Abbie found herself unable to think about waitresses or beer orders, or anything but the soulful, sexy man standing behind the bar, smiling at her.

Maybe he wasn't at all interested in falling in love with Abbie, but he certainly seemed thrilled to see her. She remembered the first time she'd walked into his bar and he'd seen her standing near the front door. He'd looked astonished, then curious, and then delighted. He didn't look astonished tonight, but there was something more than curiosity and delight in his eyes, something mysterious and penetrating, leaving Abbie with the uneasy feeling that he could see below the surface of her, beneath her clothing and her skin.

"Hi, Abbie" was all he said.

She crossed to the bar and sat on one of the stools. Lina brought her a bottle of beer and a glass. Then the waitress glanced at T.J., grinned knowingly, and took his clipboard and pen from him. "Be my guest," she offered with a mischievous smile as she took over the chore of checking the supplies.

"What did she mean by that?" Abbie asked, intrigued by the silent communication that had passed between T.J. and his waitress.

He chuckled and poured the beer into the glass for Abbie. "It means," he said, "that she knows I'm interested in you."

"Is this a typical occurrence, your being interested in a customer?" Abbie asked. Far from feeling jealous, she was relieved to think that T.J. made a pass at every woman who entered his bar unescorted. It helped her to detach herself from him; it made him less lovable.

Evidently, T.J. found her question amusing. "No," he told Abbie. "I can't remember the last time I felt the urge to get personal with a customer. I guess I'm just a transparent guy, Abbie. Lina can read me pretty well."

"Well, I'm not here to talk about that," Abbie said quickly, reminding herself of the reason she'd come to Tyler's. She took a long, refreshing draught of beer, then placed her glass on the cocktail napkin T.J. had set in front of her. "I'm here to discuss your legal situation," she announced.

"Uh-huh," T.J. grunted, finding a sponge and wiping down the bar.

"I know it's not your favorite subject, T.J., but if you honestly want my help—"

"I do," he swore, acknowledging her subtle reproach by tossing the sponge into a nearby sink. He dried his hands on a towel, leaned his forearms on the bar, and gazed attentively at her. "If I don't exactly seem happy to talk about it, it's because Thorpe called me twice today. He told me he spoke to the insurance company and they don't want to fight the suit, either. They want me to go ahead and settle."

"Well, they're imbeciles," Abbie declared firmly.

T.J. grinned. "They're also my insurance company, and there isn't a whole lot I can do to stop them from paying out their money to this kid who's suing me."

"If you want to fight the case, you might be able to stop the insurance company from settling if you can prove to them how good your chances are of winning."

"Uh-huh," T.J. grunted again, although he didn't reach for the sponge.

"What you need, T.J., are witnesses who'd be willing to submit testimony—either written or in court, if necessary—supporting your version of the incident. Can you think of any witnesses who might be able to testify for your side? Any customers who saw you serving the kid coffee?''

Racking his memory, T.J. frowned. "It was over a year ago, Abbie, and real late at night, and the place had been kind of crowded. I can't remember who was here—or for that matter who might have been paying attention to what was going on between me and the kid."

"How about your waitresses? How about Lina? Was she here that night?''

T.J.'s face brightened. "Hey, Lina—could you come over here for a minute, please?''

The waitress set down the clipboard and sauntered down the bar to T.J. "What's up?''

"Remember that lawsuit I was telling you about, the underage kid who says I served him liquor just before he was involved in a D.W.I. accident?''

Lina eyed Abbie and nodded.

"Did you see what went down that night?'' he asked. "Abbie says I need witnesses who can testify that the only thing I served the kid was coffee.''

"I don't think I was on that night,'' Lina reminded him. "That was, what? A year ago July, right? I was up in Forest Ranch helping my sister with her wedding, remember?''

"Oh, yeah,'' T.J. said. His frown increased as the implications of Lina's statement registered. "You weren't here that night, Meagan hadn't started with us yet, and Jackie never works in July.''

"Rosalie Gorman,'' Lina said, her voice weighted with mysterious insinuations. T.J. cursed under his breath and Lina laughed. "Good luck, pal.''

"You know, I've never liked your sister,'' T.J. muttered as Lina walked away. "Next time she gets married,

tell her not to do it when some kid's going to come into my
establishment and make trouble for me.''

Lina's response was a more boisterous laugh. She lifted
the clipboard and resumed taking notes on the bar's supplies.

''Who's Rosalie Gorman?'' Abbie asked.

T.J. cursed again. ''She used to work here,'' he answered. ''She lives in Lake Tahoe now—last I heard, she's
dealing blackjack at one of the casinos. She keeps in touch
with Jackie—one of my other waitresses.''

''The one who doesn't work in July.''

Seeing Abbie's perplexed look, T.J. provided her with
an explanation of his waitress's quirky behavior: ''She's
a little weird. She thinks heat lightning brings bad luck.
According to family lore, years ago some uncle of hers got
struck by heat lightning on his way to work, so now none
of them will work when there's any heat lightning. You
know what it's like around here in July, Abbie.''

Abbie knew. The days would be scorching, and at night
the air would grow heavy with an exciting, foreboding
scent, and then the sky would split and split again, dag-
gers of white energy searing down to earth. Abbie had always been enthralled by the heat lightning that strafed
Wheeler every summer—but she'd never been scared by
it. She had always thought it was Mother Nature's way of
making those hot, restless nights beautiful.

''So this other waitress, Rosalie Gorman, lives in Lake
Tahoe,'' Abbie concluded. ''That's not so bad.''

''What do you mean, it's not so bad?''

''You can arrange to have her come down here—''

''Rosalie was...a problem,'' he said carefully. ''I don't
know if she'd go out of her way to help me. She and I
didn't get along too well.''

"You could telephone her," Abbie suggested. "You could offer to prepare an affidavit for her. All she'd have to do would be to sign her name to it."

"She'd say no," T.J. predicted.

"Then maybe you could just drive up to Lake Tahoe, without giving her any warning. Just appear on her doorstep, hand her a paper, and ask her to sign it. It wouldn't take more than a few minutes of her time."

T.J. considered Abbie's idea. "It's a four-hour drive to Tahoe," he pointed out.

She shrugged. "So you'll spend the night. Or you can split the driving with a friend—"

The shadows abruptly cleared from his brow. "You're right, Abbie," he said, his sudden optimism making her apprehensive. "You're absolutely right. It's perfect. You'll come with me," he said with such utter certainty that she couldn't find it in her to protest.

Chapter Nine

"I don't know what I'm doing here," Abbie grumbled.

T.J. cast her a quick look, then turned his attention back to the road. He had rolled his window all the way down, and he rested his elbow on the ledge and leaned back in his seat, somehow managing to appear comfortable despite his tall, long-legged build. The wind tousled his hair and caused his loose-fitting cotton shirt to flutter just below the collar. As usual, he had left the top two buttons of the shirt open, and it took a vast amount of willpower on Abbie's part not to peek at the narrow portion of his chest visible where the cloth gaped.

It would take just about her entire supply of willpower to survive the next two days, she reflected with a plaintive sigh. Ever since T.J. had decided that Abbie should accompany him to Lake Tahoe to meet with his former waitress, Abbie had been scrambling—without success—for a way to get out of making the trip with him.

It wasn't that she didn't want to help him. Abbie would have been more than willing to help T.J., even if he hadn't behaved so generously toward her father over the past week, working long and hard with him to explain the fundamentals of inventory management and to produce a viable business plan that would satisfy Ed Garcia at the bank.

She knew her expertise would come in handy in getting a proper affidavit from Rosalie Gorman. Armed with a strong statement from his former waitress to support his version of what had happened at Tyler's on the night in question, T.J. might actually win his case. And Abbie wanted him to win, not only for his own sake but for the sake of justice. She wanted to see a legal case resolved in such a way that the victory belonged to an honest, deserving human being instead of to expediency or convenience.

But she didn't want to go to Lake Tahoe with T.J., just the two of them alone. From the moment he had made up his mind that Abbie should go with him, he had discussed it in terms of an overnight trip. A round-trip journey to the resort town on the Nevada border would entail too many miles of driving in one day. Besides, T.J. and Abbie might not be able to find Rosalie the minute they arrived in Tahoe. It was only sensible for them to plan to spend the night.

But Abbie didn't want to spend the night with T.J. As far as she could tell, that would only lead to trouble.

For several days, she had worked long and hard inventing excuses not to have to make the trip. "John Thorpe is your lawyer," she'd asserted, and T.J. had responded that Thorpe had no use for defense witnesses, since he wanted to pay off the plaintiff. "I'm not up-to-date on California legal practices," she'd complained, and he'd responded that the act of taking a witness's statement couldn't possibly be so different in California than it was in New York. "I'm going to have to return to Manhattan in another week or so," she'd noted, and he'd responded that she didn't have to return to Manhattan on the Sunday he was planning to leave for Lake Tahoe, or on the day after, when he would return to Wheeler. "What about my father?" she'd posed, and T.J. had informed her that her father wouldn't be lonely for one night, especially not with Faye Hinkel badgering him to come to her house for a good home-cooked meal.

"Hotel rooms are expensive in Tahoe," Abbie had pointed out in a last, desperate attempt. "And we'd have to spend twice as much reserving two rooms, because I'm not going to stay in the same room as you."

She had assumed that T.J. would give up at that point; surely his eagerness to have her accompany him on the trip was due at least as much to his desire to seduce her as to his interest in her legal counsel. But, far from surrendering, T.J. had overtrumped her final trick: "You're right—the hotels are expensive. But we won't have to stay at one. We'll stay at my place."

"What place?"

"I've got a little A-frame overlooking the lake up there."

"An A-frame?"

"A vacation cabin." At her frantic look, he elaborated. "It's got a sleeping loft upstairs and a living room downstairs—with a sofa, Abbie. We'll be on separate floors, if that's what you're worried about."

That was exactly what Abbie was worried about.

A hotel probably would have been safer. But the issue, T.J. had argued, wasn't where they would spend the night but whether Abbie trusted him. If she didn't want him to touch her, he wouldn't touch her, he swore. "Even if you *do* want me to touch you," he had added, "I won't, unless you beg me."

"Don't hold your breath," Abbie had warned—and T.J. had taken the warning as her way of granting that she would go to Lake Tahoe with him.

So here she was, late Sunday morning, sitting beside him in his car and heading for some rustic, off-the-beaten-path vacation cottage—undoubtedly the scene of numerous romantic triumphs on T.J.'s part. She must have been suffering from a temporary case of dementia when she'd agreed to this.

"What you're doing here," T.J. reminded her, brushing a wind-tossed lock of his hair out of his eyes, "is helping me to get a statement from Rosalie that will stand up in court, if it doesn't keep me out of court altogether."

"I know that," Abbie said peevishly. Given that she was with T.J. in a professional capacity, she was attired in the most conservative skirt and blouse she'd brought to California with her, hoping to exude a businesslike aura. But she wished she'd worn slacks, instead; she felt as if too much of her legs were exposed, too much of her arms and throat. She didn't want to look overly feminine. She didn't want anything between T.J. and her to suggest that she was a woman and he was a man, and that one hot, sunny afternoon less than a week ago, in the shade of a majestic oak tree, they had discovered how wildly she could react to his sexual overtures if she let herself.

"I wouldn't know what to ask Rosalie," he went on in a reasonable tone of voice. "I wouldn't know what sort of statement we need to get from her. You're my legal adviser on this, Abbie. That's what you're doing here."

"This is all well and good," she muttered, fidgeting with her purse and picturing the overnight bag she'd stowed in the trunk of the car when T.J. had picked her up at her father's house that morning. Thinking of the bag made her think of "overnight," and thinking of "overnight" made her palms grow clammy. "I have no objection to talking to Rosalie and taking her statement," she insisted.

"But you have plenty of objections to my cabin," T.J. surmised. It wasn't a difficult conclusion for him to reach; Abbie had made her opinions known to him more than once. "I've already told you, I'll sleep on the couch. And believe me, Abbie, I don't get my kicks sneaking upstairs and putting the moves on an unsuspecting woman—"

"Who said I'm unsuspecting?" Abbie shot back, permitting herself a small grin.

T.J. caught her eye and mirrored her grin. Then he turned his gaze forward again. "If you're so deathly afraid of me," he said, "we can still try to rustle up a motel reservation for you somewhere."

"It's not—I'm not afraid of you, T.J.," she claimed, unsure of whether that was the whole truth. "I just . . . I don't know. I keep visualizing this cabin, miles from nowhere, the scene of all your most sensational seductions—"

"Seductions!" He erupted in laughter.

"What's so funny?" She glared at him. "You're a good-looking single man, and you said yourself that everybody knows everybody in Wheeler. The way I figure it, you bought this cabin in the mountains so you could meet ski bunnies on the slopes and bring them back to your cozy little retreat for après-ski fun and games."

T.J.'s smile vanished. "That's not why I bought the cabin," he said quietly.

She studied him thoughtfully, trying to make sense of his suddenly subdued demeanor. "All right, I'll bite. Why did you buy the cabin?"

He kept his gaze riveted to the road. "I bought the cabin right after Mary-Jane and I tied the knot," he explained. "If I was interested in sensational seductions, it was my own wife I was going to be seducing. I happen to be an old-fashioned guy when it comes to marriage, Abbie. If I hadn't wanted Mary-Jane to be my one and only, I wouldn't have married her in the first place."

Perhaps his robust argument in favor of monogamy was supposed to reassure Abbie, but it didn't. After all, he wasn't married anymore. "Why Lake Tahoe?" she asked. "You were on your way to Chicago, weren'tyou?"

"Why not Lake Tahoe?" he countered. He accelerated to pass a sluggish truck. Once he'd steered back into the right lane, he continued, "I used to ski at Tahoe when I was a kid. So did Mary-Jane. We both loved the area, and the lake—it's beautiful any time of year. So when the Bears signed me and I suddenly found myself with some real money, I decided to buy myself the cabin I always wanted."

"Do you still enjoy skiing?"

He snorted.

She ran her gaze down his body to his legs. The man might not be a star athlete anymore, but he wasn't a cripple, either. "I've seen you jog, T.J." she commented. "If you can jog, I'm sure you can ski."

"Oh, I can, no question about it," he confirmed. The bitterness that had momentarily seized him seemed to evaporate, replaced by pensiveness. "I just...don't want to."

"Why not?" she pressed him. He so rarely talked about his injury, and when he did he usually became short-tempered or evasive. Harassing him with questions about his knee was probably way out of line, but they had several hours of driving ahead of them and they had to talk about something.

"Abbie..." He exhaled and brushed another thick, windswept tangle of dark hair out of his eyes. "Have you ever gone skiing?"

"I tried it once," she said. "When I was in graduate school, one of my roommates talked me into going to this tiny little hill in northwestern Connecticut. I snow-plowed down the beginner's slope about three times, fell about a hundred times, and had black-and-blue marks all over my rear end for a week afterward."

"Hmm," he said, lapsing into a mischievous smile at her mention of her rear end. After a moment, however, he became serious again. "To me, skiing was...it was about as close as I could get to flying. I felt so free on the slopes, just soaring down them...totally free." He reminisced for a minute, his eyes taking on a distant glow. Then he sighed deeply. "I've seen a couple of those heartwarming TV reports where they show handicapped people taking on the slopes, and I think that's wonderful and inspiring and all that. But...if I went skiing now, I would have to be awfully cautious. I couldn't take chances or turn sharp corners. One fall and I'd be wiped out, you know? My knee is held together with pins and plates and surgical thread. Half of it isn't even organic matter. One bad fall, Abbie, and that would be the end."

"Wouldn't you want to try once, just to prove to yourself—"

"Prove what?" he posed. "Sure, I could slide down a snow-covered slope wearing a pair of skis to make a point, but making points was never the reason I went skiing. I went so I could fly—and I can't fly that way, not anymore."

There was nothing belligerent or defensive in his attitude now, as there had been the first time Abbie had commented on his knee brace. She felt as if T.J. had revealed a piece of his soul, some secret part of him that he didn't often share. Perhaps sharing it with her was his way of earning her trust—and it was effective. She trusted him more now than she ever had before.

"Why haven't you sold the cabin, then?" she inquired. She felt a little bit guilty pestering him with more questions when he'd already divulged so much, but she couldn't help herself. She had just glimpsed an entirely new aspect of T.J., and she wanted to see even more.

"Why should I sell it? I like it," he replied. "It's got a terrific view of the lake."

"But—doesn't it make you sad, coming up here and thinking about how you can't fly anymore?"

He smiled. "For a while it did, but not anymore. Maybe I can't fly on the slopes, Abbie, but I've discovered that there are other ways to fly."

"Oh? What ways?"

He tossed her a swift, incisive look. "Other than making love?" He went on before she could react. "I'm an adult now, Abbie. I don't have to conquer something to feel like I'm flying. I don't have to beat another player or defeat another team, or overcome anything. I get off on simpler things now."

"Meaning, you've lowered your sights?"

"Meaning, I'm enjoying the sights, and I don't really give a damn whether they're high or low. They make me happy, and that's what counts."

The interstate began its gradual ascent out of the Sacramento Valley and into the Sierra. Abbie noticed the changing vegetation, the thickening evergreen forests and the boulders blasted in half to clear a winding route for the highway to pass through.

As the lush mountain scenery assailed her senses, she found herself meditating on T.J.'s words. In its own way, perhaps, the scenery of Wheeler was lovely, too: not necessarily the sights of rice fields and almond orchards and the staid, conventional shops lining Main Street, but the sight of people greeting their neighbors on the sidewalk, and the sight of a few laborers converging for a beer and a game of pool inside a neighborhood watering hole at the end of a long day, and the sight of a venerable oak tree rising up from a gully beside the railroad track, spreading its aged limbs over the sun-baked earth to afford a couple of joggers some cool shade and privacy.

Maybe T.J. had learned how to settle for what he could get; maybe he'd learned how to give up and make do. But Abbie didn't honestly believe that. She believed that he'd been speaking the truth. He was an adult, now. Growing up meant relinquishing some of the dreams of youth and learning to accept reality, but maturity had its own rewards. Reality could be as wonderful as dreams. And yes, Abbie acknowledged, it was possible to take flight in such moments of peace and amity.

She turned to look at T.J. He remained facing forward, apparently unaware of her scrutiny. His profile was rugged, immensely appealing. She recalled the time she'd seen his profile, minus the mustache, on television. He had been lying on the grass, so still, so horrifyingly still, his shoulders distorted with padding and his hair glued with sweat to his forehead. And even earlier, she'd grown familiar with his profile in their high school class. T.J. had sat a few rows to Abbie's left, near the window. He had always looked as if his powerful body was about to explode from the confines of the compact desk, and his gaze had frequently drifted toward the window and the football field beyond.

She imagined that he was better at "flying" today than he'd ever been before. She imagined, for not the first time, that if she were careless, she could fall in love with T.J....and she hastily steered her gaze away from him and concentrated on the telephone call she'd made a couple of days ago to her office in New York, during which one of her associates told her she was indispensable and pleaded with her to come back soon.

She'd had enough experience in doomed love affairs to last a lifetime. Any affair she embarked on with T.J. was doomed; she could see the stop sign just ahead—a stop sign and a directional arrow pointing her back to New York. She wasn't going to set herself up for the pain of losing T.J.; she wasn't going to let herself love him.

T.J. RARELY TALKED about the cabin. For one thing, it sounded so pretentious to admit to owning a second home—at least, it did in Wheeler. Nobody was wealthy in Wheeler. When T.J. signed his contract with the Bears at the ripe old age of twenty-two, he'd probably been richer than anyone else in town, including John Thorpe, Esq., and the Pendletons, a husband-and-wife team of doctors who ran a family practice out of their house. Not that T.J. cared about money, but having it, he'd discovered, had been nice.

Mary-Jane hadn't been as excited by the cabin as T.J. had. She had liked skiing, but she would rather have spent their money on jewelry. This helped to simplify their divorce settlement; Mary-Jane got to keep her diamond earrings, her three-strand pearl choker and all the other trinkets, and T.J. got to keep his cabin.

Another reason he didn't usually discuss the cabin with people was that it was so small. The deck off the sleeping loft was nearly as big as the loft itself, which was large enough to accommodate a double bed and a chest of drawers, with about a four-foot-wide aisle of walking space. The downstairs wasn't much bigger, although the downstairs deck was spacious enough to hold several lounge chairs, a picnic table and benches and a gas grill. The cabin was certainly roomy enough for T.J. when he stayed in it by himself. It was too small to entertain in, though, and if his friends learned about it they'd invite themselves up to visit him there. They would crowd the cabin, and they would crowd him.

That was the main reason so few people knew. The cabin was his retreat, his escape hatch, a place where he could be alone. Running a bar meant having to be congenial all the time, having to laugh at the customers' unfunny jokes and serve everybody with a smile—and T.J. enjoyed that just fine. But on occasion, he simply didn't want to be congenial. So, once every month or two, he'd drive to the cabin and turn off the charm. Sometimes he'd leave after Tyler's closing time on Saturday night—actually Sunday morning—and stay through till after breakfast on Monday. Other times, like this trip, he'd leave at a normal hour on Sunday and arrange for Lina to open the bar on Monday evening and run it until his return, usually by around seven or eight o'clock at night.

The cabin was his own place, his private lair, his solitude. That was why, when Abbie had asked him if it was the setting for his most sensational seductions, he'd had to laugh. Mary-Jane was the only woman he'd ever brought to the cabin—and even then, given his physical condition and the dismal state of his marriage, the trips had been geared more toward therapy than lovemaking.

If he wanted to seduce a woman, he had a perfectly comfortable bedroom in Wheeler to bring her to. He wouldn't bring her to the cabin.

He hadn't even mentioned it to Abbie right away. For the first few days that he'd been trying to persuade her to come to Lake Tahoe with him, he had deliberately kept its existence a secret. Partly he'd suspected that she would balk about spending the night with him there, and partly he wasn't sure he was ready to let anyone, even Abbie, invade his private domain. But by the time she'd started crabbing about how costly a hotel would be, he had come to the conclusion that Abbie wouldn't spoil the cabin for him. She was above all else his friend, and he trusted her. A hell of a lot more than she trusted him, he mused.

He steered up the bumpy driveway that wove through the trees, climbing higher and higher above the lake and veering past several other cozy A-frames before it ended at his own cottage. He parked the car by the deck and turned off the engine.

Without waiting for him to assist her, Abbie climbed out of the car. She inspected the triangular structure, the wall of glass facing the lake, the deck furniture and the cord of split logs stacked neatly along one slanted side wall. He couldn't read her expression, but he prayed that she wouldn't make some snide remark about how small it was. He knew she wasn't a snob, but she might be upset to think of how close their quarters were going to be, how close to her T.J. would be even if he slept on the couch and she took the loft. If she did get upset, he'd drive her straight back down the hill to the nearest motel and dump her there.

"Oh, T.J.," she said, filling her lungs with the fresh, piney scent of the mountain air. "This is beautiful."

He relaxed only slightly. She hadn't been inside, yet. Maybe it was only the surrounding forest and the lake, glittering in its turquoise splendor, that she considered beautiful.

He opened the trunk and pulled out their bags. Then he circled the house to the other side, Abbie at his heels, and unlocked the door. He had last been to the cabin in late July, and the place was a bit dusty but relatively neat. He hadn't left any dirty dishes in the sink or any towels on the bathroom floor.

"It's beautiful," Abbie said again, roaming through the sunlit living room, with its shabby but comfortable furniture. "May I?" she asked politely before unlocking the glass door that led out to the deck. She slid it open, and a gust of crisp mountain air wafted into the house.

"Do you want me to take your bag upstairs?" he asked, starting toward the open stairway that separated the kitchen and dining area from the living room.

"Not now," Abbie replied, too transported by the breathtaking panorama of trees and glittering water. "Save yourself a hike up the steps. I'll take it up later." She finally, reluctantly, closed the door and rotated to face him. "I'd like to freshen up before we go to see Rosalie. Where's the bathroom?"

"Right over there," he said, indicating a door. She unzipped her suitcase and pulled out a brush and comb, then disappeared into the bathroom, casting T.J. a smile before she shut the door.

He smiled, as well. He liked the way she'd reacted to the cabin. She clearly understood how special it was. Having her here wouldn't spoil it at all.

After a minute she emerged, her hair smoothed out and her lips tinted with a pale lipstick. "Whenever you're ready," she said brightly.

He wondered whether the reason she was so gung-ho about finding Rosalie was that she didn't want to spend an extra minute secluded with T.J. in the cabin. Then he decided he was being paranoid. Her desire to focus on business was merely part of her lawyer routine. Nodding, he took his turn using the facilities.

When he came back to the living room, he found Abbie once again staring through the windows at the view. Tucked beneath her arm was a legal yellow pad enclosed in an official-looking black folder. More of the lawyer routine, he figured. He wondered if she'd be behaving with such stringent professionalism if he told her he considered her polished looks and correct attitude unbelievably sexy.

But he couldn't tell her that. He'd promised he wasn't going to touch her. They had made a deal, and T.J. wasn't about to renege on it.

"I'd offer you something to eat or drink before we head off, Abbie, but all I've got are a few beers and some warm soda. I'm figuring we can stop at a grocery store on our way and pick up some food."

"Fine," Abbie said, crossing to the door. "I'm not really hungry. What I'd like to know," she continued as T.J. ushered her back outside to the car, "is, what kind of person is Rosalie? How should I approach her?"

T.J. grunted. They should have talked about this before they left Wheeler, but he'd been so busy trying to convince Abbie to come with him, he hadn't wanted to say anything that might discourage her. It was too late for her to refuse to accompany him to Lake Tahoe, though, and he supposed he ought to alert her about Rosalie. "She can be kind of... irritating," he said.

Abbie glanced up at him, curious. "How so?"

He opened the car door for her and assisted her into the seat. He was surprised by her reaction—or her lack of one. He had expected her to accuse him of having withheld information from her—which, he had to admit, was precisely what he'd done. However, she seemed fairly untroubled by the fact that the woman she was going to interview had just been described as irritating.

She wanted more information, and she deserved it. T.J. sorted his thoughts as he strode around the car to the driver's side. It wasn't that he wanted to hide anything from Abbie, but...well, if he told her the whole truth about what had happened between Rosalie and himself, how she'd approached him and he'd turned her down, he might come across as a world-class egotist. He had finally managed to secure Abbie's trust; he couldn't tell her about how he had invited Rosalie to throw herself at him and then had refused what she'd offered.

He was hoping that, in the year since she'd left Tyler's, Rosalie had met other men, fallen in love, found genuine happiness and forgotten about her vicious run-in with T. J. Hillyard. But on the chance that she hadn't, he had to prepare Abbie. "I think I told you," he said, starting the engine, "that Rosalie is a friend of Jackie's."

Abbie nodded. "The one who's superstitious about heat lightning."

"Uh-huh. They were classmates, they finished high school a few years behind us. Jackie's kind of trippy, and so was Rosalie." He maneuvered the car through a three-point turn and steered down the long, snaking driveway to the road that bordered the lake. "The truth is, Rosalie was a much better waitress than Jackie."

"So why isn't she at Tyler's anymore?" Abbie asked.

"She always wanted to work in the casinos," T.J. said. It wasn't a lie; Rosalie used to talk constantly about how she wanted to take one of those courses in dealing cards, and then get a job working a blackjack table in Nevada. She thought it would be glamorous. She had also thought T. J. Hillyard would be glamorous. Talk about a wrong number...

Abbie balanced her black folder on her lap and tapped her fingertips lightly together, digesting what he'd told her. "T.J.," she said calmly, "for some reason, I'm sensing that you think we're going to have a hard time securing Rosalie's cooperation. Am I right or wrong?"

He admired her poise. She knew he was hiding something from her, yet she wasn't losing her cool about it. He realized that this was part of what made her a good lawyer: she was patient. She knew better than to antagonize someone who had information she needed.

"You're right," he conceded. "The truth is, Abbie...Rosalie quit working at Tyler's because she didn't like me."

"Didn't like you?" Abbie laughed incredulously. "You're so likable, T.J."

"Thanks," he muttered. "Rosalie probably wouldn't agree."

"Okay," Abbie said, nodding again and deliberating for a moment. "I suppose we can approach her with the position that her testimony can further the cause of justice, not that her testimony can help you personally."

"I don't think she'd care one way or the other about justice."

"Which do you think she'd prefer, T.J.? Justice or you?"

T.J. glanced at Abbie. She was smiling serenely, as if she was actually looking forward to the challenge of wrangling a statement from an irritating witness. She probably was, he concluded. She probably saw this as an adventure. Finding Rosalie and prying a deposition from her was probably the most thrilling part of this trip, as far as Abbie was concerned. Certainly spending the night under the same roof as T.J. wasn't going to be the high point of it.

He was still trying, with less than total success, to resign himself to the limits she had placed on their relationship. He hadn't even tried to kiss her since the afternoon they'd jogged—and damn, she had enjoyed kissing him as much as he'd enjoyed kissing her. But if she was really all that afraid of getting involved with him, he could back off and exercise self-control as well as she could. He had promised not to attempt anything with her tonight, and he wouldn't. He had had to tune out more than a few fantasies in his life, and he'd survived; making love with Abbie was just one more fantasy he'd never see fulfilled— and he would survive that, too.

They drove across the invisible line separating California and Nevada on the eastern end of the lake, and T.J. pulled into Harrah's parking lot. By Lake Tahoe standards, Harrah's was an imposing edifice—it was perhaps the largest building on the street, clean and elegant and much tamer than the gaudy neon-lit hotel-casinos in Nevada's major cities. "I've got to confess something," Abbie whispered, touching his arm to catch his attention before he swung out of the car.

Her hand felt good on his wrist, her fingers cool and slim. He struggled not to respond. Smiling bravely, he met her vivid gaze. "What?"

"I've never been inside a casino before."

He chuckled. "In that case, brace yourself," he advised. "It's an experience."

They got out of the car, locked it and strolled around the building to the casino entrance. The opulence of the sprawling gaming room seemed to transfix Abbie; she hooked her hand through the bend in T.J.'s elbow and held on tight. Her eyes widened at the glitter swirling around her—spinning roulette wheels, flashing lights, a clanging bell as someone won a jackpot on a slot machine. She gaped at the scantily clad waitresses weaving among the tables with trays of cocktails and at the gamblers themselves, hundreds upon hundreds of them, dressed in everything from denim work overalls to sequined cocktail dresses, wielding money and chips and pursuing dreams.

T.J. knew he should be scanning the croupiers at the blackjack tables, searching for Rosalie. But he was too enthralled by the fascination lighting Abbie's face, her astonished smile and her sheer, ingenuous wonder. He recalled the first time she had walked into Tyler's; he had thought she looked so pure and childlike then, with her sweet, fresh-scrubbed features and her unassuming manner. She looked the same way now—and it did the same unsettling things to his nervous system as it had that night.

"This is amazing," she murmured, venturing farther into the casino but still clinging to T.J.'s arm. "It's so—so frenzied in here."

"This casino is mellow compared to the ones down in Las Vegas," said T.J. "Here, at least, the gambling has to compete with the mountains and the lake. There, it's gambling and nothing else."

"If this is considered mellow," Abbie remarked with a giddy laugh, "I'll make it a point to steer clear of Las Vegas."

"Good idea," T.J. concurred, meandering with Abbie among the tables, hunting for Rosalie. "I've been to Vegas twice in my life, and I hated it both times. The place is so hyper—everything happens at high speed, all day and

all night. See that guy over there?'' He indicated a middle-aged man decked out in a tuxedo and a ruffled shirt,
assuming a formidable stance at one end of a long row of
blackjack tables, with his legs spread slightly and arms
folded across his chest. "He looks like a pit boss. Let's go
ask him if Rosalie's working today."

"All right."

They started down a bustling aisle with blackjack tables to their right and crap tables to their left. Still wide-
eyed and rapt, Abbie shifted her gaze back and forth,
trying to take it all in. The only thing T.J. was trying to
take in was the identity of each dealer—and then he saw
Rosalie running the table at the end of the aisle.

She had been strikingly pretty when she'd worked for
him, and she was still a knockout. Her glossy black hair
was longer than it had been when she'd been waitressing,
and she wore it pulled back from her face in a flat barrette at the nape of her neck. Her complexion still had an
almost otherworldly translucence, although she had
adorned her cheeks with pink stripes of blusher, and her
blue eyes were artfully made up. She had on a pleated
white shirt, a tiny black bow tie, and black striped trousers. When he had first hired Rosalie, he had been overwhelmed by her beauty, but looking at her now, he felt
totally unmoved. She was just a woman, someone who
had caused him some grief a year ago.

Two players sat at her table, and she dealt the cards
with mechanical precision from a plastic storage case. Her
face was expressionless. T.J. imagined that pulling card
after card from the Plexiglas box, summing the face values and sorting out the chips thousands of times a day,
must get unbearably boring after a while.

"That's her," he whispered to Abbie, angling his head toward the raven-haired dealer. "Should we just go up to her, or what?"

Abbie stared at Rosalie for several long seconds. T.J. couldn't see Abbie's face, but he figured she was sizing the woman up, weighing various strategies before she made her move. Eventually she slid her hand from T.J.'s arm, shrugged her shoulders to straighten out her blouse and started briskly toward the table at the end of the row. T.J. followed.

As they neared the table, Rosalie had just finished a deal and was collecting the stacks of chips the two luckless players had wagered and lost. She glanced up, apparently expecting the two newcomers to ask to be dealt in. When her eyes met T.J.'s, she flinched. Then she scowled. "Fancy meeting you here," she snarled by way of a greeting.

"Hello, Rosalie," he said as courteously as possible.

Rosalie busied herself with a formal, almost ritualistic shuffling of the cards. The two players seated at the table eyed T.J. and Abbie with low-level curiosity. One of them took a swig from his cocktail glass and the other began nervously stacking and unstacking his chips.

"You wanna get dealt in?" Rosalie asked, returning the massive deck of cards to the Plexiglas box. "This table has a five-dollar minimum."

"Actually, no, Rosalie. I didn't come to play. I came here to ask a favor of you."

"A favor?" She tossed back her head and hooted. "That's funny." Her glare expanded to encompass Abbie, and she said, "Who are you?"

"I'm an attorney advising Mr. Hillyard on a legal matter," Abbie said smoothly. "We'd like to talk to you for a few minutes, if we might."

"A legal matter?" Rosalie looked panicked. "Hey, if you're accusing me of something, T.J.—"

Before T.J. could reassure her, the man in the tuxedo materialized at the table. Evidently, he had been observing the encounter, and he wasn't going to let it boil over into a full-scale altercation. "Is there a problem here?" he asked T.J. and Abbie in a deceptively obsequious voice. "I'm the supervisor. Perhaps I can help you."

"Perhaps you can," Abbie said quickly, brushing the man's sleeve with her fingertips and guiding him away from the table.

T.J. watched as Abbie conferred quietly with the pit boss. He felt Rosalie's furious stare burning into his back, but he didn't want to get into a fracas with her. He didn't want to rehash the past, or beg her for forgiveness for something that hadn't been his fault. All he wanted was to get an affidavit from her and leave.

After a minute Abbie smiled and beckoned to T.J. "Come this way," the pit boss said once T.J. had joined him and Abbie. He led them out of the casino's main room and down a back hall to a small lounge. "Please sit down," he said graciously, gesturing toward the upholstered couch. "I'll get Miss Gorman." Then he whisked out of the room.

T.J. stared at the empty doorway, then turned back to Abbie, impressed. "What did you tell him?"

She offered T.J. a cryptic smile. "I told him that if we couldn't get a written statement from Rosalie today, we would probably have to subpoena her to testify when the case enters the courts, and surely the casino would rather lose her services for a half hour this afternoon than for the prolonged duration of a trial."

"A trial?" T.J. exploded. He was more than willing to fight the case to a certain degree, but he couldn't take it all the way to a trial if Abbie wasn't going to serve as his defense counsel. "Abbie, Thorpe plans to settle before we ever get near a courthouse—"

Her smile expanded slightly. "Don't be so literal," she said. "Rosalie's boss didn't want her to leave her table to talk to us. I had to persuade him that it was in his best interests to accommodate us while we were here."

"Is this how you win cases in court?" T.J. asked, lowering himself to sit beside Abbie on the couch.

"Sometimes," she said, before swinging her gaze toward the door.

Rosalie stood there, glowering at T.J. He rose to his feet and presented her with what he hoped was an appeasing smile. "You're looking good, Rosalie," he said.

"Oh, so you finally noticed," she snapped, storming into the room and favoring him with a flinty scowl. "Well, I got news for you, Mr. Hot Stuff—you're about one year too late."

"Rosalie...come on," he protested, doing his best to swallow his own anger. "Let's not have a scene here, okay?"

"What would you prefer? Would you like to kick me in the teeth, T.J.? You seemed to enjoy doing that the last time I saw you."

"That's not true, Rosalie, and you—"

"Why don't we all just calm down?" Abbie proposed in a soothing voice. She fired a dubious look at T.J., then escorted Rosalie to the couch and sat, positioning herself so her own back was to him and her torso blocked Rosalie's view of him, as well. He realized that she was intentionally shutting him out, and he didn't like it. But Abbie had gotten what she'd wanted from Rosalie's supervisor, and T.J. supposed that she knew what she was doing when it came to Rosalie, too.

He leaned against the doorframe, listening as the two women talked and Abbie took notes. "Do you remember the night this all took place?" Abbie asked, her voice remaining low and comforting as she jotted notes on a pad. She had already mentioned the incident to Rosalie.

"Sure. I remember. That kid with the Mickey Mouse T-shirt," Rosalie said. "I kept calling him 'Mickey Mouse' in my head. It was my way of remembering which customers were getting what orders—I always gave them nicknames in my head."

"And you nicknamed this boy 'Mickey Mouse'?"

"Uh-huh. I remember him especially because he was young and he was drunk as a skunk."

"Did he order a drink?"

"He ordered a million drinks," Rosalie attested. "T.J. just ignored him, though. 'Give him coffee,' he said. So I said, 'Don't you want to card him? He looks underage.' And T.J. said, 'I don't want to card him because maybe he's carrying false proof—or maybe he happens to look ten years younger than he really is. And if he shows me valid proof I'm gonna have to serve him liquor, and I don't want to. He's way past his limit.'"

"So you didn't ask him to prove his age?" Abbie questioned her.

"Nope. I just gave him coffee. He started bitching about it, and T.J. came over and told me he'd take care of it, and the next thing we knew, the kid's throwing the mug of coffee at T.J.'s head."

Well, T.J. would give Rosalie credit for telling the truth. The kid had lobbed the mug at him, just as she'd testified. When Abbie twisted to look at him, he nodded in confirmation.

Abbie turned back to Rosalie. "Was T.J. hurt?"

"Who?" Rosalie snorted disdainfully. "Mr. Hotshot Athlete over there? Nah. The kid was too plastered to aim very well. The mug hit the floor and broke, though. It was a mess."

"And then what happened?"

"The kid bolted. T.J. started after him, but you know, he doesn't move so fast anymore, with that bum leg of his. Time he got to the front door, the kid was gonzo."

Abbie jotted some notes on her pad. "You'd swear to this version of the events?" she asked.

"It's the truth," Rosalie insisted. "Sure, I'd swear to it."

"All right. Let's go through it again, more slowly this time. I want to get it all down in your words."

T.J. remained in the doorway, listening with only half his mind to the voices of the two women as they discussed the night in question, as Abbie grilled Rosalie on phrasing and details, explaining time and again that the accuracy of Rosalie's statement was of vital importance. Half his mind listened and the other half focused on the two women—the one whom he wanted so badly it hurt and the other whom he'd rejected. He was struck again by how pretty Rosalie was, and yet how utterly indifferent he felt toward her. He wouldn't have turned her down if she'd approached him for the right reasons. But she had approached him for the wrong reasons, the worst reasons. In a sense, he'd been rejected by her.

He was grateful to her for speaking honestly about what had happened that July night a year ago. He had to thank her for supporting him and telling the truth. And yet a vision lingered in his head of Abbie impaling him with that sharp, cynical glance. T.J. couldn't escape the appalling thought that, for all he'd gained with Rosalie's testimony, he'd lost something even more important: Abbie's trust.

He should have told her, right at the start, that there was bad blood between him and Rosalie. But it had occurred so long ago, and he'd been through similar situations before, and he simply hadn't thought much of it. Rosalie had been difficult in plenty of ways; she'd had a volatile temperament, and little slights had had a way of provoking big fireworks from her. He hadn't seen the need to provide Abbie with an in-depth psychoanalysis of his former waitress.

What difference did it make? He didn't really have Abbie's trust, anyway. Sure, she trusted him enough to spend the night in the cabin with him—because the alternatives were unpalatable and because, whatever she thought of T.J., she knew he wasn't going to attack her. But she didn't trust him enough to let down her guard, to discover with him how far and how deep their friendship could go. Whether or not he had filled her in on his clash with Rosalie Gorman a year ago was irrelevant. Abbie didn't trust him.

"Okay—just sign it here," Abbie was saying. T.J.'s gaze sharpened on the two women on the couch, who were bent over the written copy of Rosalie's statement, rereading it together. "When we get back to Wheeler, I'll prepare a typed copy of this statement and send it to you for your signature. In the meantime, is this acceptable to you, in your own words?"

"It's exactly what happened," Rosalie declared.

"Great. This gives us something to work with. I really appreciate your help, Ms. Gorman."

"Forget it. I don't mind leaving my table for a few minutes." She stood and smoothed her dress shirt into the waistband of her trousers. Abbie stood, too.

"Thank you," T.J. said with as much sincerity as he could muster. He suddenly found himself hating Rosalie for having unwittingly drained Abbie of what little faith she'd had in him.

"Yeah," Rosalie grunted, giving T.J. a smile that was more a sneer. "Tell Jackie I'll be in touch."

"I will."

He trailed the two women down the hall to the casino. Rosalie headed straight for her boss, who chatted quietly with her for a minute and then ushered her back to her blackjack table. Without a word to T.J., Abbie wedged her black folder under her arm and marched through the casino to the grand glass doors leading out to the street.

He didn't have much trouble figuring out that she was angry. Well, good for her, T.J. fumed, let her be angry. If she had something to say to him, she was free to say it. And if she didn't, she could stew in her own juices. He had nothing to apologize for.

They climbed into the car and T.J. ignited the engine. Just because he wasn't going to apologize didn't mean he couldn't start a civil conversation with Abbie. Considering himself noble in the extreme, he said, "It looks as if she really came through, doesn't it."

"She was very cooperative," Abbie agreed brusquely, snatching a glimpse of T.J. and then pressing her lips together in a grim line.

He steered out of the parking lot and cruised toward a convenience store. "She doesn't like me," he noted.

"That's an understatement."

This time it was T.J.'s turn to measure Abbie with a short glance. "Look, Abbie," he said, acknowledging to himself that he wouldn't be able to stomach spending the next several hours with her if she was going to be in a snit the whole time. "If you want to ask, ask."

"Ask what?"

He coasted into the parking lot, braked to a stop and switched off the engine. Then he turned fully to her. "What happened between me and Rosalie."

"That's none of my business," she said piously.

Yet there she was, sitting no more than six inches from him and passing judgment on him. He wanted to grab her by the shoulders and shake her, but he restrained himself. "Do you want to drive back to Wheeler tonight?" he suggested, hiding his frustration behind a falsely calm voice. "We managed to finish here sooner than I thought we would."

She tossed the decision back to him. "Do you want to drive back tonight?"

"Damn it, no!" he roared, his patience exhausted. "No, I don't want to drive back tonight. I want you to admit you're mad at me and tell me why. And I want you to ask me to make it better because you really don't want to be mad at me. That's what I want."

"I really don't want to be mad at you," Abbie said, so softly T.J. wasn't sure he heard her correctly.

He peered into her face, into those round, iridescent eyes of hers, and he knew he hadn't misunderstood her. She wanted to trust him. She wanted to be his friend. She wanted to breach this rift.

He lifted her hand from the folder on her lap and sandwiched it between his. He knew intuitively that it would be easier to mend whatever was wrong between them if he was holding her, touching her. "Abbie..." He took a deep breath, then began in earnest. "Rosalie worked for me for a few months. She's—well, she's an attractive woman."

"She's gorgeous," Abbie elaborated in a dry voice. T.J. wondered if she was jealous. He had to admit that the possibility appealed to him.

"And I've got good eyesight," he granted. "She and I kind of danced around each other for a while. I sensed she was interested, and I made sure she knew I was interested."

"This is all quite intriguing," Abbie muttered.

Undeterred, T.J. went on. "Then one night, she and I found ourselves alone together, cleaning up after closing time. And one thing led to another—"

"Spare me the details, would you?" Abbie interrupted sharply.

T.J. felt her fingers tensing up against his palms. He stroked his hand over her knuckles to relax her. "The thing was, Rosalie kept talking about how I had been this idol in town. I think I told you she went to the regional high school a few years after us, and my reputation had lived on at the school, and she'd always wanted to get to know the famous T. J. Hillyard. Well, I told her that wasn't who I was, but she just kept going on and on about how I'd been so famous once and I'd played on a pro team, and I was the most well-known citizen in Wheeler, and she was just so excited to think of making love with someone as renowned and celebrated as T. J. Hillyard..." He grimaced as the memory overtook him. "And I said no."

Abbie perused him, attentive, absorbing his words and—he hoped—believing him.

"I don't like it when people cotton up to me because of who I was fifteen years ago. It bothers me. Rosalie was like a groupie, Abbie. She wanted to sleep with someone who had once had a brush with fame, and then she could notch her belt and move on. She didn't care about who *I* was or what *I* was doing—only about who I used to be. And I hate that, Abbie. I hate it. I am who I am *now*, and anyone who can't accept me for who I am now..."

He sighed. He didn't know how much of this Abbie comprehended. She hadn't been in Wheeler during the years of T.J.'s convalescence and his reemergence as an individual with a new game plan, a new life. She hadn't seen the way some people had pitied him, treating him as if his life had come to an end, as if he had nothing else to contribute, no other gifts or skills with which to justify his existence. He had been celebrated in Wheeler, but until he'd lost his stardom, he hadn't been known or understood very well at all.

"So you said no," Abbie echoed.

"She got pretty nasty about it."

"Maybe you hurt her feelings."

T.J. laughed sourly. "*I* hurt *her* feelings? You should have heard some of the things she said to me, Abbie. I mean, we're talking the kind of things that cut a man's ego to smithereens."

"You seem to have survived."

"So has she," T.J. countered. He searched her face hopefully. "Are you still mad at me?"

She held his unwavering gaze with hers. "You should have told me all of this before," she chided him.

"I know," he conceded. "I thought about telling you, Abbie—but I was afraid if I did, you wouldn't come to Tahoe at all."

"Of course I would have come," she said with a firmness he hadn't sensed in her during the past week, when they'd bickered continuously about the trip. "It just would have been better if I'd known what to expect."

"You were spectacular winging it," he praised her. She *was* spectacular, not just in her handling of a potentially stubborn witness but in everything she did. Most of all, he thought, she was spectacular in forgiving him.

"Being able to improvise my way through an examination of a witness is one of my great talents as a lawyer."

He wanted to enumerate her many great talents. He wanted to kiss her, to thank her, to love her. But he couldn't, not without destroying this tenuous peace.

So instead he said, "Let's go buy some food."

Chapter Ten

They ate their dinner at the picnic table on the larger deck downstairs: grilled steaks, a tossed salad and a bottle of burgundy. Abbie admitted without a trace of guilt that T.J. had served her a much more satisfying dinner than the noodle casserole she'd concocted for him a week ago. Even though she did assist him with the salad, he did most of the work. His willingness to cook was vastly different from what she'd been used to with Bob, who had always been very good at giving lip service to feminism and the importance of dividing domestic responsibilities equally while somehow never getting around to doing his share of the chores.

Perhaps it was because T.J. wasn't truly courting Abbie that he felt free to fold the napkins and toss the greens. Perhaps it was because he was self-assured enough not to find such allegedly feminine tasks threatening. Or perhaps it was simply because he was a fine, decent man.

She had been thinking about that a great deal this evening, ever since he'd provided her with the history of his relationship with Rosalie Gorman. Abbie's meeting with the woman hadn't gone at all as she had expected. For one thing, she hadn't known Rosalie was going to resemble a *Vogue* model. Not that appearance should matter so much, but the reflexive stab of envy Abbie had suffered the instant she'd spotted that ravishing woman dealing cards could have interfered with Abbie's ability to interview Rosalie.

She hadn't let it, though. She had comported herself with poise, trying not to compare her own rather ordinary appearance with Rosalie's, and struggling to ignore the enmity that the woman exuded toward T.J. Rosalie could never have guessed how bewildered Abbie had been, and how uncomfortable. Not until she'd gotten the deposition she had come for and departed from the casino had she dropped her facade of cool competence.

She had been furious with T.J. It was a client's job to inform his attorney of anything that might help in a case. But that alone couldn't explain the extent of Abbie's rage. She'd been upset because she had sensed subliminally that the hostility between T.J. and Rosalie had something to do with sex.

She had resolved not to let him find out how vexed she was by the idea of a love affair between T.J. and Rosalie—and then, sitting with him in his car, feeling the warmth of his hands enveloping hers and growing aware of his own anger and tension, she understood that T.J. didn't really care about what had happened between him and Rosalie so long ago. He cared only about what was happening between him and Abbie now. And that made an enormous difference to Abbie.

They didn't talk about Rosalie over dinner, or about the lawsuit at all. Mostly, they talked about the things T.J. usually did when he came to the cabin. He read, he told Abbie—action novels, spy stuff, books she had absolutely no interest in, although when he described some of the plots to her he made them sound fascinating. He told her he sometimes jogged, despite the irregular mountain terrain, and he sometimes swam at one of the beaches down on the lake. When Abbie asked him why he didn't own a boat, he laughed. "Hey, when I bought this place I was a pro athlete who'd just received a big bonus for signing with the Bears. The day I start making that kind of money with Tyler's, I'll buy myself a boat."

The view from the lower deck was mostly of trees, tall pine and redwood spires stabbing the sky. As the sun began its descent toward the western horizon, the trees threw longer and longer shadows over the deck, and eventually Abbie began to feel the chill of a mountain evening closing in on her.

"You can see the lake better from the upstairs deck," T.J. told her. "Go on up and feast your eyes before it gets too cold outside. I'll join you after I've rinsed out the wineglasses."

She climbed up the stairs, nearly stubbed her toe navigating the narrow space between the sloping walls and the broad bed, and edged past the bureau to reach the sliding door. As soon as she stepped outside, she was accosted by the glorious vista of the lake below her, deep and tranquil, reflecting the deepening blue of the evening sky and the spiked tips of the evergreens that framed it. To the east, just above the trees, sat a plump orange harvest moon.

Ignoring the slight nip in the air, Abbie leaned against the railing and drank in the scenery. If only she had a place like this to retreat to every now and then, she might not loathe New York City so much.

"Check out that moon," T.J. said.

She turned in time to see him walking through the doorway onto the deck. "Isn't it something?" she agreed as she shifted to make room for him at the railing.

He crossed to stand beside her, resting his forearms next to hers and staring out at the lush forest and the darkening surface of the lake. "I don't think I've ever seen a harvest moon here in the mountains before," he remarked. "We get them every autumn back in Wheeler, but never in the mountains. I think the atmospheric conditions are wrong."

"They're right tonight," Abbie noted quietly, deciding that the lunar phenomenon had to signify something, although she had no idea what.

Obviously, T.J. had the same impression she did. "It *is* right tonight, isn't it," he concurred, his dark gaze roaming from the moon to the lake. He edged closer to her, then bent his wrist so he could lace his fingers through hers. He gave her a minute to protest his having taken her hand, and when she didn't he said, "Let's make love."

She refused to look at him. She didn't want to see his handsome face, to acknowledge the nearness of his body and surrender to the potent glow in his beautiful eyes—at least, not before she had a chance to sort her thoughts and build her defenses. Just because the moon was surreal in its loveliness and the mountain air was bracing, just because she and T.J. were alone in his cabin and they'd managed to reach a new level of trust during the day, just because she'd been attracted to him from the moment she'd set foot inside his bar the day she'd arrived in Wheeler...

"I know," he broke into her thoughts, his voice low and intense. "I promised I wasn't going to do this to you, Abbie, and if you tell me to shut up I will."

"T.J.—"

"I want you, Abbie," he went on, not giving her a chance to say anything. But she really wasn't sure what to say, and she certainly didn't want him to shut up. "It's been good between us today," he said. "Even in my car, after we left Harrah's and there was all that tension.... It was good, and it could be better if you'd let it happen, just this one night. I know you're going to be leaving soon. I'm not asking you to change your plans or anything like that."

His thumb stroked hers in a nonverbal entreaty. She studied their hands, his so much larger than hers, so commanding as it clasped hers. She labored hard to remember all the valid reasons she had for saying no to T.J., but she came up blank. The only thought her brain seemed capable of forming was that the conditions were, in their own peculiar way, very right.

"I don't want to do a number on you, Abbie," he swore when she remained silent. "I don't want to hurt you or waste your time or hold you back. I'm not asking for the next four years of your life. All I'm asking for is tonight."

His tone was hypnotic. Or perhaps it wasn't his tone, or his gentle, beguiling words. Perhaps it was simply the magic of a golden moon, or the belief that she and T.J. had endured a long, intense day and they deserved, at last, to harvest the affection that had ripened between them. Whatever it was, Abbie felt herself succumbing. It was just tonight, one night, one chance to celebrate her affection for T.J. He wasn't asking her to stay in Wheeler, to rearrange her existence and fall madly in love with him. He wasn't demanding anything of her, except to share this one night with her.

He urged her around to face him, and when her gaze locked with his she knew she couldn't say no. She couldn't deny the inevitability of it. It was what they both wanted, what the moon and the mountains and the cool evening air had conspired to create for them: tonight, together.

He lifted her hand and pressed his mouth to the hollow of her palm. Then he released it and gathered her into his arms, holding her, touching his lips to her hair, her forehead, her temple. Frustrated by his meandering kisses, she tilted her head back so he could no longer avoid her mouth.

When his lips met hers, they both groaned. Pulling her closer to himself, he sought her tongue with his, and she readily opened to him. He wasn't talking, but his hushed, mesmerizing voice echoed inside her: *"I want you. All I'm asking for is tonight."* And without even realizing that she had spoken, she heard her own breathless response: "Yes."

The movement of her lips broke their kiss, and T.J. touched his chin to her forehead and smiled. He took her hand once more and led her inside.

After switching on a lamp fastened to the wall above the bed, he kissed her again, deeply, digging his fingers into her hair and holding her still for the assault of his tongue. It fenced daringly with hers, awakening a yearning that quickly spread down through her, causing the muscles of her abdomen to tighten, infiltrating her flesh and sending its erotic message along her nerve endings. By the time she and T.J. separated, gasping for breath, Abbie's mind had been reduced to one single thought, one single need—T.J.'s love.

He ran his fingertips along the neckline of her blouse, flirting with the skin below her throat. "Now's your chance to slap my face and call me a dirty old man," he alerted her, smiling tentatively.

"You're not so old."

He chuckled, a soft, sensuous sound that resonated against the sloping walls of the loft. "Meaning, I'm dirty?"

"Meaning, you're a man," she corrected him.

She saw the flickering light in his eyes, a sign of keen pleasure as he scrutinized the woman beside him. He slid his hand beneath her chin and lifted her face to his, but instead of kissing her again, he only gazed at her. His smile faded slightly. "I really didn't plan on this," he said solemnly.

"I didn't think you had."

He shook his head slightly. "If I'd planned it, I would have come prepared... but I didn't."

It took her a moment to realize what he was getting at. When she finally did, she hugged him. She was touched not only by his consideration but, even more, by this extra bit of proof that, as he'd just said, he hadn't counted on seducing her tonight.

"I'm protected," she admitted shyly, relieved that she'd decided not to quit taking her pills when she'd broken up with Bob. She had seriously considered stopping; at the time, she hadn't imagined that she would want to be with a man any time soon. But then, she hadn't imagined that she would meet someone like T.J.

The kiss she had expected a minute ago came now. T.J.'s tongue took hers, dueled with it, slid unpredictably over her teeth and the inner flesh of her lips. Dazzled by what he was doing to her mouth, she was scarcely aware of what he was doing to her blouse. His fingers moved nimbly down the buttons, unfastening them, spreading the fabric apart to discover the lace-trimmed slip she had on underneath. "Oh, Abbie—what is this?" he whispered, stepping back to examine the satin undergarment.

"It's a slip."

It was actually a slip that doubled as a bra. Abbie was small-breasted enough not to need both. She had always viewed her undergarments as practical, not lingerie intended to excite a man. But T.J. clearly felt differently.

"Let me undress you," he whispered.

He hardly needed Abbie's permission; she hadn't protested when he started to remove her blouse. She stood patiently as he pulled the blouse off and laid it carefully on the bureau, then unbuttoned her skirt and let it fall. He inspected the slip—and the woman wearing it. He observed the way the slinky material draped over the firm swells of her breasts, indented slightly at her waist and then dropped to a lace hem that brushed the tops of her knees. "Do all high-powered New York City lawyers wear things like this?" he asked, enthralled.

"I can't speak for anyone else," Abbie answered, "but I doubt many of the male lawyers do."

T.J. allowed his fingers to trail in the wake of his gaze. His hands skimmed teasingly over her breasts, leaving her nipples tingling and taut, and then followed the narrowing of her waist and the flare of her hips. "Who cares about male lawyers?" he posed, reaching behind her and molding his palms to the soft curve of her bottom. He pulled her to him and pressed her body to his, letting her feel his arousal through the slip, through his trousers. "I am so tempted," he whispered, grazing the crown of her head with his lips. "I am so tempted to ask you to keep this thing on...but..." Drawing in a shaky breath, he raised his hands to her shoulders and slipped the ribbon-thin straps down her arms. "I'm even more tempted to touch you."

The implications of his words aroused her as much as his fingers on her skin, gently shoving the slip down, baring her breasts, her midriff and waist and belly, catching the elastic of her panties and stripping them off in the same efficient motion.

She knew instinctively that once he gave in to that temptation and touched her, he would probably render her unable to do anything as demanding as undressing him. So she preempted him, reaching for his shirt buttons before he could reach for her, and tugging them open. He was apparently not at all disappointed by her attack on his clothing; he enthusiastically assisted her, yanking his shirttails from the waist of his slacks and shedding the shirt once Abbie had finished unbuttoning it.

She had caught partial glimpses of his chest during their jogging outings on the path by the railroad track, and what she hadn't seen she'd been able to picture, thanks to the way his perspiration-soaked shirt clung to his body. Even so, actually seeing his naked chest and knowing that tonight it was hers to caress, to make love to, sent thrills of excitement through her body. The muscles of his torso were lean and tempered, stretching beneath suntanned skin dusted with just the right amount of curling dark hair. The hair tapered into a narrow line at his navel, and her gaze followed it down to the buckle of his belt. Reading her mind, T.J. unbuckled it.

Whether it was a sudden bout of bashfulness or simply nerves, she averted her eyes as he pulled off his slacks and briefs. When she risked turning back to him, her vision snagged on the pinkish-white lines slashing across his left knee, cutting through the hair that grew over the hard muscles of his calf and thigh like roads carved into an otherwise unspoiled setting. There were thick scars, thin scars, a lattice of surgical souvenirs and battered flesh.

"Pretty gruesome, huh," T.J. muttered.

She glanced up at him. She could tell from his wary expression that he thought the sight of his damaged leg had put a damper on her passion. "No," she said unflinchingly. "No, it's not." She lowered herself to sit on the edge of the bed and traced one of the scars with her index finger. Leaning forward, she kissed his knee.

"Uh—let's not get kinky here," he cautioned, a feeble attempt at levity.

As he dropped onto the bed next to her, she straightened up and turned to face him. "You're still bitter about it, aren't you," she said, less a question than a statement. After all this time, after all the evidence she'd seen of his maturity and mellowness, he still seemed to resent her acknowledgment of his old injury.

He gave her accusation careful thought. "I don't know," he admitted.

"I'm glad it happened," she said. At his startled look, she explained, "If it hadn't happened, we probably wouldn't be here now." Abbie realized that such an opinion was extremely selfish, but if T.J. could be honest enough to confess that he still harbored bitterness about it, she could be honest enough to declare her feelings, too.

T.J. didn't object to her sentiment. In fact, he seemed amused by it, even flattered. He hoisted himself higher on the bed, pulling Abbie with him until they were both resting their heads against the propped-up pillows. Then he curled one arm around her and smiled. "I wonder why I didn't think of that," he pondered aloud. "There I was, lying on the ground and feeling very sorry for myself, and instead, I could have been thinking, 'Hey, if my career ends now, maybe in around fifteen years or so I'll wind up at the cabin with Abbie Jarvis from high school.'"

Abbie chuckled at the absurdity of his description. She cuddled closer to him, wondering why they were lying together naked in bed and talking rather than making love. They had all night to explore each other; right now, his past, his injury and his recovery were the part of him that she wanted to explore. "What were you really thinking when it happened?" she asked.

He twirled his fingers through her hair to the back of her neck, then down to her shoulder, his caresses abstract yet marvelously stimulating. "Do you really want to know?" he questioned Abbie. At her earnest nod, he grinned. "I was thinking about what a bummer it was to get pass interference in the end zone. If I had caught that ball—and I would have, if I hadn't gotten cut down by those Goliaths—if I'd caught it, it would have been six points. But when you get pass interference in the end zone, they don't give you the TD. They spot the ball half the distance to the goal."

Abbie laughed incredulously. "You weren't really thinking that, were you?"

"You bet I was."

"Weren't you even concerned about your leg? Weren't you in agony?"

"Not really," he told her. "The human body is pretty clever—it protects you from pain by going into shock. I knew something really bad had happened to me—I heard things snapping, but I didn't feel it right away." He twisted his fingers through her hair again. "I knew, though—I knew my career was over. That was my second thought, after being ticked off about the six points. I knew I was finished as far as football was concerned."

His mood was no longer prickly or troubled. He seemed to accept that Abbie wasn't with him because he was a football star, as his wife had viewed him, or even as an almost-football star, as his ex-waitress Rosalie had viewed him. Abbie was with him because he was a wonderful man who had weathered some difficult times and emerged from them stronger and wiser. She was with him because he hadn't lost hope after his first dream was destroyed; he'd had the courage and the will to keep dreaming.

"Make love to me," she whispered, astonished by her uncharacteristic aggressiveness. She hadn't spoken consciously—the words emerged from some secret place inside her soul. She wouldn't take them back, though. She wanted T.J.'s love now, when she was entranced by his goodness, his decency and honesty. She wanted him completely.

He needed no further encouragement. In one fluid motion he eased her onto her back, raised himself onto her and bowed to take her lips with his. His tongue made a heavenly raid on her mouth while his hand moved down her body in search of her breasts. He found one, cupped it, kneaded it with excruciating tenderness until she was gasping, digging her fingers into the sinewy breadth of his shoulders and moaning for more.

Her overwhelming response inspired him. Tearing his lips from hers, he shifted downward on the bed and bent to her breast. Whatever his kiss had done to her mouth paled beside the miracles he was now performing on the sensitive flesh of her nipple—tickling it with his mustache, nipping it with his teeth, cooling it with his tongue, sucking it hungrily into his mouth. She raked her fingers helplessly through his hair, frustrated by her inability to reach his chest yet reluctant to ask him to move.

He finally did move, but only to her other breast. She lay passively under him for as long as she could bear it, hugging his head to her and sliding one bent leg between his thighs. He trapped her knee, holding it tantalizingly close to him but not close enough.

"Oh, Abbie..." He lowered his head to the soft crevice between her breasts and sighed, his breath feathering across her skin. "I could kiss you like this forever."

"No," she argued, her voice ragged. "I wouldn't let you."

He lifted his face to study her, apparently unsure of what she meant. She took advantage of his new position by wriggling down beside him and splaying her fingers across the sleek contours of his chest, combing her nails through the dark swirls of hair. Once again she found herself thinking about how glad she was that he had stopped playing football. If he'd continued to play, his torso would probably be bulging with body-builder muscles, his ribs hidden beneath them, the tendons in his neck and the ridges of his collarbone lost to he-man proportions. Instead, she got to feel his rib cage, his sternum, the fierce pounding of his heart.

He was clearly delighted by the journey her fingers were making across his body. Resting his hands on her hips, he refrained from pulling her too close to himself. Obviously he wanted to give her enough space—and time—to investigate him fully.

She took what he gave her, allowing her hands to roam in a languid way over his sides, across his stomach, up to the crest of his shoulder and down his strong, graceful arm. When she ventured as low as the dark nest of hair below his navel he emitted a low, ragged groan deep in his throat, but he didn't stop her. He kept his eyes on hers, his lips close to hers, his fingers flexing gently on the soft skin of her derriere.

She let her hand skim below his navel again, and his patience crumbled. He grabbed her wrist, refusing to let her hand complete its circuit. "Do you know what you're doing?" he whispered.

"Driving you crazy," she answered, also in a whisper.

"That's right." He pressed her back into the mattress, letting go of her so he could stroke the inner flesh of her thighs, first one and then the other, urging them apart. His fingers inched higher with each caress. "Do you want me to make you crazy, too?"

"I think you already have," Abbie murmured, lifting her hips to his hand in an unspoken plea.

After a torturous instant, T.J.'s fingers found their goal. They moved on her, in her, playing through the soft thatch of hair and over the damp, sensitive skin, dancing to the edges of her thighs and back again and...yes, making her crazy. With each deft stroke he consigned her to a deeper level of insanity. She could no longer think, no longer function as a rational human being. All she could do was feel, respond, want.

Closing her eyes, she let her head sink into the pillow. She wanted to touch him, too, to caress him and arouse him and ready him, but her body seemed to be beyond her control, her hands unable to do anything but clench into fists against his chest, her legs unable to do anything but angle her hips higher against his hand. Her nervous system spun in a narrowing coil, winding through her to center on T.J., on the place where he compelled her responses...dragging her down until she feared she would leave him behind.

She moaned his name—or at least, she tried to. Whatever strange, garbled sound emerged from her trembling lips, T.J. understood what she was trying to tell him. "Yes," he murmured, sliding his hand away and rising fully onto her. "Yes, Abbie, I'm here."

With a slow, exquisite thrust, he was there, exactly where Abbie wanted him to be, where she needed him to be. She circled her legs around his hips and her arms around his waist, imprisoning him inside her, savoring him, forgetting the previous ecstasy of his caresses as she welcomed the infinitely more profound ecstasy of this, him, his body becoming a part of hers. Opening her eyes, she gazed up into his face and saw her ecstasy mirrored in his eyes, in his blissful smile.

She felt him leave her, then thrust again, his smile waning as the radiance in his eyes intensified. And again, and again, the hair on his chest brushing provocatively against her breasts as he held himself above her, his fingers tangled into her hair, his lips raining kisses on her brow, on her mouth. His rhythm was languorous as he exercised restraint, each plunging motion full and deep, each withdrawal a painful loss that could be assuaged only by his return to her.

"You feel so good," he whispered, accelerating his pace slightly. "Oh, Abbie...you feel..." He groaned and came to her again.

She wished she could tell him how good he felt, but all she succeeded in doing was to gasp and then bury her lips against his shoulder to muffle her sudden cry of rapture as her soul exploded around him. Her flesh was ravaged by fiery spasms, blazing through her, burning away what little was left of her sanity. She clung to him, desperate for the shelter his strong body could provide, the solidity and safety of him.

He absorbed her trembling sobs as her body absorbed his climax. It stormed through him, consuming him as it consumed her, causing his body to stiffen and then shudder. He subsided on top of her, sweating and breathless, and she closed her arms more snugly around him, giving back to him the comfort she had just taken from him.

For several minutes they lay that way, their legs intertwined, their hearts pumping erratically. Abbie felt T.J. begin to soften, but when she attempted to pull away he slid one hand down to her hips and held her to himself.

"Stay," he mumbled on a ragged breath. "Stay with me, Abbie."

It was all he said, all either of them said for a long time. As Abbie's mind sluggishly clarified itself, she thought about how, before they'd left the deck, T.J. had promised her that he wasn't going to ask her to change her plans, he wasn't going to ask for four years of her life, he wasn't going to hold her back or waste her time.

She also thought about how much she loved him. It wasn't a startling revelation. She realized she had probably loved him for a long while, much longer than she'd been aware of. Her feelings for T.J. had evolved. Even if they hadn't gone to bed together, she would have loved him—and now that they had, she loved him even more.

But he hadn't asked for her love. He didn't want it. All he wanted was tonight.

She felt his hands moving against her hair, his fingers wandering through the silky auburn locks in a consoling pattern. He was still on top of her, his body heavy and warm, his breath floating across her ear and the side of her throat.

But even now, after this, after he'd whispered, "Stay with me, Abbie," she knew he was already prepared to say goodbye.

Chapter Eleven

He wished he could figure out a way to make it better. Sure, the morning after was sometimes awkward, but it shouldn't have been with Abbie. She and T.J. could talk about anything, couldn't they? They trusted each other, didn't they? He appreciated where she was coming from; he wasn't going to pull a power play on her, or make her feel as if she owed him anything. So why couldn't she relax?

Why couldn't he? Drinking coffee with her at the breakfast table, which was tucked into a corner of the compact kitchen, he felt tense, strung out, at odds with himself. Last night . . . last night had been awesome. After having Abbie once, he had wanted her even more—and she had wanted him, too. They'd made love again and it had been just as intense, just as good—no, better. He had felt incredibly alive with her beside him, potent and whole, willing to do anything for her: rename Tyler's "Abbie's," give her the key to his house, gift wrap that misplaced harvest moon and present her with it . . . even let her leave him, if that was what she had to do.

Sipping his coffee, he spied on her over the rim of his mug. She looked different now than she had just a half hour ago, when they'd awakened in bed with their legs woven together and Abbie's head nestled into the curve of his shoulder. Her presence, the sweet, faint fragrance of her skin and the spill of her soft hair across his arm had worked magic on him, and he'd found himself fully aroused before he was fully awake. He had wanted to make love with her then, in the pale dawn light streaming through the triangular glass wall at the foot of the bed.

But from the way she'd responded to his good-morning kiss, he knew they weren't going to make love. She hadn't exactly spurned him, but he could tell she was holding back.

She had been holding back ever since. It wasn't just her being dressed that made her look different to him now. It was something in her eyes, something guarded and leery. As she picked at her toast and fidgeted with her teaspoon, she never looked directly at him, never gave him a genuine smile.

He set his mug down on the cramped table with a thud. His coffee was lukewarm, and he didn't really want it. What he wanted was for Abbie to explain why she was distancing herself from him, why she was waving that imaginary stop sign of hers in front of his nose.

Damn. He ought to throw caution to the wind and tell her what he felt. He ought to pry her mug from the death grip with which she was clinging to it and haul her out of her chair and give her a smothering bear hug and confess that he loved her, that he wanted her to *stay*, not just in his bed, not just with her body, but with her soul, forever. He wanted to demand that she bid all those thugs and muggers in New York City a fond farewell and stay with him.

He wouldn't, of course. He couldn't. He respected her too much—and more than that, he understood her. He had once left Wheeler himself, and fate, not choice, had brought him back. He had learned to accept that fate, even be grateful for it. But he could imagine how he would have felt if, back in the days when he had just signed with the Chicago Bears, someone had said to him, "I love you, T.J., and I want you to give up everything you've spent your entire life working for and stay in Wheeler with me."

If a woman had ever said such a thing to him, he would hate her. No matter how much he loved her, he would hate her even more for pressuring him like that.

"Do you want another cup?" he asked, standing to add some hot coffee to what was left in his mug.

"No, thank you."

He poured his coffee, turned off the coffee maker and leaned against the counter, staring at her across those few extra feet of space. "What are you going to do with the deposition?" he asked, then cursed silently. He was so eager to get her talking, he would resort to any topic. Rosalie's statement wasn't of any interest to T.J. right now, but talking about it was better than this ghastly silence.

"When we get back to Wheeler," Abbie explained, "I'll type up a draft of it. I think Margaret Schaller will let me borrow her typewriter. She lets my father use it sometimes."

"Uh-huh," T.J. said, pretending to be fascinated.

"We'll make some photocopies, express-mail them to Rosalie, get her signature, and then pass them along to John Thorpe."

"You'll be back in New York by that time," T.J. said, wondering whether he sounded disgruntled and then deciding he didn't care.

Abbie perused him, deep in thought. Whatever her feelings were about that particular fact, she obviously had no intention of sharing them with him. "If I am, you'll have to take the documents to Thorpe yourself. You can always have him call me if he needs a clarification."

"So that's it, then," T.J. muttered. "Signed, sealed, delivered."

"Pretty simple, this law business."

He studied her for a minute more, then gave up. Why push it? This conversation was straining them both. "I guess we should hit the road," he recommended quietly. "We've got a long drive ahead of us."

"I'll go get my stuff," she said, carrying her mug to the sink and then climbing the stairs.

He gazed after her, admiring the feminine shape of her calves below the hem of her skirt, remembering the way she'd looked in her lacy, clingy slip and feeling a painful twinge in his groin. He was nearly overwhelmed by the longing to race up the stairs after her, to hurl her down onto the bed and love her again, love her until she said, without any prompting, "I don't want to go back to New York, T.J. I don't want to leave you."

Right. And then Santa Claus and the Tooth Fairy would drop by, and they could all sing a few drinking songs together. T.J. had had enough experience with broken dreams to know how this one would conclude.

It didn't take long to pack up. T.J. checked the refrigerator for perishables, locked up the cabin and toted their suitcases to the car. He put them into the trunk while Abbie got settled in her seat. Then he climbed behind the wheel, started the engine, and drove away, trying to convince himself that he was glad to have dreamed this dream, even though waking up hurt like hell.

HER FATHER'S HOUSE was empty when T.J. dropped her off, a little after one o'clock. They had spent most of the four-hour drive listening to the car radio and exchanging

banal observations about how much warmer the weather
was in the valley than in the mountains. At her father's
house, T.J. got out of the car with her and gallantly carried her overnight bag up the front walk for her. Then he
stood with her on the porch, gazing down at her from his
towering height, his eyes opaque and his smile noncom-
mittal. "I'll be working tonight," he informed her. "If
you want to stop by at Tyler's later—"

"I'll see," she said, a vague answer to his detached invitation.

He stood with her a moment longer, then kissed her
cheek and bounded off the porch, moving in his lopsided
stride down the path to his car. She remained on the porch
until he drove out of sight before letting herself inside.

She walked directly to her bedroom to unpack. On the
dresser, next to the framed wedding photograph of her
parents, her father had left her a note saying "I'm at the
store. Hope you and T.J. had fun." There were also a few
letters that Marielle had forwarded from Yorktown Towers. Two were bills and the third was personal, post-
marked New Orleans. She recognized Jaime's handwriting
at once.

Grateful for the distraction Jaime's letter would provide, Abbie dropped her suitcase and tore open the envelope:

Dear Abbie,
I'm sorry it's taken me so long to answer your letter,
but since we last corresponded I have survived a
voodoo curse, a visit from my mother, a close encounter with a criminal record—don't ask, you really
don't want to know! And—I saved the best for last—
my own wedding.

A voodoo curse and a wedding. Abbie laughed faintly. She could more easily picture Jaime pulling stick pins out of a rag doll than getting married. Reeling from the delightful shock of Jaime's news, Abbie leaned against the bureau and continued reading.

Jaime described her new husband with enough superlatives to convince Abbie that the man deserved a wife as fine as Jaime.

It's funny how things never seem to work out the way you planned. Remember how I used to dream about my wedding, with white satin and orange blossoms and a huge champagne reception? Try jeans and sneakers with a free-for-all jazz jam and dancing in the street afterward. Our honeymoon was twenty-four hours of uninterrupted bliss...

A deep, pensive sigh escaped Abbie as visions of Jaime and her husband were supplanted by much-too-recent memories of the loft in T.J.'s mountain cabin. Feeling the unexpected prick of a few tears in her eyes, Abbie quickly focused back on the letter in her hand.

I guess what I'm trying to say is that sometimes, no matter how much you plot and plan, love is one thing you can't control and when you come right down to it, why would anyone want to?

"Oh, how romantic," Abbie grumbled beneath her breath. Jaime could afford to indulge in such sentimentality; she'd made herself a fabulous new life in New Orleans, and she'd found a man who wanted her as she was, where she was, for a good deal more than twenty-four hours of uninterrupted bliss.

All T.J. had wanted from Abbie was one night. They'd had their night—substantially less than twenty-four hours—and now Abbie was supposed to leave. She couldn't find fault with Jaime's assertion that love was one thing you couldn't control, but when one party was in love and the other wasn't, what alternative was there but to try to control your love as best you could?

She folded Jaime's letter back into the envelope, deciding to read it again later, when she hoped to be in better spirits. Her eyes were beginning to brim with moisture again, and she despised herself for being so horribly self-absorbed, for weeping over her own stupid affair instead of rejoicing in Jaime's good fortune.

She despised herself for weeping at all. What was it about this visit to Wheeler that had turned her into a waterworks? She had probably spent more time crying since she'd steered her rental car over the railroad tracks into town, than in the seven years since her last trip home, when her mother had died.

She stared through a blur of tears at the wedding photo sitting on the dresser. Her mother looked a lot like Abbie in the picture, young and bright-eyed and exuberant. She'd lived her life—a tragically abbreviated one—but her death was a fact, and Abbie understood that she wasn't crying for her mother anymore. Nor was she crying for her father. These tears were for herself, for having fallen in love with T.J., a man who didn't love her enough to ask her for more than one night. In all the years she'd known Bob, in all the months since she'd ended their relationship, she had never felt as utterly grief stricken as she did right now. She had never wept for him. Her tears were reserved only for the people closest to her heart: her mother, her father... and T.J.

Restless, she left her room for the bathroom, where she stripped off her clothing and took a quick, hot shower. Wrapping a bath towel around herself, she returned to her bedroom, where she put on some slacks and a short-sleeved sweater, ran her hairbrush through her hair, and tossed the skirt and blouse she'd had on into the laundry hamper. Then she detoured into the kitchen, discovered that she had no appetite and wandered down the hall to the front door. She went outside and sat on the porch, her gaze moving as if magnetized to the place by the curb where she'd last seen T.J., before he'd folded his lanky body into the driver's seat of his car and driven away.

She could go to Tyler's and see him tonight—but what for? If the place wasn't too busy, he could shoot the breeze with her for a while, and then she would say good-night, come home and crawl into bed and relive the previous night . . . and feel even sorrier for herself.

Her only other option was to avoid T.J. for the remainder of her stay in Wheeler—and to make sure that stay was as short as possible. Tonight, instead of going to Tyler's and torturing herself, she could polish the viable business plan T.J. and her father had devised for Jarvis's Hardware, and tomorrow they'd make a hurry-up appointment with Ed Garcia so Abbie could be with her father when he presented the plan and asked for new terms on the bank loan. If all went well, she could be back in her Manhattan apartment by the end of the week—maybe even in enough time to help Marielle pack up her things for her move to Chicago.

The aroma insinuated its way into her consciousness so subtly she wasn't immediately aware of it. She rested her folded arms on her knees and her chin on her arms, staring across the drying grass of the front lawn, noticing a few ripe green bulblike fruits dangling from the branches

of the walnut tree adorning the Calleros' yard across the
way, thinking about how serene this street was, how serene every street in Wheeler was—even Main Street, with
its steady current of teenagers cruising in their noisy
pickups. She thought about flying back to New York, to
the crowds and the din, the constant rumble of bus en-
gines and jackhammers and subway trains below one's
feet, the congested sidewalks and the unbroken rows of
skyscrapers blocking out the sky and the sun, the stench
of auto exhausts and incinerators and general filth . . .

And then she smelled it, the pungent scent that tinged
the air, hauntingly familiar. The rice fields were burning.

How could T.J. have thought the burning fields stank?
she wondered, inhaling the smoky aroma. It was a strong,
tangy scent, but she liked it. It made her think not of pollution and waste, as did so many of the odors of New
York, but of harvest, regeneration, renewal. The farmers
harvested what was valuable and burned the rest, and
from the rubble a bountiful new crop would emerge next
spring.

What a marvelous process it was. Abbie wished human beings could recycle their lives as easily as the farmers recycled their fields. She had derived great happiness
in the past; she'd won cases, seen justice prevail, helped
to restore the egos of a few victims and even salvaged the
souls of a few criminals by persuading the courts to sentence them to drug treatment centers or counseling pro-
grams. But perhaps she had harvested all that could be
gathered from that season of her life. How appealing it
would be to burn what was left, just burn it and bury it,
making her all the more fertile for the next season of her
life.

The sound of an approaching car broke into her rev-
erie. Focusing on the street, she saw not a car but an old

white van with Fifty Years of Know-how painted in bright green letters across the side. Abbie glanced at her wristwatch and was startled to discover how long she'd been daydreaming on the porch.

Her father pulled into the driveway and waved to her. She stood, stretched the stiffness from her back and neck and stepped off the porch to meet him on the walk.

"How was Lake Tahoe?" he asked, slinging his arm around her shoulders and ushering her back up the walk to the house.

How was it? Wonderful. Dreadful. She couldn't begin to answer that question. "We got the deposition from T.J.'s old waitress," she told him.

"Mission accomplished," Roy Jarvis said with pride. "What else can you expect from a top-notch attorney?" He held the front door open for Abbie and followed her inside. "There were a few things for you in the mail today," he said. "I swung by around lunchtime to make sure the bank hadn't sent another of those dunning letters—"

"Mr. Garcia promised he'd put a hold on the notices until you finished writing your business plan," Abbie reminded him.

"Yeah, well, just in case, I thought I'd take a look. They usually come on Mondays. Anyway, I'm happy to say everything in the mailbox was for you. You might as well move in, if you're gonna be getting so much mail here."

His offhand joke caused something to twist painfully inside Abbie. For a minute all she could think about was how nice it would be to move back into her childhood home, to burn the remains of her life in New York and plant new seeds here in Wheeler. She heard T.J.'s low, husky voice whispering, *"Stay with me, Abbie..."* and then she forcefully shook her head clear.

"I heard from my friend, Jaime Faber," Abbie remarked, accompanying her father into the kitchen.

He rolled up his sleeves to wash his hands at the sink. "The short one with the artist mother, right?" he guessed. He had met Abbie's friends during his visits to New York.

"That's right. Only she's not Jaime Faber anymore. She's Jaime Gerreau."

"She got married, did she?" He shook off his hands and dried them on a dish towel. "That's real nice. Give her my best."

Abbie nodded. She watched her father swing open the refrigerator door, inspect its contents and pull out a package of sliced turkey. "Sandwiches okay?" he asked. "I didn't know when you were going to be getting home, so I didn't plan for a big dinner or anything."

"Sandwiches are fine," said Abbie. Even though the only things she'd consumed all day had been a cup of coffee and a piece of toast, she wasn't particularly hungry.

While Roy fixed the sandwiches, Abbie set the table. She wondered how often he ate sandwiches for supper when she was away—and how much longer he would have to eat those suppers by himself. "Did you have dinner at Faye's house last night?" she asked, keeping her tone light.

"Yeah." He didn't look at Abbie when he answered, but pretended to be engrossed in the jar of mustard.

"What did she make?"

"Pot roast. You want a Coke, Abbie?"

"No, thanks," she said, watching as he pulled a bottle of cola from the refrigerator and carried it to the table.

She filled a glass with water for herself and took her seat, waiting for her father to say something more about his evening with Faye Hinkel. His terse answers fed her curiosity, but she wanted to give him a chance to volunteer more information before she embarked on a full-fledged interrogation.

He took a bite of his sandwich, chewed, and washed it down with a swig of soda. "What happened, Dad?" she asked, her concern building as he continued to avoid making eye contact with her.

"What happened when?"

"Last night at Faye's."

"Nothing," he said, then took another bite.

Ignoring her sandwich, Abbie leaned forward, bearing down on him. "Dad, tell me. Did you and Faye have a falling out? Did you have a fight or something?"

At last he stopped eating and met Abbie's steady gaze. "No, we didn't fight. We had a pleasant time, Abbie, all right?"

"But...?" She knew her father well enough to realize that he wasn't giving her the full story.

He relented with a wistful smile. "But something's missing, Abbie. I wish it weren't so, but it is. Something's missing."

"What?" Abbie asked compassionately.

"I don't know, sweetheart. I like Faye. She's a fine woman, she's attractive, she's kept herself in good shape over the years, she's good company. And it's not like I don't want to marry again, Abbie. I loved your mother, but she's been gone a long time and I'd like to find somebody else. Marriage is just about the best thing there is, if it's meant to be. But..." He sighed, his smile growing even more poignant. "It's not meant to be for Faye and me. What can I say? The spark just isn't there."

"Oh, Dad," Abbie commiserated, reaching across the table to squeeze his hand. "I'm sorry."

"Don't be," he reassured her. "We gave it our best shot, and now we know. I love Faye as a friend—but we can't force what isn't there."

"Love is one thing you can't control," Abbie murmured.

"Hmm?"

"It was something Jaime wrote in her letter. She said she and her husband don't seem at all suited to each other, but they love each other and that's all that matters."

"I reckon the spark was there for them," Roy remarked. "They're lucky souls, Abbie. I had that spark with your mother, and if I never find it again, at least I had it once. It's so rare—when it's there, you've just got to thank your stars and hang on for as long as you can, because it's too precious to waste."

"You're right," Abbie said with conviction, shoving back her chair and rising. "You're right, Dad. It's too precious to waste. Can I have the key to the van?"

Roy appeared startled by her abrupt request, but he reached into his pocket, pulled out the key and handed it to her. "Where are you going?"

"To find out if I'm a lucky soul," she said, dropping a kiss on her father's cheek and then racing out of the room.

Somewhere along Route 20, she coasted onto the shoulder and stopped the van, giving herself a few minutes to sort her thoughts. She, Abigail Jarvis, assistant district attorney for the City of New York, Borough of Manhattan, was actually contemplating marching into a bar, throwing herself at the proprietor and asking him whether he would mind if she gave him more than one night. She was contemplating kissing her career goodbye, her apartment, the hectic life and alleged glamour of New York, in order to move back to a somnolent farming town in the middle of a flat, arid valley, miles from the nearest theater or museum. She was contemplating doing all of this because she thought there might be a spark between her and T.J. On the slim chance that there was, she wanted to give it an opportunity to ignite.

She was contemplating giving up everything she'd ever dreamed of for a man who had made love to her with the understanding that she would be out of his life soon enough, a man who had not once mentioned anything about love or commitments or promises for tomorrow.

On the other hand... She drummed her fingers nervously against the steering wheel and inverted her thoughts, hoping that by viewing everything from the right perspective she would find the proper course of action.

On the other hand, she rationalized, she had spent four years with a man who had mentioned love quite glibly, who had made all sorts of promises, most of them having to do with the commitment he would make tomorrow—except that tomorrow never came. And would moving back to Wheeler really mean giving up anything so fantastic? Her apartment in Yorktown Towers was much too expensive for its size, and she hadn't had the time or energy to go to a museum or a play in nearly a year, and as for her career... well, Wheeler was sorely in need of a second lawyer. John Thorpe ought to be spending his days fishing in the Sacramento River, not trying to cram simplistic settlements down his clients' throats.

One other thing she was giving up: her dignity. Was she truly willing to go to T.J., the one-time heartthrob of Wheeler, the affable, approachable guy who ran the best bar in the region and prided himself on knowing nearly every available woman in town, and tell him she wanted to trade her burned-out dreams for the chance of a future with him?

Yes. She was willing. She revved the engine, pulled out onto the road and drove to Tyler's.

The parking lot was nearly empty—two pickups, an ancient VW Beetle and T.J.'s car were the only vehicles outside the bar. Abbie pulled the van into a space between the trucks, sucked in an anxious breath and climbed out.

She hesitated near Tyler's front door, trying to summon her courage. To the west the sun sat just inches above the horizon, glazing the flat expanse of farmland with an orange glow and casting into stark silhouette the few trees dotting the agricultural landscape. Because the air was hazy with the smoke from the burning fields, the sun looked unnaturally large, a huge amber sphere bathing the earth in its final warmth. It reminded Abbie of the harvest moon, that same vivid color and magnified size. In less than an hour, it would be gone, replaced by night.

Sobered by the thought, Abbie drew in another deep, steadying breath and entered the bar. Four young men were hunched over the pool table, armed with cue sticks and open bottles of beer. Lina stood behind the bar. From the jukebox came Bonnie Raitt's gutsy voice, crooning "Love Has No Pride." That song seemed to be playing every time Abbie came into Tyler's. She wondered whether there were any other records in the jukebox.

"Hey, Abbie," Lina hailed her. "What can I get you tonight?"

"T.J.," Abbie said automatically, then colored as the implication of what she'd said sank in. "Is he here?" she asked hastily.

"He's downstairs, unloading some stock," Lina informed her. "I'll go get him." She disappeared down the back hall.

Abbie stood by the bar, waiting. One of the farmhands called to her in a nonthreatening greeting. Reminding herself that in Wheeler it was generally safe to acknowledge a friendly stranger, she smiled and nodded at him. He resumed playing pool, and she stared at the neat rows of liquor bottles lining the shelf behind the bar, listening to Bonnie Raitt sing, "I'd do anything to see you again," and speculated on whether her pride would survive this confrontation with T.J.

After a few minutes he appeared in the hallway with Lina. She was jabbering something to him, her braid swinging ebulliently with every step. Although T.J. was listening to her, his eyes sought Abbie. The instant he saw her, his mouth curved in that familiar lazy smile of his. "Hey, Abbie," he said.

What on earth was she doing here? The mental debate she'd engaged in on the shoulder of Route 20 went totally forgotten as she digested T.J.'s greeting. What bothered her about it was its very ordinariness. Nothing in his relaxed grin implied that less than twenty-four hours ago she had been with him in his secret hideaway, that he'd spent the night in her arms, loving her with a passion so intense that merely thinking about it caused her blood to heat up. Nothing in the way he uttered those two simple words resembled the sound of his voice, raw and vulnerable, whispering, "Stay with me..."

"Hello," she said, hoping she didn't sound as frightened as she felt.

T.J. wiped his hands on a towel and appraised her. He had on his usual work outfit: a pair of jeans and a cotton shirt with the sleeves rolled up. For an irrational moment she wished he had worn something else, something less attractive—but anything he wore would look attractive on him.

As he moved closer to her, she noticed that his left leg was moving less flexibly than usual. Probably all that driving hadn't done it much good—and two days without jogging. If she lived in Wheeler, she would remind him that he had to jog more regularly... and then she'd turn into a nag, and he would hate her....

What was she thinking of? What was she doing here?

"If you need me, let me know," T.J. was instructing Lina. Abbie watched him pull two bottles of Olympia from a refrigerator under the bar. He carried them to the corner table at the back of the room where she and her father had sat the night she'd gotten him to tell her about the store.

She joined T.J. at the table, lowering herself slowly into her seat so she wouldn't look as if she were on the verge of collapse. He twisted off the caps, handed her one of the bottles, and dropped onto the chair facing her. "How are you?" he asked, at long last allowing her to sense something personal in his attitude toward her.

She surveyed her surroundings: the birch paneling, the unlit candle enclosed in a tinted glass bowl at the center of the table, the unused ashtray. The bottle of beer before her, the one before T.J., his strong, gentle, sensuous hands wrapped around the damp brown glass. "Is this the official heart-to-heart table?" she asked.

T.J. weighed her words before answering. "Are we going to have a heart-to-heart talk?"

"I hope so," Abbie said, feeling her courage slipping away and struggling to keep a grip on it, and on herself.

She swallowed and lifted her face to his. He was gazing at her, his eyes dark and unreadable, his mustache soft and velvety looking, his lips slightly parted, reminding her of how good his mouth had felt on her... *Wrong. Keep a clear head,* she cautioned herself.

Swallowing again, she presented him with a limp smile. "T.J., what I'm going to say I can say only once. After that I'm going to fall apart and run away. So please don't laugh at me, don't make fun of me, don't stop me till I'm through and then, keep your answer short and sweet, okay?"

Again he took his time absorbing her words before he responded. The corners of his lips twitched upward. "Do you always browbeat your witnesses?"

"Don't laugh at me," she repeated. "If you do, I'll leave right now."

"I won't laugh," T.J. swore, permitting himself not even the trace of a smile.

She took one final breath, then blurted out, "I love you."

"Abbie—"

"No, hush. Let me finish while I'm on a roll, okay?" She knew that if she stopped, she'd never get started again. "I love you, I want to quit my job in New York and move to Wheeler and spend more time with you. I'm thirty-four years old and it's time to simplify my life, to figure out what I want and go for it. I want to get married and have children, I want to practice law, I want to be able to live someplace where the odds of getting mugged are minimal. I love you and even if last night hadn't happened, I would have loved you anyway. If you say no, say it and we'll pretend I never said any of this." Running out of steam, she groped for her beer and took a long, bracing gulp of it.

T.J.'s silence weighed unbearably on her. She took another long sip of beer, figuring that if worse came to worst she could get drunk and pass out. If he didn't say something soon, passing out might begin to seem like a reasonable plan of action.

"Am I allowed questions?"

She risked glancing at him. He wasn't smiling, and for that she was thankful. His thumbs ran restlessly up and down the sides of his bottle, filling Abbie's mind with more erotic imagery and making her nod quickly and drink a bit more beer.

"You said you wanted to move to Wheeler. Exactly where do you want to move?"

She wasn't certain what she'd expected him to ask, but that wasn't it. She raised her eyes again. His gaze was so tender, she couldn't help but take heart in it. Shoving her beer from her before she drank any more, she said, "I was figuring I could stay with my father until I find a place of my own. If I can't talk John Thorpe into retiring and letting me take over his practice, I'm going to have some income problems initially, but if need be, I'll commute to Sacramento—they've always got jobs for lawyers there. Then I'll see what I can afford in the area. Housing costs can't possibly be as high here as they are in New York."

"You don't think your father will mind having you living with him?"

What was T.J. getting at? Was he trying to talk her out of her plan? "To tell you the truth, T.J.," she answered, "I think he'd be thrilled."

"So do I," T.J. agreed. His thumb wandered up and down the bottle again, tracing a line through the condensation on the cold glass. "You've never been to my house, Abbie," he pointed out. "Kind of strange, isn't it? You've been to the cabin, but never to my house."

This time, it was Abbie's turn to remain silent. She waited; she knew he had more to say.

"It's a nice house, Abbie. Bigger than your father's. Plenty of room for a nursery or two."

"Two?" She wasted time with the trivia, afraid to grasp the import of T.J.'s statement.

"I think each kid should have his own room, don't you?"

"Two" was definitely not trivia. T.J. was about ten steps ahead of her, and she strove to catch up. "T.J.," she said judiciously, measuring each word and giving him ample opportunity to correct her if she had misconstrued his statement, "you've been married and divorced. You ought to think very carefully about what you're implying here."

"What am I, an idiot? We both know what I'm implying, and I'm sure as hell thinking carefully." She detected a hint of a smile returning to his lips, but he valiantly suppressed it. "You've been through a rough one with a guy, too, Abbie. And if I'm not mistaken, you gave him four years. You're giving me only one answer, one minute, on the spot, yes or no."

"That's right," she confirmed. She'd learned an important lesson with Bob—not the obvious lesson that if you gave a man four years he might just take every second of them and then answer no, but the more important lesson that if you truly loved a man and he truly loved you, neither of you needed four years to figure it out. Abbie had spent four years anguishing over Bob because *she* hadn't been sure. She was sure about T.J., though. She was as sure of her feelings for him as it was possible to be. And if he wasn't as certain as she was, she'd leave. She'd be devastated, but she'd leave.

"Well. You've got me backed up against a wall," T.J. complained, shrugging. "You used to do this to Mr. Daniels in our social studies class, lecturing him and sounding off and not giving him a chance to get in a word edgewise. The thing is—" he let go of his bottle and took her hand "—what you used to do in that class took a lot of nerve . . . and it still does. And the other thing is, you were always right . . . and you still are."

She squeezed his hand, afraid to hope for too much, afraid to believe the spark had caught until she saw the flame and felt its warmth. She gazed into his eyes, searching . . . and then she saw it. She saw the love glowing in them, brighter than any spark, warmer than any blaze. She saw it and she knew that she had done the right thing in coming, the right thing in opening her heart to T.J.

"You know," T.J. went on, "it's not every day a woman walks into my bar and proposes marriage to me."

"I'd be willing to bet I'm not the first," Abbie mused.

"You're the first I've ever said yes to," he murmured, lifting her hand to his lips and grazing her knuckles. "You really want to give it all up for me?"

Abbie was surprised by the doubt in T.J.'s voice. Had he been as worried about her feelings as she'd been about his? If there was any question in his mind, any question at all, she would gladly spend the rest of her life reassuring him.

"I love you, T.J.," she swore. "And I'm not giving a damned thing up."

"Oh, yes, you are," he warned, tugging her out of her chair and pulling her onto his lap. He ringed his arms around her and kissed her soundly. "Maybe you happened to notice that stink of burning in the air this afternoon. You're giving up the freedom of not having to smell that."

"I did notice," Abbie said, returning his kiss. "And I love it."

"You're a very strange lady," T.J. whispered, brushing his lips over hers.

From the bar, Lina shouted, "T.J.? Did that shipment of peanuts ever get here?" But T.J. was too busy kissing Abbie to answer.

ABOUT THE AUTHOR

Prolific, insightful, intelligent—these all describe Judith Arnold. Since 1985 she has been contributing to American Romance, and in those three short years has written fourteen novels for the series. Her stories combine a unique blend of sensitivity and believability in a voice that speaks to the modern American woman.

She lives in Connecticut with her husband and two young sons.

Books by Judith Arnold

HARLEQUIN AMERICAN ROMANCE

149–SPECIAL DELIVERY
163–MAN AND WIFE
189–BEST FRIENDS
201–PROMISES*
205–COMMITMENTS*
209–DREAMS*
225–COMFORT AND JOY
240–TWILIGHT
255–GOING BACK

*KEEPING THE FAITH SUBSERIES

HARLEQUIN TEMPTATION

122–ON LOVE'S TRAIL

Don't miss any of our special offers. Write to us at the following address for information on our newest releases.

Harlequin Reader Service
901 Fuhrmann Blvd., P.O. Box 1397, Buffalo, NY 14240
Canadian address: P.O. Box 603,
Fort Erie, Ont. L2A 5X3

ATTRACTIVE, SPACE SAVING BOOK RACK

Display your most prized novels on this handsome and sturdy book rack. The hand-rubbed walnut finish will blend into your library decor with quiet elegance, providing a practical organizer for your favorite hard-or soft-covered books.

Only $9.95

Approximately 16" x 8" when assembled

Assembles in seconds!

To order, rush your name, address and zip code, along with a check or money order for $10.70* ($9.95 plus 75¢ postage and handling) payable to *Harlequin Reader Service*:

Harlequin Reader Service
Book Rack Offer
901 Fuhrmann Blvd.
P.O. Box 1396
Buffalo, NY 14269-1396

Offer not available in Canada.

BKR-1A

*New York and Iowa residents add appropriate sales tax.

Lynda Ward's **TOUCH THE STARS**... the final book in the Welles
... the final book in the

The Welles Family Trilogy

Lynda Ward's TOUCH THE STARS... the final book in the Welles
Family Trilogy. All her life Kate Welles Brock has sought to win the ap-
proval of her wealthy and powerful father, even going as far as to marry
Burton Welles's handpicked successor to the Corminco Corporation.

Now, with her marriage in tatters behind her, Kate is getting the first
taste of what it feels like to really live. Her glorious romance with the
elusive Paul Florian is opening up a whole new world to her.... Kate
is as determined to win the love of her man as she is to prove to her father that she is the logical choice to succeed him as head of Corminco....

Don't miss TOUCH THE STARS, a Harlequin Superromance coming
to you in September.

If you missed the first two books of this exciting trilogy, #317 RACE
THE SUN and #321 LEAP THE MOON, and would like to order them,
send your name, address and zip or postal code, along with a check or
money order for $2.95 for each book ordered (plus $1.00 postage and
handling) payable to Harlequin Reader Service to:

Harlequin American Romance

COMING NEXT MONTH

#261 THE TROUBLE WITH THORNY by Lori Copeland

Chelsey Stevens was in a tizzie. As the director of Rosehaven, it was her job to keep the retirement home running smoothly, but Thorny Bradford, a new resident, had the place astir. And Thorny's son Greg wasn't any help, either. He merely overwhelmed her with his charm.

#262 NATURAL TOUCH by Cathy Gillen Thacker

As a pediatrician, Sarah thought she knew all about children. But when her best friend died and left Sarah guardian of three kids, she found out how wrong she was. Attorney David Buchanon thought Sarah to be a loving, giving woman, but did she have what it took to turn a household into a family?

#263 LOST AND FOUND by Dallas Schulze

When Sam rescued Babs Malone from kidnappers, he intended only to collect the reward and part company with the heiress. But kidnapping was only the tip of a nasty iceberg threatening Babs, and for the first time Sam found a reason for heroism—but no guarantee it would keep them alive.

#264 FIREDANCE by Vella Munn

Smoke jumper Lory Foster battled forest fires that ravaged the Northwest forests. Mike Steen battled those blazes from his specially equipped chopper. Together, they gambled everything on one glorious weekend on the drifting currents of Idaho's Snake River.

HARLEQUIN SIGNATURE EDITION

VIOLET WINSPEAR

HOUSE OF STORMS

Editorial secretary Debra Hartway travels to the Salvador family's rugged Cornish island home to work on Jack Salvador's latest book. Disturbing questions hang in the troubled air over Lovelis Island. What or who had caused the tragic death of Jack's young wife? Why did Jack stay away from the home and, more especially, the baby son he loved so well? And—why should Rodare, Jack's brother, who had proved himself a man of the highest integrity, constantly invade Debra's thoughts with such passionate, dark desires...?

Violet Winspear, who has written more than 65 romance novels translated worldwide into 18 languages, is one of Harlequin's best-loved and bestselling authors. HOUSE OF STORMS, her second title in the Harlequin Signature Edition program, is a full-length novel rich in romantic tradition and intriguingly spiced with an atmosphere of danger and mystery.

Watch for HOUSE OF STORMS—coming in October!

HOFS-1